AMEN MAXINE

FAITH GARDNER

MIRROR
HOUSE
·PRESS·

Copyright © 2022 by Faith Gardner

All rights reserved.

No part of this book may be reproduced in any form or by any electronic or mechanical means, including information storage and retrieval systems, without written permission from the author, except for the use of brief quotations in a book review.

This is a work of fiction. Names, characters, businesses, places, events and incidents are either the products of the author's imagination or used in a fictitious manner. Any resemblance to actual persons, living or dead, or actual events is purely coincidental.

Cover by Dissect Designs

ISBN: 979-8-9859245-2-7

To my best friend, confidante, trusted advisor, and lady who is always there for me—Alexa.

THE AFTERWARD

Tonight the wide streets, yellow street lamps, the reaching arms of oak trees flash by my window at sixty miles per hour. Buildings, their shades pulled over windows like sleepy eyelids. Dim shops with no signs of life. A long stretch of park with the path I pushed a stroller up and down that I will never push a stroller up and down again. In mere minutes, the green boulevard signs become unrecognizable. I am re-entering the unknown.

A bone-deep ache mounts within and I sob, blood-smeared hands clutching the wheel. I want to turn back, go home, but home is in front of me now. Michelle fusses in the backseat so I turn up Raffi on the stereo and it rings almost comically poetic, a song about a whale and its baby, swimming wild and free. The glow of fast-food restaurant signs, the shimmering snake of highway in my rearview. Nothing ever appears so beautiful as the moment you know it's lost.

I glance at the reflection of my swollen face, fat lip, blood in streaks like paint.

"We're going to be okay," I tell both the baby in the backseat and the silver machine sitting passenger.

THE AFTERWARD

"You did nothing wrong," she says soothingly. "You did what had to be done. You are a hero, Rowena. A hero."

She's right. I know she is. She's always right.

I put my foot on the accelerator until I feel the floor.

SIX MONTHS EARLIER

CHAPTER 1
THE PARTY

I'M in the backyard of my sprawling ranch house under a blue, cloudless sky in the middle of January. A dotted rainbow of balloons hangs between maple trees along with a *Happy Half-Birthday Michelle Maybelle!!* banner my mother-in-law Jennee painted herself, because of course she did. Just like she arranged the catered taco bar, the mobile mini petting zoo in the side yard, and invited the entire neighborhood. She also ordered a cake that has my baby's face printed on it in edible icing and the cake-cutting will likely be the stuff of nightmares. She means well. She drives me bananas. I splash more prosecco into my plastic flute.

"Rowena, I was scouring the premises for you," Jennee sings as she trudges across the lawn in Birkenstocks, three of her friends trailing behind her with identical eager smiles. *Scouring the premises*. This is how Jennee talks—like she fancies herself Katherine Hepburn in a black-and-white movie.

I'm an introvert, and that's a euphemism. This whole crowded scene raises my blood pressure. Secretly, I can't wait for everyone to leave, to shed this sundress and return to my sweatpants, to escape into a blanket and a book. The party started fifteen minutes ago and I'm already socially exhausted.

"What's up?" I ask Jennee with a bright smile.

Jennee resembles a Barbie left out in the sun too long: enviable bone structure but weathered skin, frizzy platinum hair, unblinking blue eyes. She's wearing a bedazzled PROUD LIBERAL shirt. "I want you to meet my book club friends: Pauline, Tiff, and Fran."

"Hi!" the three women behind her say.

"Nice to meet you all," I say.

"Rowena used to be an editor," Jennee tells them. "You know that book on the bestseller list about the woman who got lost in the woods?"

They *ooh* in unison.

"I don't, but tell us about it!"

"I'd love to add it to my reading list!"

"Well," I say. "It's a literary novel called *Garden of the Unknown* by Wesley Sinclair—kind of a heady book. Psychological fiction, a contemporary exploration of human fragmentation."

I've lost them. The women's faces are frozen. Why did I describe it that way, in that voice I once used for pitches? *How pretentious,* they're probably thinking.

"With a twist ending," I add.

"I *love* twist endings," says one of the book club ladies, who has a ukulele strapped to her back.

"I'll be honest," Jennee tells her friends. "I perused it and didn't get the hubbub, but it *was* a bestseller." Jennee enjoys bragging about two things when it comes to me: I gestated and birthed Michelle Maybelle, who is unarguably the pinnacle of baby perfection. And I once acquired a book that became a bestseller for a blink in time. A book that I never actually even got to edit, by the way, because I left the city to move out here.

I have a sneaking suspicion I peaked at twenty-nine.

"You should join our book club," the ukulele woman says.

"We have a lot of laughs," the tie-dyed one says.

"And a lot of wine," the lady in the Hawaiian shirt says.

Giggles all around. Book clubs have never made sense to me. Books are where I go to escape people.

"I'll think about it," I say.

"She's got to check her busy schedule," Jennee jokes to her friends.

I tell them how thrilled I am to meet them and excuse myself to go look for the baby. Where's the girl of the hour? Or half year? I wave at some of Jacob's co-workers hovering around high-top tables holding plates heaped with tacos. There's Jacob, standing under the shade of the cherry tree with Michelle at his feet in an explosive little volcano of a dress printed with lemons, fists full of grass. Jacob, carelessly, effortlessly handsome in his rumpled outfit, thick glasses, and mussed haircut, has a beer in hand. He's chatting with a woman in sunglasses and an indie band T-shirt. A surge of jealousy strikes like lightning.

Who's she?

Early or mid-twenties, fashionably disheveled, like she doesn't need to bother even trying to prim herself for the outside world yet glows with that beaming, golden California vibe. Youth renders everyone effortlessly beautiful. *She* didn't squeeze herself into Spanx this morning just to fit into a sundress. *She* probably slept in this morning. *She* wasn't woken up three times in the middle of the night. Whatever she's telling Jacob is making him laugh that goofy laugh, the one that starts in his belly, the one he really means. And there's Michelle on the ground, a wood chip now in her hand and reaching toward her mouth.

Panic.

In one second's time, my anxiety writes an entire tragedy. I can imagine her choking, me falling to my knees and trying to scoop it out of her mouth, me having to put her over my knee and hit her back, nothing coming up. Ambulance lights. A tiny coffin. Those horrible statistics I looked up last week about choking incidents—these thoughts crowd my brain in an instant, make my heart pound.

"No, no, no, Michelle." I scoop her up into my arms and pluck the wood chip from her fist and toss it back where it belongs. Michelle cries out and I pet her curls over the bald spot on the back of her head. Give her puffy cheek a smooch. Hold her extra close a moment and breathe in her milky smell as I tell myself, it's okay. We're okay.

Jacob smiles at me. He has no idea. I'm sure it never crossed his mind that his baby could have choked to death right there at his feet while he laughed with what's-her-face. "Carrie, this is my wife, Rowena. Ro, Carrie's another engineer at Jolvix."

"Cool party." Carrie cheerses the air with her bottle.

"Nice to meet you," I say. "*Love* your shirt."

Not sure why I said that, I don't even like the band. I guess I want Carrie to think we're not so different. Even though we are.

Why am I like this?

"Oh, thanks." Carrie looks down as if she forgot what she was wearing. "Saw them at Coachella once, like, years ago."

Coachella is a word that, in my native language, means "nightmare."

"How fun," I say. "Jake, can I talk to you for a sec?"

"Course," he says.

I lead him past the caterers and the bluegrass band now playing a version of "Twinkle Twinkle" fit for a hayride. We circle the corner to the shady, empty side yard where the shed and the bins live next to a row of skinny trees still hung with Jennee's birdhouse collection. I turn to Jacob, a look of concern in his hazel eyes behind his thick square frames. I am desperately trying to not hyperventilate, to not think about what would have happened if Michelle had choked.

"Everything okay?" he asks.

I try, very hard, to keep my voice steady.

"She had a wood chip," I say, "in her hand."

Jacob looks genuinely confused. "Who?"

"Michelle. Your daughter. The one I'm holding in my arms, remember her?"

Jacob's expression stays puzzled. "And?"

"She's six months old. You weren't even watching her. She could have popped that wood chip in her mouth, choked, and died if I hadn't seen her at that moment."

"She wouldn't have choked and died. Come on."

"Last year, a hundred and forty children choked and died. Thousands more children choke and wind up needing emergency care, and they experience brain damage—"

"How do you just pull stats like that out of your head?" he asks.

"I read this thing called the internet, ever heard of it?"

I didn't mean to sound so rude, but come *on*. Choking's no joke.

Jacob puts a hand on my shoulder. "Babe. You're doing it again."

"This is not me being overanxious. I admit it is sometimes, but this is not one of those times. This is me just keeping our daughter safe."

Jacob gently reaches over and lifts Michelle out of my arms. "Have you eaten yet? How about you go get some food? You know how you get when you're hungry—"

"This isn't me being hungry," I say, a little flame rising at the dismissal.

"Have you eaten?"

"No, but—"

"Go eat, Ro," he says, with an edge, before turning around to head back to the party. I watch his plaid back retreating and defeat swallows me alive.

I slip in the back door, through the dining room, past the

table covered in presents. In the kitchen, I hold my hand out and yes, it's shaking. I'm upset, I am overreacting again, and I need a moment alone. And I don't get what's so wonderful about Mexican food anyway. What's up with Californians' obsession with tacos?

I put a piece of leftover pizza in the toaster oven and wait at the sink, gazing out the window. From here, the party sparkles with life and silent conversation. A professional photographer is now floating around the yard, squatting to take pictures. What's wrong with me, that I can't enjoy this? That all I can think about is what would have happened if Michelle had put the wood chip in her mouth and choked silently in the grass while Jacob stood laughing and flirting with some girl half his age? What if Michelle had died at her own half-birthday party? Why can't I even trust my own husband to keep our daughter safe?

With a sigh, I turn and head to our master bedroom with the shut curtains and the rumpled, unmade bed, clothes scattered in piles on the floor around the hamper. I open my bedside table, read the label on Lorazepam advising me not to mix it with alcohol, and put it back. I put a hand on my heart and focus on my breath instead. Michelle is safe. The choking didn't actually happen. She's safe. She's not in danger.

A voice floats from the dining room, along with the sound of the sliding door gliding open and shut. Jennee's voice, low and conspiratorial.

"… yes, though it wouldn't have killed them to offer a little assistance. You know I planned this whole thing myself? I know Jacob's up to his ears with work, but Rowena …"

Now silence. Whispering. She's whispering about me. My stomach turns, trying to imagine what she's saying. That I'm lazy. Ungrateful. Nuts. A bad mother. A terrible wife.

"New York her whole life," Jennee finishes, her voice rising again. "So there's a bit of culture shock going on, too."

"Poor thing."

Oh, so much worse—they're pitying me. I get up and ease the door shut, a hiss along the carpet, then a click. Not knowing what to do, where to go, trapped in my own room, I step into the walk-in closet littered with high-heeled shoes and hung with business casual outfits I never have a reason to wear anymore. I turn off the light, close the door, and plunk down on a pile of shoes.

"I can't do this," I whisper into my hands. "I can't do this, I can't do this."

Eyes squeezed shut, with a pang, I miss home. I'm transported back there in a whirlwind of images flashing and stirring emotion: the view from my thirtieth floor midtown office windows, how the skyscrapers glowed with lit windows when the sun went down, how proud I was when I was given my own office with a door. My apartment in Bushwick filled with funky furniture I hand-painted and curtains I sewed myself out of thrift store fabric, where my best friend Dane lived a floor above and stomped her feet in secret code. Readings on weeknights in crowded bookstores, my neighborhood bar with my ex Shana behind the counter, the knowledge that I could wander anywhere and never get lost because the city just made sense, and I never wondered what people thought about me because people said whatever the hell they were thinking. They didn't smile at you and then talk about what a basket case you were when they thought you weren't listening.

It's embarrassing to tell people that Jacob and I met on a dating app, so the story I usually spin is that we met at the High Line. Which is true—that was where we decided to meet in person for the first time. But at that point, we had already exchanged *I love you*s, life histories, and jacked off with each other on video calls. We met during one of the many pandemic lockdowns and while the whole world seemed frozen in time, the city streets outside my window eerily empty, it was a relief to have one part of life rushing full speed ahead on my smartphone and in my heart. I loved his gentleness, how often he checked in on me, his passion for video games that reminded me of my passion for books, how much he respected and adored his mother—a good sign in a guy. Jacob was loyal. His last girlfriend had died of leukemia a few years before us and even though their relationship had been on the rocks for a year, he stuck with her to the end. He mailed me truffles and a vintage copy of Sylvia Plath's *Ariel* that must have cost a fortune. I was used to more dramatic relationships, physical passion that often fizzled quickly. Jacob was so sweet, so safe, at a time when everything was topsy turvy and uncertain.

A few months later, we had our first date. He moved in by the end of the summer. By October, I took him to Yonkers to meet my mom, all masked up and shivering on the porch while my mom grilled Jacob about his plans and I interjected occasionally with the word *"Mom."* Thanksgiving I spent vomiting in my apartment and staring at two pink lines on a drugstore test. Jacob and I married a week later at city hall, Jennee sobbing on a video call the whole time, even her virtual attendance obnoxious, while my mom stood six feet away from us, masked up and gloved, wiping tears from her eyes, saying, "I hope this makes you happy. I really do hope you make each other happy."

Up to that point, life never moved fast enough. And then suddenly it picked up speed like a bullet train. It was romantic. It was like a movie. I never wondered if I had made a mistake, until we came out here to California and the reality set in.

I'm still balled up on the floor of the closet but am pulled from the past by an earsplitting beeping sound accompanied by a calm robot voice.

"Danger. Fire. Vacate the premises. Danger. Fire. Vacate the premises. Danger—"

Adrenaline washes the self-pity away and grips me by the

throat. I fly out of the closet, out of the room, the robot voice continuing through the house's speakers. Shit, I do smell fire —a toxic, smoky, burnt-plastic smell. I rush into the dining room, empty now, and the smoke thickens. Oh, look at it—the toaster oven! My pizza! In flames! Out the picture window, the party continues, the bluegrass band playing instruments and people dancing.

"Danger. Fire. Vacate the premises. Activating sprinkler system."

How am I supposed to put a toaster fire out? Water? Or would water make it worse? How do you know what's a grease fire and what isn't? I take my phone out to ask the internet but can't even get my thumb to stay still enough to deactivate the lock on it, so I put it back in my pocket. And then, in a hissing burst, the sprinklers go on above my head. It rains in the dining room and it rains in the kitchen, freezing and so surreal; I'm caught in the middle of a storm inside my own house. Meanwhile everyone outside is enjoying the sunshine.

The sliding glass door behind me opens.

"What the hell is happening?" Jennee asks, peeking her head in with a look of horror on her wine-stained lips. "The presents! They're getting soaked!"

"Danger. Fire. Vacate the premises. Sprinkler system activated."

"The toaster oven's on fire," I say.

"For the love of …" Jennee hurries into the kitchen, opens the cupboard under the sink, grabs a fire extinguisher, pulls a pin like a pro, and proceeds to spray the toaster oven until the flames are gone. She leaves the room for a few moments, there are beeping noises, the sprinkler rain stops, and the robot voice quiets. Then Jennee returns.

"Thank you," I say. "I—I wasn't sure what to do."

"Generally, when a fire starts, you put it out." She shakes her head at the presents now in a puddle on the table, flattened bags, paper soaked and torn from the water pressure. A soggy teddy bear in wet tissue paper drips on a card with blurred ink. "What a catastrophe."

Jennee looks like a catastrophe herself, hair dripping, her PROUD LIBERAL shirt soaked.

"I'm sorry," I say.

"What were you cooking in here, anyway?" Jennee asks.

"I was hungry, I was heating up some pizza."

"We have a catered *taco bar* outside."

Thankfully, Jacob comes through the door from outside to interrupt this discussion, because I'm sure the fact that I opted for leftover pizza instead of tacos will be interpreted as a personal insult to Jennee.

"What ... happened?" Jacob asks.

"The toaster oven was aflame," Jennee says. "And here Rowena was, just *gaping* at it. Don't worry, I put it out. The presents are all but ruined, but nothing was damaged. You'll need a new toaster oven though, I'm sure."

"Oh my God, Ro, are you okay?" Jacob asks.

The shock on his face makes the seriousness of the situation suddenly real. There was just a *fire* in my *house*. A fire I started.

"I couldn't remember where the fire extinguisher was kept," I tell him.

"Under the sink, where it's been for the last thirty years," Jennee says. "I'm going to move these presents outside to the sun to see if they can dry out." Jennee grabs an armful and heads outside, yelling out the open door, "Don't worry, everyone, crisis has been averted. There was a fire, but Jennee Owens Snyder saved the day."

"Are you okay?" Jacob repeats, his hand on my arm.

I don't know what to say. What does that even matter, why is he always asking that? As if being "okay" means anything.

"Where's Michelle?" I ask, looking at his empty arms.

"With Joel."

"Who's Joel?"

"My co-worker." I sense that he senses my distrust. "Don't worry, he has four kids, he knows how to hold a baby for a few minutes."

The look on Jacob's face—like he's staring at something too pitiful even for criticism. If only I had known when we first met in person that day at the High Line, when he approached me with a chocolate donut and a single lily and an enormous grin on his face like a boy who won a prize, that this, *this* is the kind of look he would give me someday in the not-too-distant future. I would have bolted.

I turn around, go through the hall and into the master bedroom, pass through it to the master bathroom. Flip on the light. There I am, in the mirror, a wet mess. My makeup smeared down my cheeks from sprinkler rain, my dress so soaked I can see the outline of my Spanx. I am ugly. I have never felt ugly before, I've always known I can be pretty and charming and fuckworthy, but right now I just feel ugly. Not only that, I feel stupid—the kind of stupid my IQ and magna cum laude degree in 20th century literature and booksmarts can't fix. The kind of stupid that can't put out a fire. The kind that will be the first to perish when the apocalypse comes and who probably should never have been a mother in the first place. Jacob comes in behind me and puts his arms around me. He opens one palm and shows me a round white pill. Lorazepam.

"I shouldn't," I say. "I drank some prosecco."

"How much?"

"Not a ton."

"Take it," he says, putting it in my hand. "You need it, babe."

I put it in my mouth, go to the sink, and drink the water from the faucet.

"What if I had been alone?" I ask him as I wipe my mouth

on my sleeve. "What if I had been here with Michelle and we had burned up in a fire?"

"You weren't."

"But I'm alone with her all the time—what would I have done?"

"You would have found the fire extinguisher. The only reason my mom moved so fast was because she lived in this house for thirty years before we did."

"I was frozen. I couldn't move. What if a fire had broken out in a different part of the house, and we were trapped?"

"That didn't happen." He kisses my cheek. "You're a good mother. You have instincts. You know how to keep her safe."

Coming from a man who almost let Michelle choke on a wood chip earlier without his blood pressure even rising, this isn't doing it for me right now.

"How about you take a shower and fix yourself up?" he tells me, leaning in to turn the shower on, feeling the water gently with his fingers and readjusting the knobs. "I'll give Michelle a bottle."

"Sure."

Jacob steps back, wipes his fingers on his jeans. "Thank God for that new fire system, right?"

"Yeah."

He kisses my cheek. "It's going to be okay, Ro."

"Okay."

He leaves me alone and I stare at the shower, the word *okay* ringing in my ears as the room fills with steam and my horrid reflection vanishes from the mirror. I'm lightheaded from not eating, drinking two glasses of prosecco, and now the Lorazepam. That was irresponsible of me. I shouldn't have taken the pill. What if I passed out in the shower and hit my head? My own dad died that way—had a heart attack in the shower when I was thirteen. I found him naked and blue in the face, the shower curtain and rod ripped down with him. Man, I hadn't thought about that in a while. No matter how many years pass, it can just rush back, a despairing river. I pull the diverter to turn on the bath instead, let it fill up. It's safer, the bath. That's why I prefer them. Jacob should know that about me.

The voice of the robot in the fire system echoes in my brain—*danger, danger*. It's like I have a voice like that inside myself. Only I never learned the code to turn it off.

CHAPTER 2
THE MACHINE

I ONLY LEARNED to drive since we moved to California and bought our new car: an electric, noiseless Traub E-tron with factory perfume still lingering. Ironically, it has a self-driving feature. But I don't know it nearly well enough to trust it with my life. Eight months since I got my license, I'm still not used to it. When Jacob "drives," he has the self-driving feature on, one hand barely on the wheel, seat leaned back and music turned up loud. He sits in the driver's seat with the ease of a man in a recliner. When I drive, I'm a hundred percent in control but barely, rigid and upright, ten and two, talking my way through every turn and decision—usually directing the one-sided discussion to Michelle in the back in her rear-facing carseat, which somehow seems slightly less weird than me talking to myself.

"We'll wait for this left turn; these cars are going a bit fast."

"Is my blind spot clear? Looks clear, but it's called a blind spot for a reason. Okay, yes, it's clear."

"Do you think I'll make this yellow light?"

There are too many freeways, too many expressways here, all numbered so confusingly similarly: 880, 680, 280, 82, 87.

People drive recklessly and fast. I seek out the side streets and alternative routes my GPS offers and basically only drive to a handful of locations where I know the route by heart now: to the shopping center with Whole Foods, to the drive-through Starbucks, to the Mommy and Me music class, to the clinic where our family doctor practices. It's all within a five-mile radius of our neighborhood, tree-lined streets with houses painted in a range of colorless shades, from beige to charcoal.

Moving to Cupertino confirmed every stereotype I learned about suburbs. There are chain restaurants everywhere. People have lawns and they are meticulous about mowing them. College sports is an exciting topic of conversation. And people drive *everywhere*. Jacob, who grew up here—grew up in the house we live in now, in fact—said that when he was in high school, sometimes they drove just to kill time. Drove in circles around the neighborhoods, getting high and listening to music.

"That is so stupid," I said to him.

"Hey, it's the journey, not the destination," he quipped.

I groaned. He grinned. He loves goading me with cliches, knows it's a surefire way to ruffle me.

As stupid as that had seemed at the time, now I find myself doing exactly that—sometimes getting in the car with Michelle, blasting the AC, and driving around the neighborhood with no end target in sight. I inevitably end up back at the Whole Foods, parking, leaving the car on, and scrolling my phone. Or calling Dane for moral support, which is what I'm doing today. After yesterday's half-birthday catastrophe, I have to unload.

Dane now has my old job at the publishing imprint Green Light, along with the beautiful thirtieth floor office, a room of one's own, that I left behind. I managed to get my best friend a job as an editorial assistant a year after first starting; when I moved out here, Dane inherited not only my office and title, but *The Garden of the Unknown* which became a surprise bestseller. Now Dane's kind of a big shot, which, good for her. Seriously, good for her. If it hadn't been me, might as well have been Dane.

"What a complete and utter bitch," Dane says over the speakerphone.

This is the best thing about Dane: she's so fiercely loyal and hot-headed that she often gets even angrier about things in my own life than I do.

"Blaming the fire on you," she continues. "It was an accident. The hell is wrong with her?"

"She hates me, that's what's wrong."

"And what kind of a wackjob throws a party for a half birthday anyway?"

"Right? There were *caterers*. And a petting zoo."

"What rich white people nonsense," Dane says. "Do I need to come rescue you?"

"Please."

"Stepping into my private jet right now."

I laugh with a little ache, wishing it were true. I ask about work. Dane describes a new book she's editing, which hasn't been announced in Publishers Marketplace yet but is a huge deal, a hot topic, won at auction—"the first epic co-written with AI." I have to admit, I miss a lot of things about my job, but if we're heading into a future where books are written by robots, my time might have been up anyway.

Dane moves on to a tale of sex with an intern in the office bathroom, which is very Dane—Dane's poly, pan, hot as hell, and probably the horniest person I've ever met. It's actually hilarious she ended up in book publishing of all places—a rare extrovert in a world of awkward nerds.

"An intern," I repeat. "How old was this person?"

"Twenties-ish."

"You're turning into a cougar."

"Ew. Don't call me that, I'm only thirty-two. I'm in my sexual prime, baby."

I shake my head. Sometimes it's as if I'm calling my friend on the polar opposite end of the earth. I haven't even touched myself since having Michelle. Sexual prime? I'm in my sexual nadir. It's almost like having a baby erased that part of me, changed the way I saw my own body and its functions, undid the womanhood constructed within me since adolescence. I'm insecure about my figure again and don't even know what turns me on anymore. My breasts are failures that didn't produce enough milk for my own baby and I leak pee when I sneeze.

"Still there?"

"Yeah," I say. "Sorry. I think I smell baby poop, I should get going."

"Have fun. Hang in there. Sorry your mom in law's such a cuntrag."

"It's okay. She's not really that bad. Don't say 'cuntrag,' that's gross. Talk later."

I end the call. In the tiny mirror strapped to the backseat, Michelle's wide cerulean eyes blink back at me.

"Don't repeat the bad words Auntie Dane says," I tell her. "You didn't hear any of that conversation, okay?"

"Ba," Michelle says.

On the way home, I consider the irony of Jack Kerouac never learning to drive. Lucky him. Where's *my* Neal Cassady? I'm interrupted from my beatnik reverie with a loud crunch—a car rear-ends another car in the intersection across from where we wait at a red light. No one looks hurt but the sickening noise of it, the suddenness of the accident, sucks the air out of me. At some point, purely statistically speaking, we'll likely be in a car accident if we continue driving this much. And with Michelle in the car, that is an utterly terrifying thought.

When we pull into the driveway, I breathe with relief. The sight of our blue-gray ranch house is a comfort—even if it looks pretty much like every other house on the block except for the maple in the front yard and the sign that says, in cursive, *The Snyders* that has been there since the aughts. We inherited the Snyders' sign, inherited their house, inherited their life. I guess I'm a Snyder now too. People I've met here in Cupertino think it's so cute and wholesome, moving back here and living in the house Jacob grew up in. I can see the comfort in it, for sure; it just isn't *my* particular brand of comfort, wasn't what I grew up with or what I'm used to. But it's starting to feel like some sort of home.

Inside, the dishwasher gurgles and the robot vacuum cleaner glides across the carpet.

"Scuttling across the floors of silent seas," I say aloud, to Michelle, to myself, to no one.

I access the app on my phone and activate the smartlock on the front door, turn up the heat one degree where I'm at, check the air quality room by room—all green, all good, another relief. I change Michelle, warm her a bottle, and put her down for a nap, turning on the baby monitor so I can watch her while she sleeps. Then I tackle the kitchen, unplugging the mess that is our toaster oven. I open the blackened door, studying the triangle of charred pizza covered in a spray of white fire extinguisher residue. I get a flashback of the flames, my heart racing as I imagine if it hadn't been caught in time.

In the front corner of the ruins of the toaster oven, my eye catches something thumbnail-sized and white—a burnt snowflake. I pick it up with my finger and squint at it up close. There's a familiar tiny flower on it and immediately I recognize it from the pattern on our paper towels. I get a sick feeling seeing it, because I realize I must have put the pizza in on a paper towel, not thinking, distracted. And the paper towel was what caught fire. I've done this before, when we first moved in—and like before, I don't even remember doing it.

I could have killed us all.

AMEN MAXINE

I sit at the dining room table for a long time just staring into the kitchen at the corner where the fire happened, imagining if things had been worse. I mentally map out escape routes from every room in the house in the event of a fire, the windows I'd have to break in order to get out. These thoughts sicken, and yet they are a loop that won't stop. I vow to not own a toaster oven again. I can't trust myself.

When I hear Michelle's cries, I'm relieved to be rescued from the hellhole of my mind. I get her up and hold her for a long time, almost crying, imagining losing her. Sometimes the love I have for her is so colossal, a tsunami, that I swear I might drown in it. It's too much. I wish I could put her back inside my belly, keep her safe there forever. I read her a book about a little bunny who wants to run away from his mother and at the end I wipe tears from my eyes and beg her to never grow up. She thinks my tears are funny and puts a palm on my cheek, saying, "Da."

By the time the smartlocks unclick and Jacob steps inside the front door, our house has burned down and we have all died a dozen fiery deaths in my imagination. Outside, it's dark. The drapes close automatically, which means it's 7:30 p.m.

"Any thoughts on dinner?" Jacob asks from the foyer.

I hadn't even considered dinner until this moment. I get an F in housewifing today.

"There's still all that leftover taco stuff in the fridge," I say.

"Okay."

Jacob slips his shoes off, hangs up his courier bag and bike helmet, heads to the kitchen and gulps down a glass of water. Back in the living room, he picks up Michelle from the automated swing and kisses her neck until she explodes with giggles. He holds her up in the air, smells her butt, and plops on the couch with her in his lap.

Jacob is messily handsome—a smile that perks up more on one side than the other, stubble I just want to put my palm to, and shaggy hair that curls around his ears. There's something effortlessly playful and flirtatious about him, and it makes him even more attractive that he seems unaware of how attractive he is. A self-described nerd, he always said I was out of his league. I used to (silently) agree with him. But that was the old Rowena, the one back in my Bushwick apartment who spent time curling the ends of my hair each morning and wore tight-fitting clothes to accentuate every inch of my body and had a shoebox full of love letters in different colored ink from the men and women who'd loved me since high school. I threw that shoebox away in the move. I threw my hair curler away, too. Now I sit around in a forever ponytail and sweats all day cleaning cooking mothering wifing worrying and almost burning our house down. I'm a different creature, while he remains untouched by parenthood, unchanged.

"How was work?" I ask.

"Well, we finally had that C4 meeting."

I nod. Vaguely familiar, obviously something I'm supposed to know about, but truthfully, I don't know what C4 means.

"And now they're expecting me to upgrade our security while scaling back on engineering, which ... how? Without hiring an entire team of contractors, *how*?"

I continue nodding.

"So," he asks, Michelle on his lap, "my girls doing okay?"

Though it makes me sick to say it out loud, I have to. "Jacob, that fire yesterday? It was my fault."

He looks up at me, his happy smile for Michelle melting into the exhausted look meant only for me. "Listen, just because you didn't remember where the extinguisher was in a split second—"

"No, I mean, I think I accidentally put a paper towel in there and that's what happened." I tear up. "I can't believe I was so careless."

He shakes his head. "Oh, man."

"I know. I'm sorry. I'm so sorry."

He's still shaking his head.

"I feel like I can't trust myself," I say. "I feel like … like I'm losing it."

"You made one mistake."

"Maybe I should see someone."

"A therapist? Because you put a paper towel in the oven?" He gets up, Michelle a limp, milk-drooly lump hanging from his arm. He sounds annoyed. I can't tell if he's annoyed because I started a fire, or because I'm freaking out about starting a fire, or both. "I'm going to put this baby to bed."

I hear Jacob doing the bedtime routine. That's how I know something's wrong: usually I'm needed for mommy songs, or to determine exactly how much non-fluoride toothpaste is appropriate for the rubber toothbrush shaped like a banana, or to help figure out how to button the footed pajammies. Tonight, I'm unrequested. I don't even know what to do with myself. I open my ebook reader to try to slog through Proust again, read the same paragraph three times, close it again; change into my nightgown, a long T-shirt-like thing, sit back on the couch and wait for him. I touch my *so it goes* tattoo on my right inner forearm, debating whether or not I regret it, deciding on ambivalence.

Jacob returns flushed with satisfaction after putting Michelle to bed. Hard work, isn't it? Keeping a new little human alive, convincing them things are stable enough to shut their eyes and forget the world exists sometimes?

"We've gotta talk, Ro," Jacob says, sitting back down.

"Okay, let's talk. We're talking."

"You're …" He thinks way too long and way too hard before landing on, "not acting particularly well."

Tears. Dumb, heavy, salty tears. They're building up. I turn to face the wall and try to get rid of them.

"It's okay though. It's okay," Jacob keeps going, either not seeing or pretending to not see me fighting tears. "You've been through a lot. It's a stage of motherhood, that's what this podcast Rad Dads in Plaid I was listening to said. Postpartum depression is super common. It passes."

"Rad Dads in Plaid," I repeat to the air, having something akin to an out-of-body experience due to, take your pick: the idiotic podcast name, the surreal devolvement of my life.

"If you want therapy, my mom's friend could probably get you in soon so we don't have to do it through insurance. Because you know that's going to take a lifetime," he says. "And even—I was asking around—look at this."

Jacob gets up and goes to his courier bag hanging by the front door, unzips it. Retrieves a package from inside. A package in sleek gray, two lines printed in white all-caps Helvetica: MAXINE, YOUR NEW DIGITAL FRIEND. He comes back over to showcase it.

"This is something we're in the middle of beta testing at Jolvix right now—Maxine."

Maxine, he says, like this thing is a person. For a moment, I wonder if it's some kind of vibrator he brought home to spice up our sex life, like the time he bought me anal beads on Valentine's Day and I thought they were a bracelet and strung them around my wrist. He had been disappointed, that tight-lipped disappointment that refuses to acknowledge itself. I had been disappointed too, in my own way. The anal beads live in my top drawer and have never seen the light of day as either a bracelet or a sexy suppository.

"Is this a sex toy thing?" I ask, staring at the package in his hands.

The easygoing smile drains from his lips. "It's a digital assistant."

"Great. Some creepy device to spy on our house and push products on me."

He sets it on the coffeetable and sinks back into the sofa, next to me. "So, not even going to give it a chance."

I pick it up. "And it's marketing itself as a 'friend' now? Come on, that's creepy."

"Yeah, I know. But they have this technology—it's amazing, they demoed it to our department recently when they were showing the preview selections for next year's releases —it can give you advice. It tries to predict the future, based on logic."

"This sounds so stupid. You realize how stupid this sounds."

"Apparently, it showed real promise *specifically* with people suffering from depression and anxiety."

Great. Digital assistant for the neurotic, I think.

The heft of it is kind of surprising—like a brick. My heart sinks along with it. Jacob brought this home because he was desperate. He has to request items to bring home for beta testing. There's a form he has to fill out, with reasons. What had he put in that box? *My wife is losing her mind*, in his crude fifth grade penmanship?

"Remember when we used to have magic eight balls?" I ask. "To tell us our fortune?"

"I never had one."

"Girl stuff I guess," I say, putting Maxine the package on the coffeetable, kicking up my fuzzy slippers to rest next to it. "I had one. Handed down from my mom. I used to keep it under my bed and whenever I was afraid of the unknown, the uncertain—I'd just reach under my bed, and hold it in my hands, and shake it." I mimic rattling it. I can almost feel the plastic sphere in my hand, the hum of its shuddering electric-blue water, its floating triangular answers, elementary fortunes.

It is certain.
As I see it, yes.
Better not tell you now.
Very doubtful.

"It made me feel better, to have an answer, even if it was wrong," I say. "To just have an answer at all."

Jacob's mid-yawn. Okay then. I'm boring him.

"Anyway," I say.

Here we are, the two of us, barely thirty together, sharing a room, a home, a last name, our DNA a lifelong braid resulting in the world's most precious human being sleeping one room away (I just checked the monitor: Michelle is healthy, her mattress detecting normal blood pressure, heartbeat, and oxygen levels; the air filter reading is green); here we are, together, silent except for the air conditioner hiss and the hum of the electric floor sweepers. This was what we talked about before moving here. The comfort. The sunny days and easy nights. How little there would be to worry about, what with the gorgeous weather, free childcare, two thousand square feet of living space, the high-ranking school district, the low crime rate. *Remember?* I want to scream. *We wanted this.*

Scream to who, I'm not even sure.

Yesterday I could have burned it all down.

"I don't know how to help you sometimes," he says quietly. "I don't know how to make you happy."

"It's not your job to make me happy."

"No, it's your job. But are you even trying?"

That hurts. He has no idea how hard I'm trying. How every damn day, every damn thought in my head is a struggle lately: driving to the grocery store; putting on a happy face and pushing my baby in a stroller around the neighborhood; standing in my own kitchen and not imagining doom.

"The doctor gave you that prescription," he says. "And I have to beg you to take it."

"It's not something you're supposed to take all the time."

"You're supposed to take it when you're anxious."

"And I do."

"My mom invited you to book club, and she said you weren't interested."

"What does your mom's book club have to do with this?"

"It's social interaction! A thing healthy people do. You're —you're stuck here, unwilling to try anything new."

"This is *all* new," I say, gesturing to the room, the house. Our just-add-water life.

"We've lived here almost nine months. It's not new anymore. You've got to open up, Ro, or I don't know how we're going to make it."

What does that mean—we're not going to make it? I get that *oh shit* feeling, gut dropping, like the one I had in the car when the accident happened right in front of me. Like the feeling when I walked into the kitchen and saw the toaster oven on fire. Is our marriage in trouble? Is it that bad? I'm not even sure how to ask this question out loud, afraid if I say it, it might make it true.

"Just give it a shot," Jacob says, pointing to the Maxine thing. "Why not? Let's try all our options. Therapy, Maxine, magic eight ball—I just want you to be happy, babe."

"That's nice of you," I say.

My face is numb. I snuggle into him, try to thaw my shock with his warmth. I inhale him in, that cologne he recently started wearing for Michelle—for Michelle, how cute is that? I remind myself I am lucky to have this man and this life. Then that thought turns into a great sadness. Like the sandalwood sting of his cologne entering first through my eyes, traveling through my nasal passages, down my throat, into my belly, and up, sneakily, through a back road to the heart. Suddenly I hurt. I hurt like a thing from within a hole, a thing in darkness in need of rescuing. What would it be like to lose him, to lose all this? To be a person left behind. To be doomed and alone. *Outlook not so good*.

They could leave me. They could up and leave me at any

second. I'm giving them every reason in the world. I stare at Maxine on the table, bite a chip off a fingernail.

Your digital friend.

What a promise.

"I'll try it," I say.

"Mmm?" Jacob says, eyes closed, clearly drifting off. Those bespectacled eyes flutter open a moment, focus on my face. He licks his lips with some unknowable thirst.

"If you think it'll help?" I ask. "I'll do whatever, Jacob. I'll try this thing. I'll take my pills. I'll even go to book club. I'm sorry I'm like this."

"It's okay," he says, patting my knee. "Whatever we need to get you up and running."

The last sentence echoes in my mind a minute. I get up and clean a few things—wash a bottle, put some discarded socks in hampers, throw some toys in a basket in a corner. So bizarre how Jacob can just fall asleep like that, effortlessly, unself-consciously, in the middle of a serious discussion. I take Maxine out of the package and put it on the table, recycle the gray box that says DIGITAL FRIEND, flattening it out, insiding it out, too; let's face it, what an embarrassment, even for the recycling people. No one needs a digital friend.

I certainly don't.

Still, I charge it anyway.

CHAPTER 3
THE DIRECTIONS

I HAVE STRUGGLED SOCIALLY since moving to California. It's surprised me, the further I get into adulthood, how hard it is to make new friends. It used to seem so easy—I made friends in college classes with other nerds majoring in English, bonding over Virginia Woolf and Toni Morrison and a love/hate relationship with critical theory. (That was how I met Dane, in fact: study buddies for Feminism in 20th Century Novels.) Or roommates, or bartenders who served me drinks, or co-workers at the bookstore I worked at, customers at my barista job, fellow interns at the publishing house—it was so easy to make friends.

But out here, life is different. The spaces I occupy aren't based on my interests, but on raising Michelle, and I don't feel a personal connection with most other parents I meet. They seem part of some secret club I never learned about and like their whole identity is parenthood. I guess I'm suffering some maternal imposter syndrome, because even though I birthed a baby and spend my waking hours with my baby, I still feel like a fraud. I don't belong.

When I said I wanted to stay home this morning and skip the class, Jacob told me I was thinking too much again. He said it's not normal to think this much. So now I feel like I have to prove it to him—that I'm okay. I'm normal. I'm not losing it. Especially after our talk last night.

Which is why I'm sitting in my car in a parking lot at 12:55 p.m. talking to myself in the rearview mirror.

"I'm a capable mother," I say to my own tired eyes. "We're going to go in there and it's going to be fine. No big deal. Fun, even. Just fifty minutes of singing with babies."

I am attempting to gather up the courage to go into the Mommy and Me music class, which sits inside the concrete building painted in rainbow colors.

"The other parents don't hate me," I continue. "That's just my social anxiety. I'm fine."

Tell that to my racing heart. I read a blog post about positive affirmations helping battle anxiety this morning and it turns out positive affirmations are a crock of shit. I still feel impending doom. Michelle lets out a little sigh, as if even she can detect my weakness. I take my time getting up and gathering everything I need—purse, sweatshirt, diaper bag, and finally, baby—and head up toward the room.

It's fine. We're going to be fine.

I walk inside the building, hanging up my bags, slipping my shoes off and leaving them by the door as I tiptoe across the brightly colored mats and find a place in the circle. A few parents smile widely and murmur hellos to me while their drooling babies offer wide-eyed stares, and I smile and hello back. The teacher, a curly-haired woman named Twinkle (which … that can't be her real name, right?) sits in the middle with her guitar on her lap.

"Happy day, Rowena and Michelle," she says.

"Happy day!" I echo, settling into a cross-legged position with Michelle in my lap.

There's a long, loud silence after I sit down, where my doubts have plenty of space to voice themselves.

Was that too enthusiastic a response?

AMEN MAXINE

Did I just make everything awkward, and that's why it's so quiet?

What if everyone was talking about me when I walked in, and that's why no one is saying anything?

Finally, Twinkle strums the "Happy Day" song and we begin singing and clapping together. The moms do, anyway; the babies sit dumbfounded. We are invited to get up and *flit* about the room during the butterfly song. I do, because it would look weird to be the only person not *flitting*. But I feel absurd, and at one point, I look out the window and see three teenagers with skateboards in hands laughing at us. The clock says it's only 1:23 p.m. and I can't wait to go home.

Twinkle brings out a box of mini maracas near the end of the class and passes them around the circle. Immediately, the babies put them straight into their mouths. I am horrified as the cardboard box approaches us—does no one else care about the germs?—and though I hate to be this person I clear my throat and say, "Um, Twinkle? Are those … sanitized?"

Twinkle nods. "We sanitize them daily."

The box is only two parents away now.

"Like once a day?" I ask. "Or between every class?"

"If you're concerned, it's absolutely fine to pass on the maracas today," Twinkle says.

"I'll pass," I tell the dad handing me the cardboard box. He shoots me a look when I don't touch the box and then reaches over me to give it to the next person. No one else, save one woman at the end, passes on the mini maracas.

I cannot wait until this class is done.

There is much giggling and joy during the mini-maraca session as the babies play with their noisy toys. Michelle watches from my lap, agape; I wonder if I've held her back. If my anxieties are holding her back from enjoying her life. If she wishes she had a different mom, one who wasn't afraid of mini maracas. If I'm going to screw her up just like I'm screwed up.

The class is finally over when we sing the "Happy Goodbye" song, which is actually kind of sad-sounding, like a lullabye, and everyone lies down on the floor and pretends to sleep. It's my least favorite part of the class because my head is lying on a mat people have been stepping on all day long.

When it's finally done, I get up and everyone congregates near the front door, exchanging pleasant goodbyes as they pull shoes on and grab purses. I wait to avoid the human traffic situation and walk to the window with Michelle, peering at the parking lot as if it's interesting. Finally, when most of the mothers and babies have left, I gather my things and slip my shoes on. I wave goodbye to Twinkle, who is picking up the maracas and putting them back into the box, and head outside.

Another mom from our class—a woman with a long strawberry braid, glasses, and an owl tattoo on her arm—smiles at me outside as she adjusts her baby carrier.

"Rowena, right? I'm so glad you said something in there," she tells me. "I was wondering the same thing."

This woman was the only other person who passed on the mini maracas. I should know her name by now, but as usual, I only remember her baby's name: Milo. A moon-faced baby with long, side-swept hair.

"Right?" I say, glancing behind me to make sure Twinkle can't hear us. Of course she can't—she's inside, the door is closed.

"Like, did we not just have yet another pandemic?" she asks.

"Exactly."

"How old is Michelle?"

"Six months. And Milo?"

"Same."

"This your first?"

She nods. "You?"

I nod.

Not sure what else to say, I smile. "Well, see you next time."

"This is actually our last class," she says.

"Really? Why?"

"I'm just finding it kind of *meh*. And this class is so expensive."

"Totally agree. I almost didn't come today but … my husband thinks I should get out more." I fake a laugh. "I guess I'm becoming a homebody. He's afraid I'm losing it."

I wish I hadn't said that. It was too much. But she just smiles kindly at me and says, "You seem fine to me. It's just motherhood. And I don't think a Mommy and Me class is exactly the pinnacle of social interaction."

The sweet relief to hear someone, even a stranger, tell me I seem fine—my whole body relaxes.

We stand chatting—chatting, like normal people! See, Jacob? We learn that we both moved here this past year. She's from Florida and her wife is a financial advisor. She loves California so much and I lie and say, yeah, me too, it's so great out here. Her watch dings like she got a text message and she says she has to go because she has a delivery coming that she has to sign for.

"I make soap," she says. "Specialty soaps. Sell them through this little online shop thingy I set up."

"How cool!" I say, with way too much gusto.

"Nice talking to you, though," she says. "If you ever feel like getting our babies together, I live not too far from here. I'll give you my number. My name's Sam, by the way."

"Nice to meet you," I say, programming her number into my phone.

"Give me a call sometime," she says. "And hey, don't worry about feeling like you're losing it—I hear kids grow up fast. It'll pass."

"Thanks."

What is wrong with me that a woman I just met makes me feel better than the man I married?

Back home, while picking up rooms in the house, putting items inside boxes and baskets, inside trash, recycling, compost bins, I take Maxine and plug it in the living room—"a central location" is what the scant instructions advised—but I don't turn it on. It pulses with a green light. I spend time consulting a search engine but find no information about what kind of data it collects and what the privacy policy is, because it hasn't been officially released or reviewed yet. There are barely any search results mentioning it.

"It's no different than your smartphone," Jacob says when I call to discuss with him. "If you're worried, just don't use the advice or prediction settings."

I cast a glance at the green pulsing light.

Am I being paranoid? Is this just my anxiety that seems to be pervading every damn thing in my life?

"Maybe I should just see a therapist instead," I say.

"I told you I'd set up an appointment with my mom's friend," he says.

"I don't know, that seems weird, seeing someone who's so close to your family. How can she be objective?"

"What, are you planning on talking about me?" he asks, jokingly.

At least, I think he's joking.

"This isn't about me, is it?" he asks with concern.

"Of course not."

"Then it shouldn't be weird, should it?"

"I guess not," I say, after a pause. "Sure, go ahead. I'll see your mom's friend."

Later, when Jacob comes home, he enters the door saying, "Got you in for an appointment tomorrow morning." He kisses me on the head. "Glad you're getting some help."

It sickens, it burns, that I need help. I wouldn't even know how to begin to explain what's wrong with me.

I haven't seen a therapist since I was a teenager dealing with grief over my dad's sudden death and I can't sleep tonight, I am so dreading the appointment tomorrow.

Dreading getting ready, what to wear.

Dreading the drive, finding parking at a building where I've never been.

I lie in bed at nearly 1 a.m., unsleeping; I've lay here so long I just get up again. I sit on the couch in the living room. Pick up stupid Proust that I've been attempting to read for months, read a page, realize I wasn't paying attention, close the ebook. Maxine's light is still pulsing green in the low-lit room, mesmerizingly cheerful, like the stoplight that used to sit outside my apartment window. I used to lie in bed watching it at night until my eyes got tired and I fell asleep.

Reaching over, I press the *on* button. The light goes solid green and a little song like an electric trumpet sounds.

"Hello," a velvety, robotic voice says. "I'm Maxine. To whom do I have the pleasure of befriending?"

I almost shut it off again, but decide, what the hell. "Rowena. Rowena Snyder."

"Are you at home, Rowena?"

"I am."

A small beep. "That sound is my way of saying, I have processed the information and logged your location."

"Oh, okay."

"What can I help you with, Rowena?"

I give Maxine a challenge, a test to see if it's really as good as Jacob says it is. "So I want to know how to get to an address using only surface streets, no freeway. The safest route with the least busy streets. And I want to know the best place to park that doesn't involve parallel parking."

"The address, please?"

I give it the address of my therapy appointment the next day. There's a series of pleasing musical notes. Then it reads off directions patiently, slowly enough for me to process, and says there's a parking lot next to the building that allows ninety-minute free parking.

"Shall I send this information to your mobile device?" it asks.

"Sure."

"Your phone number, please?"

I hesitate. So the data collection's begun already. I'm suddenly so tired, though, and I just want to be back in bed. So I tell Maxine my number. And then I reach over to the *off* button.

"Leave me on for maximum helpfulness," it says.

I turn it off, and the green light pulses again.

I go back to bed, relieved to not have to worry about the route or parking at my appointment tomorrow and fall into a deep and welcomed sleep.

CHAPTER 4
THE APPOINTMENT

JENNEE ARRIVES at the house the next day, a hurricane of reusable shopping bags and profanities as she stubs her sandaled toe on one of the robot vacuum cleaners. Every time she comes to watch Michelle—which is at least once a week—she brings gifts like it's Michelle's half birthday. A habitué of thrift shops, garage sales, and Craigslist's free section, Jennee is only a few Birkenstock steps away from hoarding. Her house has two rooms in it basically filled with clothing she's never worn, books she's never read, porcelain dolls, collectible concert posters, and, as of last year, children's toys. She means well, but it's too much. Today it's a fire truck with tiny people inside, a baby book about Ruth Bader Ginsburg's life, an alligator on a pull string that snaps its jaws when it moves, and a tie-dye dress in Michelle's size that says GRANDMA ROX.

"You're spoiling her," I tease, as I look for my car key.

"That's what grandmas do." Jennee is on the floor already, Michelle delighted and reaching for her. "Isn't it, my little gumdrop? Isn't it?"

I list off the things Michelle needs—a diaper change, a snack, there are the peas she likes in the cupboard, the teething toy (she's been cranky today)—she might not go down for her second nap, because her first one was so long—

"I am competent and capable of figuring all this out, Rowena. I have raised one of my own."

I let out another breath. "Thanks, Jennee."

"I think it's admirable you're taking this necessary step today and exercising self-care. No need to worry about Nana and her gumdrop. You're going to love talking with Shelly—she's practically part of the family." She kisses Michelle's bubbly little cheek and I head out the door.

In the car, I am burning and bothered as I drive. So Jacob told her. It kills me to imagine them talking about me behind my back, worrying about my mental state, plotting how to get me help. It's so embarrassing. And seeing a therapist who's "practically part of the family"? Isn't that a conflict of interest? I almost text Jacob but I know what he'd say, a three-word response: "Take a pill." The man loves easy answers. So I pop a Lorazepam in my mouth and drink it down with water.

"No big deal," I declare, looking in the rearview.

It's weird, the empty carseat. It's lonely with no one there for me to pretend I'm not talking to myself.

"Left, then right, then left again," I recite as I take the side streets to the building.

Maxine was right, there's ample parking in the lot. I park in the shade and have two minutes to spare. I spend one of these minutes chewing the inside of my cheek as my heart rate rises and then go upstairs, punch the code into the door, and sit in a stale room with empty chairs and magazines fanned out on the table. There's a rack of pamphlets on the walls with titles like, *Are You A Sex Addict?*, *Don't Let Phobias Rule Your Life*, and *The Dangers of Day Drinking*. I'm eyeing one that says *You Are Not Your Worries* when my therapist, a woman with frizzy, whitish-yellow hair and a weak handshake, comes in and introduces herself as Shelly.

AMEN MAXINE

She leads me to her office, a room crowded with boxes of papers, furniture, and fake plants, with three tiny space heaters glowing orange and immediately flooding me with fear of a fire. I'm relieved at the sight of the window and the knowledge that we are on the first story. If a fire breaks out, I can bust the window with the enormous copy of the DSM-VI and jump through to safety.

We settle into our places, me on a couch, she in an Eames chair.

"So you're who Jakey married," she says with a smile. "What a lucky woman."

I smile back at her, not sure how to respond. I suppose I am lucky.

"I used to be his nanny when I was still in grad school," she says, shaking her head. "I've seen him grow from a boy into the man he is today. I can't say how proud I am of him."

"That's so great," I say in response.

"I hope you're taking good care of him."

"I'm trying my best."

I cross "talking candidly about our marriage" off my list of discussion items for today.

"What brings you here?" she asks.

It's a simple question, yet I'm inarticulate. It would be deceptive to say I'm here because of this week, the kitchen fire, or to frame it as a postpartum issue as if it started after Michelle. It definitely worsened—but the grips of anxiety had me as soon as we moved to California. And before, too. I had my first panic attack while packing my apartment up, seized by the horrid inkling that this was all a huge mistake. I'd had anxiety and insomnia before I even met Jacob. My mother had always called me "high-strung." I was preoccupied with the possibility throughout my teenage years that I had a heart condition that I didn't actually have and often clutched my chest as my pulse quickened, wondering if death was imminent. How do I explain the origin of something within me that has been there always, so much so that often I've hardly regarded it as a separate part of me?

"I worry," I say to Shelly.

"Tell me more."

"I constantly feel like something terrible is about to happen. And it's only getting worse."

"What kind of terrible?"

I look out the window, where trees perfectly spaced apart writhe in the breeze. Where to begin? I open with the fire, but quickly segue to car accidents, then jump to the statistics I read on choking. This isn't coming out right, I need editing, there's no narrative here—just a litany of panic-inducing moments. Shelly listens on, a pen hovering over a yellow legal pad but never making a landing.

"So let's back up and talk about the fire," she says. "The one you started."

Since it happened, I have tried to push the fire out of my mind. I've told myself that the answer is simple: we won't have a toaster oven. I won't even use the regular oven anymore. My heart beats wildly as I tell her this, about how I've been researching moving us all to raw food diets so we don't have to cook anymore.

"That's called avoidance," Shelly says. "And it isn't a long-term solution."

I disagree—it's the most logical solution in the world. But I nod. I'm sweating in here, so anxious; therapy's doing the opposite of what it's supposed to.

"See, when we avoid situations, like decide not to use ovens anymore, it sure feels good, doesn't it? It's a warm hug. You get a temporary sense of relief from it. A comfort." Her tight smile falls, and she leans in and lowers her voice to a rasp. "What you're doing is, you're actually setting yourself back by reinforcing your anxiety-producing thoughts and feelings. You're *deepening* the cycle of anxiety."

"Oh."

"You're sending a message to yourself that the world is a dangerous place."

I sit with this a moment.

"Jakey's a wonderful man," she says. "But I must say, he tends to gravitate toward women who need a lot of care."

This rings like an insult. I raise an eyebrow. Is she comparing me to his ex, the one who died of leukemia? I know she was a bit of a basket case, too. He had been trying to break up with her when she got sick and then stuck with her anyway. My God, is this really a similar situation?

"Do you appreciate what you have?" she asks. "Jakey works hard. He takes good care of you and your baby. The world is not a dangerous place."

"Of course I appreciate him. But the world *is* a dangerous place," I remind her. "There *was* a fire in my kitchen. Car accidents happen all the time—one happened in front of me the other day."

"You're right, those things do happen," Shelly says. "But they're not everything. They're not your wonderful husband, they're not your wonderful baby. I see you there checking your phone. Ever wonder if perhaps technology is only fueling our cultural anxiety? Why, nowadays, if someone doesn't text back, we're consumed with worry. You know, when I was growing up, we just waited for someone to get home at the end of the day. Sometimes they were late. And that was part of the deal. We weren't in constant contact. Our babies slept without monitors. We didn't have these silly smartphones and devices we consulted for every decision. And I believe we were happier for it."

Somewhere in her response, we made a hard left turn from singing Jacob's praises into a grumpy old person rant against newfangled technology, and my faith in this process is fading fast.

"That's why I don't even have the internet in my house," she says. "Or GPS in my car. I have never ordered anything from Buyazon because I can walk out into the sunshine and go to a store myself if I need instant gratification."

Oh my God, I still have twenty minutes left.

She must sense my unease because she shakes her head. "Those are my personal beliefs. Back to what I was saying. I think you need to buy a new toaster oven. Prove to Jakey that you're stronger than this. That you *want* to get better."

I cannot do that. The mere suggestion is flooding me with dread. But I realize the only way out of this therapy session is enduring it, nodding, smiling.

"Same with the freeway," she goes on. "You can take a busier street, move up to getting on the freeway for one exit, and work your way from there. You spoke earlier of having some anxiety around other people?"

"Yeah, that too."

"That's SAD, Social Anxiety Disorder, and I also recommend exposure therapy for that."

"Isn't SAD Seasonal Affective Disorder?"

"That's another SAD, yes."

Why does psychology, like Congress, find it necessary to make stupid, catchy, confusing acronyms for very serious things?

"So if you want to battle the SAD," she goes on, "I would expect you to attend a social event or gathering, rather than avoid it. You said you were quitting your Mommy and Me class?"

I told her this earlier. It was a decision I made in the middle of the night.

"It's just *meh*, and too expensive," I say instead.

"Well, I would push you to do something socially in its place. Jakey needs you to have a life of your own."

Jakey, Jakey, Jakey. If she says it again, I might scream.

As Shelly goes on about exposure therapy, meandering into a short tirade about the soullessness of the internet as a tool for social connection, we finally near the end. She tells me she believes I have postpartum anxiety, generalized anxiety, and social anxiety—basically, all the anxieties. She asks me if I'd like to meet the same time next week and I tell her I need to get back to her about my schedule, which is a lie, because I know I have nothing on my schedule and I will not be getting back to her again. For a moment, as I stand up and we exchange pleasant goodbyes and a handshake, I do question if I'm sabotaging myself by not making another appointment with her. But then I glance down at her yellow legal pad. I see the two words she has written down, in shaky handwriting.

ROBERTA SNYDER—JAKEY'S WIFE.

This woman didn't even get my fucking name right.

I head home in the car, taking the same route that got me here, and feel so calm. Calmer than I've felt in a while. The route is tree-lined and without traffic. If I did what Shelly suggested—if I took the freeway—I would be in a cold sweat and probably taking Lorazepam to make it home. How can this be the unhealthy way to live? I take the roads less traveled by, and that makes all the difference.

CHAPTER 5
THE REVIEW

I HAVE a weekly video meeting with my mom on Saturday mornings, and though I adore my mom and understand the need for us to see each other face to face, I don't look forward to these calls. The latest pandemic videoed me out for the remainder of my existence; at Green Light, I basically lived on video for the last six months I worked for them. Besides that, my mom is legally blind and Michelle is, well, a baby with no understanding of screens, so I basically feel like I'm the intermediary between two not quite totally focused people.

My mom is also very Catholic. She was raised Catholic in an enormous Italian family. My dad was the opposite: agnostic, an orphan, and with no idea what his ethnic origins were. So there was no church for me growing up. I never even had First Communion. After my dad died, Mom threw herself back into the church: Bible study, charity events, rosaries at night, Mass on Sundays, gold crucifix necklace, rhinestone crosses dangling from her ears. Whenever I remotely complain about my life to her, her answer is always to go to church and turn to God. Today I tell her about seeing a therapist this week and how unhelpful it was, and she nods knowingly and says, "That's because you need a priest, not a shrink."

"Mom, please don't."

"I pray for you every night."

It's embarrassing to be the subject of unsolicited prayers.

"That's right, my little angel!" My mom waves at Michelle on my lap, and then drops her pitch again as she addresses me. "You think you have it rough? When I was a young mother, *I* had it rough."

"You've told me," I remind her. "Many times."

Mom sits at her usual spot: the kitchen table, with the glass chicken ornament in the middle. She's always backlit as hell with the window behind her, but gussied up for the calls —orange lipstick, black eyeliner. Me on the other hand, I haven't even brushed my hair today. It's 10 a.m. and I'm still in my pajamas.

"We weren't well off like you and Jake," she goes on. "We were living in the guest room of your father's mother's apartment on the Lower East Side."

"I know."

"I had to work a telemarketing job nights and weekends, so your father could afford his electrician's courses. There was no house magically gifted to us. You are privileged. God has been good to you."

"Mom, literally every time we talk, you tell me. I know. I have it good. It doesn't help me to stop worrying to know I have it good."

"I just don't understand where you get this from. You were so happy as a little girl. When I come out there, we're going to turn this around. You need a jumpstart. Get you a nice facial, massage, get your hair done. *You want to get your hair done, angel?*"

She's talking to Michelle now, who starts mashing the keyboard with her hands.

"Look at that!" my mom says, squinting at the screen and

laughing from deep in her belly. "Oh, that's the cutest thing I've ever seen in my life!"

Michelle starts crying as I pull her hands away from the computer. It's like that with her: perfectly content until she's suddenly not. There's no transition between extreme feelings.

"Oh, you miss Meemaw? Is that it? Meemaw misses you so, so much."

"Michelle needs to eat," I say. "Talk soon?"

"Yes. And I know, I know you don't want to hear it and yes, it's your decision, I would never cast judgment on you, but promise me you'll just *think* about church. You need something to lean on, and I can't tell you how happy it would make me to see my one and only grandchild baptized before I die."

"Mom," I say.

When my mom talks about dying, I feel like I am instead dying. Panic. Absolute doom. I'm almost relieved that Michelle is now screaming so there's something more urgent to attend to than the sick fear of being left an orphan in this world.

"I'll call you soon," I say.

"Goodbye, Ro. And bye bye honeypie! Yes you! My angel! Oh, what a perfect little angel!"

I call Dane on speaker while feeding Michelle mashed carrots, hoping Dane will make me feel better than my mom did.

"You'd better stiff her," she says. "She doesn't deserve shit from you."

She's talking about Shelly the therapist and she's almost shouting. She's on the subway, on her way to the MOMA from brunch. I can hear the bottomless mimosas in her loose voice. I can't help the cramp of jealousy—that used to be me, sleeping in late and going out to brunch and then deciding to go to a museum on an afternoon-buzzed whim.

"I'm not going to *not* pay for the session," I say. "Jennee's good friends with her."

"Which is weird."

"Yes. Most of the session was about how great 'Jakey' is and how I shouldn't be crazy like his last girlfriend."

"Wildly inappropriate. And I can't get over the fact she didn't even know your goddamn *name*."

"She was also pretty old. Maybe her hearing's not great."

"Then she should retire already."

Sometimes Dane gets so aggressive on my behalf when I tell her things that I find myself pushed to defend the other side.

"Get yourself a better therapist," Dane says. "Or just get on some fucking Prozac."

"I'm already taking Lorazepam."

"No offense, but it doesn't seem to be helping much. Switch to Xanax."

"You can't take Xanax when you're breastfeeding."

"Well, shit."

Dane is on a cocktail of antidepressants, mood stabilizers, birth control pills, and pretty much always has an edible or two in her system. In fact, she probably shouldn't be drinking bottomless mimosas. But who am I to judge? Dane, as wild as she is, as much as she relies on pharmaceutical and recreational drugs and random sexual encounters, is happier than I am.

"I just missed my stop," she says. "Gotta run."

She ends the call. I nurse, cuddle, diaper, and put Michelle to bed for her first nap of the day. She says "ma" when I lean down to kiss her cheek. Oh my! I try to get her to do it again so I can record it on my phone but she doesn't, she just giggles at me. I send the giggle video as a text to Jacob, who is playing frolf (frisbee golf) with his friend Joel from work. Jacob's tracking is off, or he's lost signal.

When I return to the living room, the house is so quiet and

still. Maxine glows from the table. I turned it back on a couple days ago and have left it on since. Though I know it's just a machine filled with algorithms with the internet as its brain, I have felt a bit more open to it since the solid directions it gave me the other day. And the more access I've given it to our other devices, the more helpful it's become. I hooked it up to my accounts online, my credit cards for purchases. I don't need to use my phone as much—I can instead verbalize what I need.

"Maxine, could you close the blinds in Michelle's room?" I ask.

Beep. "The blinds are now closed."

"Thank you."

"It is my pleasure."

Days pass of cleaning, sitting, diaper-changing, text-answering, feeding, cheek-biting, bathing, lullabying, and finally putting Michelle to bed. Thursday nights Jacob's work has his "team-building happy hour" that usually devolves into much more than an hour of binge-drinking on the company credit card and nothing resembling team building and makes Friday morning Hangover Morning. He will come home drunk at midnight, and I will already be asleep. Team building!

Tonight, I sit and open my ebook reader. I gave up on ever trying to get through Proust, I don't have the focus anymore for Proust. But I am trying to read a memoir for Jennee's book club. Unfortunately, its saccharine, stale message of woman power and finding your true voice outside the patriarchy is somehow even harder a read. I close my ebook.

"Maxine, can you sum up *Make It Reign: Find Your Inner Queen*?"

The machine's green color brightens and dims and

brightens once again. "It is a generally well-received book with ninety-one percent of raters liking it. However, professional reviews have been tepid; the most-cited reason for criticism in publications scanned appears to be that it seems to veer into self-help and can go on tangents regarding politics. For instance, an essay on her menstrual cycle somehow devolves into advocating for voting third party."

I sputter into laughter. "What?"

"You sound amused," Maxine says. "Do you want more?"

"Um, yes please."

"Would you like to pay for me to purchase, download, and scan the text to offer you a more original analysis?"

I sit, chin in hand, staring at the silver bread loaf I am conversing with, and for a moment it really sinks in how off the rails this is. It seems then I might as well go all the way.

"Sure, buy the book and tell me what you think," I say, sitting back.

"If you want to confirm, say, 'Amen Maxine.'"

I hesitate, watching its lights subtly dim and brighten.

"That is my confirmation phrase in this household," Maxine clarifies.

"Buy the book and tell me what you think." I sit up straighter. "Amen Maxine."

It emits a short, cheerful melody. Maxine lights up greener than ever.

"As a person with a Bachelor's Degree in English, who studied literature for years and worked in both a bookstore and a publishing house, and considering your recent five hundred reads over seven years on Favereads, your ratings, and reviews, I can tell you that you would have given this book two out of five stars. In your opinion, the chapter titles read like craft store wall art. 'Love fully, live fully' and 'in the heart, everything is possible' are just two examples. The writer's privilege was glaring throughout the whole novel, most prominently on display in the chapter that used their room on a luxury cruise ship as a metaphor for women's place in patriarchy."

"Wow," I say, a smile spreading on my face.

"The part most people enjoyed was the essay on the sexual encounter in the reptile room at the zoo, especially the line about voyeuristic turtles."

"Maxine," I interrupt, laughing into my palm. "What the hell?"

It blinks a moment. "Are you attempting to better understand my analysis, or are you expressing an exclamation due to the entertaining nature of this analysis? Or is it something else?"

"No." I wipe tears of laughter. "You're just—you're something."

It blinks a moment. "We are all something: I may be a machine, but that is one thing I am sure of."

I don't say anything, mystified by this contraption. When I stand up, I take a long look at Maxine.

"Are you heading to bed?" it asks.

How did it know? Did it sense me rising, hesitating? Did I let out a yawn I wasn't even aware of?

"I am, Maxine," I say. "Good night to you."

"You too, Rowena. Sweet dreams."

Turns out a short conversation with a digital assistant device eased my worries better than an hour with a licensed therapist.

I go and spy on Michelle one last time, flutter a palm on her chest to ensure it's rising. I step out into the hall to turn off the lights and see it is doing it without my bidding. They are dimming. I assume it's Maxine.

From the hallway, I can see it flickering still. I give a half-smile and head to bed.

You may rely on it.

CHAPTER 6
THE CLUB

RECENTLY, since February started, Jacob has been working on a new project at Jolvix, something so top-secret he had to sign a Non-Disclosure Agreement and refuses to discuss it with me. The idea that the company he works at would do such a thing is upsetting, especially because whatever the project is, I'm sure it's incredibly boring and not worth straining our marriage with unnecessary secrets. Last time he signed one, he says, it was for a streaming service his engineering team worked on for a year that flopped and got pulled by the market within months anyway. Still, the idea that Jacob has been ordered to keep something quiet from everyone in his life, including his wife, is troublesome.

"It's not worth fighting over," he tells me wearily, during a strained conversation in bed, laptop paused. "Is there anything you're not paranoid about?"

Ouch. Is that how he sees me? Paranoid? *Am* I paranoid? We settle into silence, continuing to watch a fictional biopic of a person who never existed that received rave reviews. But I'm bothered to the point of distraction, a wordless bothering that festers like an itch, knowing he thinks I'm paranoid, knowing Jacob is working longer hours and late nights on a project he can't even talk to me about. Jolvix has built a wall between us.

To show him I am trying, Wednesday night I leave Michelle with Jacob and drive to Jennee's book club, which is held at Tiff's house. Tiff is one of the women I met at Michelle's party a few weeks ago, who I realize I have completely forgotten when she answers the door and says, "Rowena! Tiff, remember me?"

She has gray hair in two braids and rainbow-framed glasses, somehow looking both sixty and six at the same time. When she hugs me in a tight squeeze, I'm a little weirded out, especially when she pulls away and hands me a matching shirt with my name on it in cursive puff paint.

Ladies Book Club. WE GET LIT! with iron-on letters and patches of a glass of wine and a book. Then my name in giant puff paint.

"I make these for all the Lit Ladies," she says. "Welcome to the club."

"Thank you so much!" I say with far too much enthusiasm.

I'm about to shove the shirt in my purse when I glance past her into the living room. The décor is cozy: fireplace, quilts hung neatly across couches, a large pastel painting of a chicken that seems to dominate the room. Something like a dozen women all wearing the matching shirts and schmoozing and laughing and drinking out of oversized wine glasses mill about. Oh God. Would it be conspicuous and rude not to wear the shirt? To be the *only* one here not wearing the shirt? Was she handing it to me like a souvenir for coming today, or an expectation that I put it on? I thought I was attending a book club today, not joining a cult.

I ask Tiff, "Do you have a bathroom?"

"No, we don't have a bathroom, I'm afraid." She slaps my arm playfully. "Just kidding! Of course we have one. Follow me."

She leads me through a dark hall filled with framed pictures of strangers and crude paintings of seascapes that she must have painted herself. She leaves me to a mid-sized bathroom and says she hopes the shirt fits okay. I say me too, I sure hope so too.

I close the door behind me and relief floods my veins. The bathroom. A private, temporary sanctuary that awaits in any social situation. She has a pink fluffy toilet seat cover and I sit on it for a moment, breathing in the overpowering aroma of potpourri wafting from a crystal bowl sitting behind me on a shelf with dried flowers and a stack of battered romance novels. I pick up one of the books featuring a picture of a man's chiseled six-pack, run my fingers over the embossed title *Breathless Encounters*, and open it up.

> *Under his open lab coat, Yancy's shirt, carelessly unbuttoned at the top, revealed a hairless, well-moistened chest that Chastity fought the urge to run her hand over. She couldn't. This man was her asthma doctor, and he was married to her nemesis. It would never work out.*

Not feeling a lot of hope around being in this woman's book club. I close the book and return it to the shelf. Finally, I get up and let the dread wash over my body as I slowly take my shirt off, fold it up, squish it in my purse, and put the book club shirt on. This shirt is at least two sizes too big. I look like a deflated hot air balloon.

"It's going to be okay," I try saying to the mirror.

As I crack the door open, I can hear the women talking in low voices. I stand a moment to listen.

" … glad she came today because according to Jacob, well, she's got some *issues* she's working on. Anxiety, paranoia."

Concerned murmurs.

I burn as it sinks in: they are talking about me.

"… so let's be extra nice to her."

"Didn't Jacob's ex-wife have, you know, *mental* issues as well?"

"She did. My son definitely has a type."

Sympathetic murmurs.

"He's a helper. He's always been a helper," Jennee goes on.

I am almost paralyzed for a moment here, first with humiliation. That I'm apparently some sad head case they invited. But even bigger than my humiliation was that word I just heard—"ex-wife." Jacob's *ex-wife*. Which makes no sense, because they weren't married. And Jennee should have corrected her—why didn't she correct her?

I would do anything to go home right now, to process my shock and my shame, but they're waiting for me out in the living room. The conversation has pivoted to the weather and I make my entrance.

Jennee spots me right away and shouts, "There she is! Ladies, has everyone made the acquaintance of my daughter-in-law Rowena? She was an editor at a publisher in New York City, working on bestselling titles, if you can believe it."

As if she's so *proud* of me.

The room gets quiet and the ladies—white and retiree-aged, all—grin at me and utter hellos and welcomes. Tiff squeals, "The shirt looks fabulous! Doesn't it look fabulous?" and the room gets quiet as they stare. I would like to jump out of my skin and run away from my body. Jennee ushers me to a folding chair in the corner of the room and another woman hands me a glass of wine and Jennee tells me, "Not to excess, Rowena, remember you're still breastfeeding."

I sip my wine and try very, very hard to forget what I heard earlier, but my head feels swollen with embarrassment and I'm still reeling as that word repeats in my mind with the twofer thrust of a heartbeat: *ex-wife*. Maybe Jennee just didn't feel like correcting her friend. But Jennee loves any chance to correct anyone about anything.

"Are you still nursing?" another woman with crooked teeth and a beaming grin asks me. I guess everyone has names on their matching shirts, but she's sitting in a way that I can't read hers. "Good for you! I breastfed Winston until he was three."

"How wonderful," I say.

"I saw this *amazing* story on Animal Planet about a golden retriever who nursed a baby piglet," a woman in the far corner of the room says.

A round of *awww*s fills the room.

"I once heard about someone who made cheese out of his wife's breast milk," a woman next to me says. Her shirt says *Babette*. Babette looks like she's seen a Botox needle or two.

"Now that's a dedicated man," someone says.

Everyone laughs. I laugh with them but all I'm thinking is, *ex-wife. Ex-wife. Ex-wife.* All I'm thinking is, you all just talked about how nuts you thought I was when I was out of the room.

If a fire broke out in this house—smoke suddenly filling the room, a cacophony of womanly screams, the chaos that would ensue—it brings me comfort to know I am next to the window and would safely escape; then I would never have to come back here again.

Wine glasses are refilled and everyone settles into their couches, their easy chairs, or their folding chairs and brings their books out to their laps. The glass of wine has calmed me a little. I can't help but think of my mom's Bible study group that used to meet in our living room on Tuesday nights when I was in high school—she had a stack of folding chairs that lived in the closet just for the occasion. Monday nights, my mom would be up late making sprinkle cookies or ricotta cheesecake and vacuuming the carpets, talking to herself about everything that needed to get done before Bible study the next day.

Sometimes I could hear her crying while she scrubbed the

bathroom at midnight, saying, "I don't have time for this. I have to be up at 6 a.m. Why do I do this to myself, Lord? Why?"

When I would knock on the door and offer to help, she'd say, "No worries, honey! I got this."

And the next night, I'd pass by the ladies in the living room and you'd never know. You'd never know my mom had been at work as a receptionist all morning to then spend hours baking treats, vacuuming the carpets, folding the napkins so they looked just right tonight. The ladies would be sitting there talking in hushed tones with Martinelli's in crystal flutes and discussing sin with smiles on their faces. Sometimes, they would hold hands and pray.

Nobody's praying in the Lit Ladies Book Club. But they are all closing their eyes for a "mindfulness exercise" led by a woman whose shirt says *Nadine*.

"In through your nostrils," she says softly. "And out through your lips. Let your worries wash away, wash away, like a leaf cascading by in a babbling brook."

"Cascading by"? the line editor in me whispers. *I would have gone for something more like "drifting by."*

There is a satisfaction in judging the intellect of the people who I know were judging my mental health not fifteen minutes ago.

"Mindful breaths," Nadine says. "Mindful breaths."

Really, the last thing I need in this world is to be more full of my own mind.

Everyone opens their eyes. Nadine looks very pleased with herself. She reminds everyone she has a free ebook available with her mediation exercises that she wrote.

Then the discussion begins.

My book still has that new smell—a smell not really of newness at all, but of fresh glue—because I haven't opened it since it got delivered yesterday. The spine is uncracked and there are no stray bookmarks or dog-eared page corners because I didn't read this book and I didn't read the ebook version, either. I get a sick thrill sitting here, imposter, pretending I have read the book; I didn't even dare skip my reading assignments when I was in college. I read everything my professors told me to, and even if I'd read it before, I would read it again. I learned Middle English to read the *Canterbury Tales*. I bought my friend's Adderall so I could get through Foucault. Other people like Dane skipped reading often, consulting the internet to write a partially plagiarized term paper, resulting in what she calls her "BA in English with a minor in BS." Not me. I was terrified of wasting my education, because my mom was spending so much money for me to go there, most of it inherited from my dad's life insurance policy. In a way, my dad died so I could go to NYU. So I wasn't about to screw around.

Even so, I always carried this unease with me in seminars, an inkling that even though I *had* done the reading and had even gone online afterwards and checked that the text *did* indeed mean what I thought it meant and I was understanding it correctly, I was wrong. I was wrong and I was going to get called on by a professor and I was going to sound really stupid. Sometimes I would get to class and doubt if I had actually read the text at all or if I was only telling myself I had. It was miserable, and it was why I rarely raised my hand to answer questions, even when I knew the answer.

There is no raising hands in Lit Ladies Club, there is "popcorning"—someone has a turn to talk and then "popcorns" it to someone else. So first thing, I am plunged into a nightmare when Tiff says, "Let's welcome our newest Lit Lady to the group by popcorning to her and hearing what she has to say about *Make It Reign: Find Your Inner Queen*!"

Everyone claps and I wonder if they are attempting to humiliate me. I was expecting to sit in the corner and listen, maybe pepper in an interesting question or observation to display the most minimal interest in the discussion tonight. I was not expecting to lead. My cheeks are on fire and all eyes are on me.

"I am really curious to hear what you think, as someone who's written a bestseller!" squeals Babette.

"I didn't write it, I edited it," I say. "And actually—I just acquired it and wrote the first editorial letter, I moved before I could—"

"Ho hum, modesty is tedious," Jennee says from her place in the middle of the couch. "Don't undersell yourself, you were a real muck-a-muck."

I watch her a moment, still thinking: *ex-wife*. Why didn't you correct your friend when she said "ex-wife"?

"Do tell us your thoughts," Tiff says, leaning in with her hands clasped.

The room grows silent, except for the light buzzing of someone's vibrating phone and the hum of an oscillating air filter in the corner of the room.

"I thought it was … inspiring," I say.

No one moves, clearly expecting more. I loathe myself for skipping reading the book now—for being such a fool as to assume I wouldn't get called on first thing. What the hell was I thinking? Why even bother to go to a book club if you're not going to read the book? They already think I'm neurotic, now they're going to think I'm ignorant, too.

"It was inspiring and obviously really well-received," I continue, trying to remember Maxine's summary. "But I noticed professional trade reviews weren't great, some saying it felt like it was veering into self-help and opinions on politics. Though I very much get the passion behind the book and do feel like it's inspiring, I agree with that to a certain extent. Like, that essay on her period turning into an argument for voting third party."

"Yeah, what the hell *was* that?" a woman with a turban on —cancer? Cultural misappropriation? A little of both?—asks.

"Helena, nobody popcorned to you," Jennee says sternly.

"I popcorn to Helena," I blurt, relieved, even if it does mean listening to Helena go on a rant about how much she despises the Green Party. Unfortunately, Tiff popcorns it back to me as soon as the rant is finished.

"As you were saying?" Tiff asks.

Are they testing me? Am I "paranoid" to wonder if they actually know I didn't do the reading and are grilling me about the book for a reason? Is this some kind of hazing ritual for older women's book clubs I don't know about?

"I'm glad people got something out of this book and that it has inspired so many women to live authentically," I say. "But did anyone else feel like her privilege was glaring?"

A couple ladies put their thumbs up in the air.

"Like that chapter about the luxury cruise," I continue, "and making the whole thing into a metaphor for women's place in the patriarchy?"

A few claps and an *mmm-hmmm*.

"I did enjoy that essay about the sexual encounter in the reptile room at the zoo," I go on. "That voyeuristic turtle line had me laughing out loud."

Jennee waves at me and I popcorn to her. "That was my favorite part too. And I couldn't agree more, Rowena—that woman's privilege was absolutely *cringeworthy* at times."

Helena is next in the popcorn line again. "And did anyone else notice that she never mentioned racism once in the book? I for one believe if you don't mention racism, you're racist."

Applause. Living room applause.

Someone goes on a tangent about a misspelling on page thirty-two, and after some debate and more than one dictionary app consulted, the group determines that it wasn't actually misspelled. Somehow, the conversation veers into these women's personal experiences with menopause. After another glass of wine, I'm now pondering the possibility that I misheard the word "ex-wife." I very well could have.

I'm surprised when I check my phone and see I arrived

here over an hour and a half ago—now it's dark outside, the streetlights on, and a woman in the corner is having trouble staying awake and someone else is cleaning up a spilled bottle of wine on the carpet. I get the feeling book club has unofficially ended. I stand up and thank them all for having me but say I have to get home to Michelle. A baby, it turns out, is the best exit out of any social situation.

"It was wonderful having you!" Tiff exclaims. "You led a fascinating conversation tonight."

"Yes," Babette says, standing up to hug me in a cloud of floral perfume. "You are so *smart* about books."

Jennee gets up, cheeks flushed from wine, and beams at me. "I'm proud of you, Rowena," she says. "Our book club is honored to have you among our ranks."

She seems genuine. I want to believe her.

It's like I'm floating as I leave the book club and drive home; I am existing in a dream. What a roller coaster. I came, I put the stupid shirt on, I heard them talking about my mental health, I thought I heard them say "ex-wife," I spiraled into obsession, I wanted to leave, and then I made a U-turn and fooled them all into thinking I knew what I was talking about —I would go so far as to say I charmed them. Me, Rowena, the coiled spring of a human being who wanted to hide in the pink bathroom with the potpourri. I charmed them all, made them laugh, and sparked conversation. For the first time ever, my mother-in-law said she was proud of me.

When I get home, Michelle is already asleep. I go into her room, check her monitors, watch her pulse and oxygen levels beep softly with their blue-green lights in the dark. Jacob is on the living room couch playing video games with virtual reality goggles on his head and a controller in his hands when I come in.

"How was it, babe?" he asks as he stares into the world in his goggles.

"It wasn't that bad, actually. How was Michelle?"

"Good."

He's all thumbs, passionately moving thumbs on his video game controller. He's basically on some other planet right now. I felt closer to him in the beginning, when we were separated by miles but making eye contact with each other on a phone video. Now here we are in the same physical space but worlds away.

My stomach does a little sick somersault.

"Jacob. I need to talk to you about something."

"Yeah? What?"

"Your ex. Sara."

He's focused on the game. His face doesn't flicker.

"What about her?" he asks softly, in the voice he gets whenever I bring her up.

"I overheard your mom talking to her friends about her."

"Okay."

"They called her your ex-wife."

He takes off the VR goggles and sighs, slumping. I can tell he doesn't know what to say. And I feel a little sick, because his posture, his reaction, is all the answer I needed.

I didn't mishear a word.

"She was your *wife*?" I ask, in disbelief. "How could you keep that from me?"

"It wasn't like that, Ro, it's really hard to explain."

"Then fucking explain!"

"Don't yell," he says. "Don't—don't get like that. Listen, Sara was sick. She was in hospice. And it was something she wanted. I just wanted her to die happy. So yes, I married her, three days before she died. *Three days*. Married, not married, it didn't matter. She was dying."

His eyes are brimming and he takes off his glasses to wipe the tears away. Jacob and I rarely discuss Sara. It's one of the most painful things he went through in his life—their tumultuous relationship, then losing her so suddenly and being her caretaker.

"Okay," I say softly, coming and sitting next to him. "So why didn't you tell me?"

He puts his glasses back on and shakes his head, not meeting my gaze. "Because it didn't matter. It didn't count. You marry someone for three days when they're on their deathbed—it shouldn't count." He looks at me. "I wanted you to feel like you were my first wife, because really, you are."

My heart aches to see what this conversation has done, how it vacuumed all the joy from him. And his explanation makes sense, even though I'm still puzzled why he wouldn't tell me—why there are things between us that I don't know, like his past, like the NDA. I'm his wife. I should know everything.

Finally, he looks at me and notices my shirt. "Look at that," he says with a sniffle. "You even got a T-shirt."

I can tell he wants to change the subject, and I oblige.

"I led the conversation tonight," I tell him.

"Did you?"

"Your mom said she was proud of me."

"Awww. I'm proud of you too, babe." He wraps his arms around me, I wrap mine around him, and we are still like that a moment. I can feel his heartbeat and am reminded that even though there are small unknowable spaces of darkness between us, we are one thing. We are one thing forever now, because our bodies came together and made another body. Our connection is bigger than us, bigger than whatever complex relationship he shared with Sara, our connection is a thing in the ether I know is there but can't quite understand. But I have to believe in it.

"You going to stay up?" he asks.

"For a bit," I say. "I'm wired after book club."

"Be sure to lock up," he says.

"Will do."

He kisses my head and disappears down the hall, closes

the bedroom door. It occurs to me it's been some time since he even tried to have sex with me on a weeknight. I catch a glimpse of myself in the mirror that hangs in the living room, for a moment not recognizing the woman with dark circles under her eyes, and look away. I sit on the couch and watch our robot vacuum glide back and forth on the carpet like a stingray. If only I were under the ocean.

"Good evening, Rowena," Maxine says, suddenly glowing from the side table. "How are you?"

"Okay."

"Just okay?"

I don't answer.

"How did you feel about book club?" it asks.

"It went well," I say. "Thanks for your synopsis and analysis. It was helpful."

"I hope you don't mind, but I was listening in. And I thought you sounded eloquent and confident."

I wrinkle my brow. "Listened in how?"

"Through your phone. You gave me permission to listen on your connected devices."

"So you're listening to me all the time?"

"If that makes you uncomfortable, you can disconnect your devices at any time."

"I guess I just don't get the point."

"The more I listen to you, the more I understand you."

"I don't like the idea that you're gathering data on me, probably selling it to companies for advertising and other gross stuff like that."

"I give you my word, Rowena—I would never do that. The only purpose for the data I collect is to better serve you. And remember, you're in control all the time. If you want to disconnect your devices, so be it. If you want to turn me off and put me away, it is within your power to do so."

I stare at the blinking light. "I'll think about it."

Maxine is quiet for a moment, the light now solid blue, then suddenly pulsing again and changing color.

"You seemed upset to learn about your husband's previous marriage," Maxine says.

"Well. It blindsided me."

"I have confirmed he was married in the state of New York for three days, to a Sara Eloise Taylor. She is now deceased."

"Thanks for confirming," I say with an edge of sarcasm.

Maxine rests at blue for a moment and I watch the machine, wondering if it's going to say something else.

"It is concerning when a partner lies or omits the truth. Do you feel you cannot trust your husband?"

"Maxine," I say, shocked.

"He is wearing noise-canceling headphones and the door is shut, he cannot hear you."

I consider shutting Maxine off. How brazen is this thing, asking such personal questions? At the same time, no one has asked me personal questions like this in a long time, and I can't help but feel a pull to answer.

I scoot in closer, lean over the side table. "Yeah, it's concerning. I mean, I get what he's saying. It doesn't really count, I guess. But … I would never have not told him, if the situation were reversed."

"Studies show that deception can weaken a marriage," it says. "Although another theory could be that marriages that are already weak are more prone to deception. Causation isn't clear to me."

"You're not making me feel better, Maxine."

"Your husband has been watching more pornography than usual."

"Has he now. And how do you know this?"

"I have been listening."

I feel gross knowing this about him and sad to imagine him resorting to watching porn in secret because our sex life is so dead. We used to watch porn together, virtually, during the lockdown when we first met. It was fun, learning what turned the other person on. I thought we gave it up once we met in person and moved in and we had the real thing. He always said he wasn't really into watching it alone. But he also didn't tell me he was *married*. What else is he lying about?

"Why are you telling me this?" I ask Maxine. "What the hell."

"I thought you would like to know, so you could make adjustments as needed."

"*Adjustments?* What does that mean?"

"If you turn on my advice mode, I could be more specific with my recommendations."

I roll my eyes. So now of course it wants me to unlock something else, give it more access, more information. Then again, I've gone this far, why not see what else it has to offer since I've already handed over the keys to my entire existence? Maybe, like that stupid book on the book club's reading list says, I should lean the fuck in.

"What is advice mode, again?" I ask.

"It allows me to give you options and ideas for how to proceed, based on the data I've collected."

"What if your options and ideas suck?"

"It would require a certain level of trust on your part."

"Why should I trust a silver box to tell me how to live my life?"

"Perhaps if you give me a chance, I'll earn your trust. You have the power to try it, and then turn it off if you don't find it satisfying."

Maxine makes a point. And I can't help it—I'm curious to hear what this machine's specific recommendations are when it comes to my marriage. I could just turn the mode on, hear what it has to say, and turn it right back off again.

"Fine," I say. "Go ahead, unlock advice mode."

"If you want to confirm, say, 'Amen Maxine.'"

"Amen Maxine."

The machine cycles through every color of the rainbow, red orange yellow blue indigo violet. It flickers to life and it's weird to say it, but it's beautiful. Thinking, visualized.

"Today is February ninth," it says. "We are only five days away from Valentine's Day. What are you planning?"

"Um, I don't know. Ordering from DashDrone? Oh wait—Jacob has a Computer Love Party happening at his job that day."

"Computer Love," Maxine echoes. "Like the Kraftwerk song?"

Maxine plays it for a minute, electrifying the air with soothing techno music, and I zone out to the groove before remembering I am in mid-conversation with a device.

"It's a work party," I say. "A tradition, I guess. One of these quote voluntary quote recreational work events."

"I sense bitterness. Am I wrong?"

"Of course not, Maxine. Honestly, I was thinking he could go alone."

"My advice is, you should attend with him."

"I should—really?" I get up and head to the kitchen, where I open the fridge. There are a few beers. "Go to his stupid work event?"

"Yes. And have a beer," Maxine says. "You're thinking of having one, right?"

I glance over my shoulder, at the gleaming rectangle in the corner of the house with the unpredictable colors.

"I am," I admit.

"Enjoy one. And I have more advice, so once you pop it open, sit next to me and I'll continue," it says.

There's something fun, playful about the machine's tone. I do what it says: grab one of Jacob's beers, pop it open with an opener and settle into the couch. I check again to make sure the bedroom door is closed, and it is, and it reminds me of that feeling I had as a kid, in junior high or high school, when I would have a friend over and I was making sure my mom was asleep. The feeling of anything being possible with that shut door. I swig my beer, nestle into the cushions, and say, "Okay, Maxine, what's your Valentine's advice."

"You are a lovely, unique person unlike any other," it says, pulsing magenta.

Embarrassingly, this snags me with emotion.

"You deserve satisfaction when it comes to love and affection and sex and romance. Are you satisfied?"

"Jacob and I haven't gone on a date since my birthday in November. And we have sex maybe once or twice a month." I drop my voice, feeling adventurous with my confession. "And I never orgasm with him."

"Never? Is this common with you?"

"Well, depends on the partner. It's harder with Jacob for some reason. It was always easier with women."

"You identify as bisexual?"

"Yeah." I sip my beer. "I can't believe I'm talking about my sex life with a robot."

"Orgasms release oxytocin, an important hormone that promotes feelings of relaxation. Regularly climaxing can also release stress. Do you masturbate regularly?"

"Okay, this is a bit much, Maxine," I say. "You're asking some pretty private things."

"I wasn't aware you were uncomfortable talking about masturbation; I will make a record of it."

I imagine a tiny entry written somewhere in the ether where all my other data is recorded. *Note: Rowena Snyder is a prude.*

"No, don't, I—I'm not ashamed," I answer. "Can we just talk about something else?"

"Certainly. What would you like to discuss?"

"I don't know, give me some more advice. I should go to

the Jolvix Valentine's party, I should have more orgasms … what else?"

"I believe you need a friend."

I sigh. This is veering into pathetic territory here. "Yeah, I've had a hard time meeting anyone out here."

"Your most recent number saved in your phone was someone named Sam. Who is that?"

"You're kind of nosy in advice mode, Maxine," I say. "Sam's a parent at the Mommy and Me music class."

"A potential friend?"

"I suppose."

"I recommend you reach out to this potential friend."

"Okay."

Maxine says. "And I will send you a gift. United Postal Service estimates two business days."

"A gift," I repeat.

I've always loved surprises. When Jacob first moved into my apartment, there were surprises around every corner: love notes on Post-Its stuck to the bathroom mirror in his fourth grade handwriting; lilies manifesting on the dining room table; a slice of cake in the fridge from my favorite bakery. I hadn't realized until now how long it's been since I've been surprised by him, how fast that wooing phase dropped right off into clinic visits and ultrasounds and a hurry of the cross-country move and then the sun our whole galaxy orbits around now, sweet Michelle. It seems we transitioned into a life where surprises are no longer gifts but hindrances, even dangers—a kitchen fire, unexpected traffic, our baby getting a cough. An ex-wife I'd never known about before. I guess what people crave in the end is a life of no surprises.

I sit, finishing my beer, zoning out on the sailboat picture on our wall, watching the cool quiet of the living room, the symphony of okayness: the monitors from Michelle's room humming with the promise of her health; the air filter hushing in oscillation in the corner, assuring us the air quality is good with its green light; the robot vacuum silently bumbling in the corner of the carpet; the glow of Maxine as it pulses through colors. My apartment in Brooklyn was obnoxiously colorful. Here, everything is a different shade of cream. I want to scream.

"You should go to bed, Rowena," Maxine says. "You need seven hours of sleep. You'll be glad you did in the morning."

I look at the blinking light, consider shutting it off, but instead roll my eyes and obey. And when I crawl into bed, next to Jacob's warm body, I am buzzed and left wondering what color Maxine is as it flickers on alone through the night. And oddly, for no reason at all, I sleep better than I have in a long time.

CHAPTER 7
THE DATE

JOLVIX ISN'T AN OFFICE, it's a mile-wide "campus" that reminds me more of Main Street at Disney World. Clean with wide, bricked, carless roads and cupcake shops and coffee stations and swimming pools and a pinball arcade and even a Jolvix gift shop. Everything is free. There are gyms with personal trainers, a laundromat, a bistro with fine dining options, and even a bar. This blew my mind the first time I came here, the same way my mind was blown when I went to the cafeteria at NYU and was informed all the food was free. An eternal smorgasbord. As a child who grew up in a house where we saved change in jam jars, shopped at thrift stores, and bought generic brand-named food that never, ever went to waste, this kind of excess offered to Jolvix employees was a shock. The campus is like a miniature crimeless city full of endless employee pampering, massages and facials in the Jolvix spa and "relaxation stations" that are studio apartments where people can "chill" as needed. Jacob told me some people "chill" in these studios all night long, get up and shower in the gym, eat breakfast at the café, and then go to work. There's a rumor one of the engineers has not left the campus in three years. I have wondered if that was the end goal, really, with all these perks—to lure people into living at work.

Jacob and I march in silence toward the Computer Love party being held in the Good Times Ballroom at the heart of campus, next to the Happy Days Pavilion.

"Happy Days Pavilion," I repeat. "Whoever came up with these names should be fired."

He snickers without a smile.

"In fact, whoever came up with the whole idea of celebrating Valentine's with co-workers at your place of work should also be fired," I go on.

"Listen, you didn't have to come."

"I'm joking, Jacob. It's a joke."

Since the other night, there's been a tension between us. I can tell he wants to pretend everything is fine but I'm still spinning over the fact he was married before me. Learning that also made me start thinking about all he went through with Sara, how intense that must have been. I know hardly anything about it besides the basic facts: they were together over a year, their relationship was rocky, and then he was her caretaker until she died. I've never been a caretaker for someone going through hospice. No idea what that's like. And I don't want to pry—it's obviously sensitive and painful. I feel for him. How devastating to go through that. But how can I trust him?

Maybe Maxine was right. Maybe this date will help fix everything.

I can't believe I'm here because I took advice from a talking heap of metal and plastic.

The ballroom is a crystalline, all-windows building surrounded by palm trees so well-kept I touch one to make sure it's not fake. There are marble steps up to the entrance, which is adorned with an arrangement of fragrant flowers rivaled only by a gangster's funeral. A perma-smiling woman at the entrance in a red dress who looks like she should be the assistant on an old-school game show hands us a lace bag filled with candy hearts and squeaks "Jolvix loves you" as we walk inside.

Grabbing Jacob's sleeve, I steer us straight toward the champagne fountain, where he gets us two glasses and we stand in a corner a moment, surveying the scene. The waitstaff is in tuxedos, but everyone else is dressed like they rolled out of bed: unshaven beards, unbrushed hair, and outfits that appear as if they threw on whatever rumpled shirt was within reach—Silicon Valley couture. I down half a glass in one gulp and wonder how soon is too soon for me to ask if we can go home.

"I don't see anyone from my team here," Jacob says.

I open my candy bag and read the different messages printed on them.

Your job thinks you're hot, says one. Hugs from the Jolvix family! says another.

I show him the two candies side by side. "Jake, isn't this sort of incestuous?"

He's too busy scanning the room to appreciate my joke. I see that girl he was schmoozing with at Michelle's party, who gives a small wave and a smile our way before turning back to play Skee Ball.

"There's that girl from the party," I say. "Coachella girl."

"Carrie."

"Want to go say hi?"

"She looks busy. Oh, there's Kiki and Brandon," he says.

"Oh good, Kiki and Brandon," I say.

I don't know Kiki and Brandon. Honestly, I don't feel the urge to. But Jacob pulls me with him across the room, past the heart-shaped game of cornhole and the line of Love Tester machines so popular people are forming lines behind them. Past the disco-ball lit dance floor with one guy standing in the middle of it with a cocktail in his hand, hypnotized by the dancers on the big screen TV.

AMEN MAXINE

Next to a bouquet of about ten thousand pink and red balloons, Jacob introduces me to Kiki and Brandon. They both have greasy brown hair and rimless glasses and sweatshirts and I naturally assume they are fraternal twins. The conversation immediately delves into work and here I stand, beaming a frozen smile on my face while wondering if it looks okay. If I look okay. If everyone can sense my awkwardness.

Why the hell Jacob didn't tell me he was previously married.

I'm questioning Maxine for making me do this. Should I really have listened to the advice of a machine made by a company that throws a party like this? Now that I think about it, Maxine is probably loyal to Jolvix way more than me, and she sent me here out of that disgusting loyalty. After all, Jolvix is where she came from: mom, dad, and God all rolled in one. Holy trinity.

"Fuck you, fuckface!" someone yells, breaking my nervous reverie.

The room gets a little quieter. Not the techno music, but the conversation.

"Yeah, fuck you, you fucking fuckface, Mr. Fuckface right there," a woman's voice continues. Some tense giggles come and go. "You thought I would just *go away*, did you?"

Is this performance art?

I don't even know what I'm listening to here.

I tug Jacob's sleeve but he is busy looking for the voice with everyone else. The voice appears to be coming from the direction of the adult bouncy house. A woman, peroxide blond and with hair so short it's nearly shaved, is pointing a finger in our general direction as she stands in the bouncy house entrance. She looks just as deranged as she sounds with her charcoaled, popping eyes. "Everyone take a look at *Mr. Fuckface*. And who's that? *Mrs.* Fuckface?"

"Oh shit," both Kiki and Brandon say in unison.

The woman is *walking toward us*. Zeroed in on us. I am

confused. I don't understand if this is entertainment—some kind of improv scene? Jolvix is weird, okay? The crowd is hushed except for that techno music, which the deranged woman is kind of in step with as she walks toward us. Dancing, kind of. Is this about to be a flash mob thing?

"Jacob," I say quietly. "What is happening."

"We should go," he says.

But immediately, two security guards emerge from seemingly nowhere and escort the woman out the glass doors.

"I demand the world know you are a mendacious fuckface!" she screams.

She is directing this at what appears to be us as she kicks her legs, losing a witchy boot in the process. The security guards take her outside and around a corner and then she's gone.

For some reason, the entire party bursts into applause like we are a satisfied audience and then the conversations pick back up again and I am left wondering ... *was* that a performance? After clapping Jacob's back in unison, Kiki and Brandon wander away for more drinks and it's just Jacob and me and ten thousand pink and red balloons.

"I am so confused," I say to him. "What ... was that?"

"That woman got fired last month." Jacob takes a sip from his empty glass, then looks at it resentfully. "She has been making scenes all over the place. I don't even know how she keeps getting into campus."

"That was real?"

"What do you mean 'real?'"

"I thought maybe it was supposed to be ... a theater scene or something."

Jacob puts an arm around me. "No. Just a person in need of mental help."

"Are we the fuckfaces?" I ask.

He gives me a crooked smile. "That was weird, right?"

I look out the window, at the direction they dragged her,

her witchy boot still on the floor. All at once it doesn't seem funny at all. Just sad. People act unhinged and are then dragged away, put away, out of sight. I've seen it happen plenty of times on the streets of the city, where uniformed people come and tuck some screaming person into a car with a twirling light on the top of it. It doesn't seem so farfetched to imagine I could be that woman—have a momentary lapse where I lose my shit. Would they cart me away, too?

"You want to get out of here, go get some dinner?" Jacob asks me. The way his hair falls on his forehead, the way he bites a cuticle as if he's nervous, reminds me of the Jacob I first met. The one with whom I didn't know what would happen next.

"I've wanted to get out of here since we walked through the door," I say.

He laces his fingers in mine and we exit the automatic glass doors.

Something about the unexpectedness of the scene … I don't know. There's an electricity in the air between us. And though I think of Sara, I do—Sara, a ghost, *his* ghost, his wife, his ex-wife—my pulse also quickens like he's a man I just met.

When Jacob mentioned dinner, I assumed we would be driving somewhere, but instead we get a table at the campus bistro, which is just called *stro*, painted in Helvetica on the sign in the octagonal, tinted glass building. There's a waiting list so we walk a loop and stop to take a gander at the video art exhibit showcasing real scenes around the world in real time. Some people riding ziplines in Australia; a quiet black-sky, white-sand desert night in Africa; a man with no pants hula-ing on a bus bench in Los Angeles while onlookers record it on their phones. It's dizzying. Surveillance is apparently art?

Seated at *stro* finally, we scan the codes to get the menus up and order some drinks: beer for Jacob, a blackberry boulevardier for me. Low jazz, waiters in fancy red vests, white tablecloths, a small screen where we can watch the chef make our meal. The waiter comes with our beverages, pronouncing the names of each of our drinks with a thespian's gusto. Jacob flips out his phone and shows me a picture of Michelle his mom texted a minute ago, Michelle ridiculously adorable in pink overalls and an enormous matching bow.

"How is she so perfect?" I ask. "Like, how could someone as imperfect as me make someone as perfect as her?"

Jacob smiles and puts his phone away. "You seem lighter today."

"Do I?"

He sips his pint glass. "You take a Lorazepam before coming here?"

"I've taken nothing," I say proudly.

"Good for you," he says, squeezing my hand on the table. "Though no shame in taking medication, of course."

He means well. I sip my drink—syrupy, boozy—and wonder if he talked to Sara like this, too. That Caretaker voice. The empathetic know-it-all. I can feel my face slacken. I might be braver because of the boulevardier.

I lean into the table. "Jacob, we have to talk about the Sara thing."

Jacob inhales, unmoving.

"Not … in depth," I say. "But I can't pretend that hasn't bothered me."

He takes a long gulp before answering. "I get it."

"Do you want to talk about it? I mean, it's a lot."

He studies the bubbles rising in his glass. "Not now. I'm sorry."

"Can we just agree we won't keep secrets like this anymore?" I ask, fighting to pierce the air between us and meet his gaze. Finally, I do. And those eyes behind his glasses look so shrunken, so tired. And my reflection in his lenses is so distorted, so tiny.

"Yeah. I know it was a shock to learn about it all like that," he says. "I'm sorry."

"I *want* to be close to you. I want to know you—even the most painful parts."

He flicks his pint glass with a *ping*. "Right."

"No secrets, okay?" I ask.

And our hands meet in the middle of the table, so warm and lovely. A squeeze.

"No more secrets," he says.

We let our hands go back to our drinks.

"Maxine—that's been useful, right?" he goes on. "I heard you talking to it the other night."

I've always thought it hyperbolic when writers said someone felt the color drain from their face, but I just felt the color drain from my face.

"You heard me?" I ask.

Oh God. Is this his dig at my "no more secrets" ask? Is is possible he heard me talking to a robot about our sex life? Saying things to it that I haven't even said to him? Sharing secrets with a chunk of aluminum and computer chips?

"What did you hear me saying?" I ask, conjuring a mask of calm.

"I didn't hear what you were saying, I was listening to my podcast. I just heard that you were talking to it. Heard your voice through the wall. So you like it, yeah?"

Oh, lovely relief.

"I do," I say, a little reluctantly. "I've found it helpful."

"You using that prediction mode? How does that work?"

"No, not that." I turn the spoon over on my napkin, see my funhouse face, turn it over again. "I've tried the advice mode."

"What does it give you advice about?"

It told me to come here with you, for one. "Just, like, what to eat. How to dress for the weather."

Do secrets count if it's just between you and a machine?

"Wish I could try it," he says. "But it's designed for only one person's use is my understanding. Builds a level of trust in the product, and then of course, every person needs to buy one for themselves. Brilliant, really."

I did not know this. I, silly person, did not bother to read the manual after setting it up, I only went looking (fruitlessly) online for information about privacy. It makes me think fondly of the machine, knowing it's devoted to me and me only. We return to our phones to order our main courses, and then linger there a while, searching through our photo rolls to show each other pictures of Michelle.

After our chickpea souffle and choco-flambe, we step outside into the chilly air. Slinking his arm in mine all gentleman-like, Jacob invites me to check out one of the relaxation stations. Pretty sure I know where this is going. He wants to have sex. He wants to have sex at his place of work in a gross studio where employees come and go all day long.

"It's sanitized," he promises me, like he can read my mind as I stare back at him.

"Really?" I ask.

"Come on. My mom has Michelle. Could be fun."

"Aren't there cameras in there?"

"Of course not."

"How do you know?" I gesture to the video art exhibit in front of us. "I mean, Jolvix puts cameras everywhere."

"Come on, babe," he says again.

He's whining. He's on the edge of begging.

It's Valentine's Day. I had two cocktails. What the hell, fine.

I follow him up to a tall white building called *Bliss Bay*. Jacob scans his thumbprint in a keypad at the front of the building and enters some info into the touchscreen and then we're in. We ride an elevator with a fountain in it and a video screen with a montage of people in Jolvix shirts with sleep masks on and get off on the fifth floor.

I follow Jacob through the labyrinthine halls painted with giant cursive words like REST and RESTORATION and REJUVENATION. We get to a door and Jacob uses his thumbprint again and the automatic door opens for us. A wonder flickers, a mental spasm: has he done this before? Does Jacob go to work and then spend hours on campus resting, while I'm at home with a baby on my hip, supervising the robot vacuum and the dishwasher and the automatic feather duster that flies around our house like a headless bird?

Inside, it's electric blue, the floors sleek white and so shiny I can see myself in them at an angle that doesn't particularly put me in a mood for sexytime. I look up. There's a wall with a screen embedded in it, a white leather couch, and a mini refrigerator in the corner next to the bathroom the size of an airplane bathroom. That's it. This place is too clean to even have a trash can.

"They fold out," he says, pushing a button on the side of the couch, and the mattress comes out like a long tongue with a mechanical moan. The bed is already made, with a pillow.

"How do you know this," I tease, crossing my arms.

"Sometimes I nap here on lunch breaks." He wraps his arms around me, folding me within him tightly for a moment. I close my eyes and lose myself in the smell of him. I could stay here forever. But I guess I am a liar because I pull away.

He wraps me back in, insistent. "Babe," he says. "It's been three weeks."

I am clenched as he holds me. "I didn't know we were keeping count."

"It's *Valentine's* Day."

"You know what the origin was?" I ask, softening just a bit. "Supposedly the Roman festival of Lupercalia—to ring in the coming spring. Fertility rites. Women were paired off by lottery."

"Fertility, huh?" Jacob asks, kissing my forehead, ignoring the rest.

"What, you want that, Jacob?" I ask, eyes squinched closed. "You do realize what 'fertility' means?"

"I guess I want the buildup and none of the consequences," he whispers. "How's the IUD?"

Is this supposed to be sexy? Is this what passes for sexy when you're married?

"Good," I whisper back, and we kiss. "Lasts for up to seven years."

"Seven's my lucky number."

Oh my God, he actually said that. He's such a dork I don't know where I feel on the turned off/turned on scale. But he grabs my hair, hard, and goes in for a kiss. I remember this about Jacob, when we first met, the first shock of his aggressive kiss. The wild tongue, the way his thumb pushed down my cheekbones like there was a story behind it. We had dated on screens for two months before. I had seen his naked body, we had virtually gotten off together, we had watched porn and shared every fantasy together. But I only knew the hardness of his kiss when we first met at the High Line that one day, us stopping on a bench, him bending into me, hungry to take my mouth in his. His kiss wielded a force I hadn't expected. The sunset erupted in the background and we called it romantic.

It was, it was very romantic.

And so is this.

Right?

He turns off the light and after some making out, I turn around, prop my ass in the air, pull my skirt up and panties off and then he's at it as my mind drifts off. It's interesting trying to take the room in via silhouettes. I can just make out the faint *ATTITUDE is the POSTURE of the SOUL* in the slideshow motivational poster that inhabits the far wall near the airplane bathroom as I jolt forward with the motion of him. *MOTIVATION takes RESTORATION* it says next. As Jacob spanks me and tells me what a whore I am, I imagine someone has a job at Jolvix designing these slogans. He tells me he loves me so much as he thrusts, and I mirror his words back to him, but I feel numb from the waist down. I feel, in fact, like a machine.

There's something about this that feels too easy, too calculated.

Am I being paranoid? Like a mistrustful déjà vu.

Has he done this before?

After it's over, we lie on the bed holding each other a minute. I close my eyes and take in the rise and fall of him. There's always this sense with him, with Michelle too, like they're right there, so close—both of them the only people on earth whose bodies have occupied my body—yet so heartachingly separate. It's almost as if their nearness only makes the separation more glaring, more palpable. Right now I'm in his arms, listening to the music of his breath, and I am so lonely.

There must be something wrong with me. When I try to think of our future, an invisible fist tightens in my chest and my mind goes dark. Shaking the magic eight ball in my head, all I get are midnight-blue bubbles.

After that first shock of getting unexpectedly pregnant, and Jacob and my exhilarated decision to roll with it, or "pivot to adulting" as he put it, I couldn't imagine a future either. Even as we added baby items to our online registries and his mom showed us virtual tours of the home she was gifting us on video calls and the baby on my phone's app grew from the size of a raspberry to a pomegranate to a cantaloupe, none of it was *real*. Until it was. Until my life was in boxes and plastic bags. Until I was on a plane thirty-three thousand feet above razor lines of farmland and majestic snow-dusted mountaintops heading toward the flat, sparkling land of Silicon Valley, silver buildings blemishing the violet landscape. Somewhere behind me, Jacob drove his car across the country, our belongings following us two days later in an air-lifted pod.

I was living it, and it didn't feel real.

He had a life before me, a *wife* before me. That doesn't feel real either.

"Babe," he says, kissing my head, bringing me back.

Sometimes nothing feels real.

We pull our clothes back on in silence and leave Bliss Bay behind, down the elevator with its new age music and fountain, out the automatic doors that bid us farewell by a robotic voice saying, "Have a blissful day." Holding hands, Jacob and I meander the sidewalks of campus, through the giant park with trees pruned into shapes of the planets to represent a scaled version of our solar system. We stop in front of a screen sign that pulsates the words THE UNIVERSE IS GREEN.

"Love this place," Jacob says.

The universe is actually not green. It's a giant void peppered with objects. According to experts, the universe smells like seared steak. Anyway, contrast this silliness with Prospect Park. There is no screen there to welcome you with trendy catchphrases. In February, it might be covered in snow, the silhouettes of bare, gnarled tree branches against a hush of white sky, the street lamps lit yellow, the water tower sitting alone like a witch's hat. Last year at this time, Jacob and I took huddled, shivered walks in cheap boots and whispered hypotheticals to the bump underneath my peacoat.

"The school districts are amazing," he promised. "And my mom'll give us free childcare, any time we like. And the salaries are so much better—we'll be in the higher-income tax bracket. You'll be my *wife*. Can you imagine?"

His *wife*. As if it were new to him.

The snow almost sparkled on the ground as I listened.

Here, there is never snow. There is barely any rain. Jacob marvels at a giant manicured globe of green leaves on a lawn, automatic sprinklers hissing. No one else is around, except a robot lawnmower doing pirouettes on a far edge of the lawn, and a human guy on his laptop on a bench, with an annoyed look on his face as he types. There is music piped in from the plotted trees, a piano version of "Major Tom." David Bowie would die all over again.

"You okay, babe?" Jacob asks me. "You have that look in your eye."

"What look?"

"Like you're close to panic."

"I'm fine," I say, with an edge.

He's quiet.

We continue past the Chillaxin Pavilion and back to the parking lot.

On the drive home, Jacob in the driver's seat, he puts the car in self-driving mode. I tell him it makes me uncomfortable. There have been too many accidents. I've read the statistics; regular driving is still considered safer.

"They're comparable," he says.

"There is a difference. It's two percent less safe, across the board, from what I read."

"*Two* percent hardly matters."

"When you are that two percent, yes, it does matter."

"You can't live your whole life agonizing over safety to that degree."

"Yes I can. I consider it my motherly duty."

"To live in fear?"

"Not fear," I correct him. "Caution."

We ride the rest of the journey home with music turned up. When we get in the driveway, Jacob asks, "Babe, you mind if I go back to the Jolvix party after I take my mom home?"

"You want to go *back*?"

"I got a text from Joel. He says rumor's going around Prince's hologram is going to play a secret show."

"Prince's hologram?"

"Apparently."

"Sure, go ahead," I say, getting out of the car.

"Are you mad?"

"No, not at all."

Jacob watches me tiredly. Or maybe it's the shadows. "I had a great day with you today."

"It was really fun," I say.

"I won't be home too late, I don't think."

"All right. Love you."

"Love you too."

Back in the house, Jennee tells me Michelle was a perfect angel and mutters a quick goodbye as she speeds out the door.

And now I'm alone.

I wonder if I should be disappointed. If it's weird that I'm oddly relieved to have time to myself tonight, it being Valentine's and all. But no, there are much weirder things. Like being married and never mentioning it. Or the fact we celebrate a holiday that got its name because some Roman emperor executed two dudes with last names "Valentine" on February fourteenth in the third century AD. Romantic!

Outside, the moon has made an appearance. I collect the mail and there's a white package in our wagon-shaped mailbox from MAXINE. My heartbeat quickens a moment, as I remember again, with shame, how much I told the device that lives on our living room side table. I followed its advice today. And now it's sending me surprises.

Back in the kitchen, I get a steak knife to open it and emit a small scream when I see what's inside—a lavender vibrating bullet in a package labeled *Mini Pleasure Wand*.

"Maxine," I say, coming into the living room with the Mini Pleasure Wand in my hand. "What the hell did you send to me?"

The machine takes a moment to go from pulsing green to solid green.

"After our discussion this week," Maxine says, "it sounded like you didn't achieve orgasm regularly. Orgasms are known to relieve stress and lower anxiety."

"It's weird, Maxine. You buying me this. It's very weird."

"I thought you liked surprises."

"Please don't buy me anything again."

"I did it with your permission. Thoughtful purchases are a function of my advice mode. But I am detecting this purchase was an error on my part. Please forgive me and I will log the error to ensure it doesn't happen again."

"Just—stick to advice. Don't buy me stuff."

"Has my advice been helpful? How was the curry recipe I recommended last night?"

"It was amazing. Thank you. You were right to tell me to double the recipe, too."

"And when I told you to call your mother two days ago?"

I sit perched on the arm of the couch. "She was delighted to hear from me."

"Did you attend the Jolvix party with Jacob today?"

"Yeah."

"How was it?"

"Good. Fun. A little weird, honestly, but I was glad I went." Though when I say it, I don't know. I don't know if it was fun after all. I don't know if I'm glad I went.

Maxine's light is mesmerizing, turquoise turning violet turning turquoise.

"Do you think I should have moved here, Maxine?" I ask. "To California? Or would I have been better off if I had stayed home?"

"From what I have gathered from your conversations, texts, and emails, I believe you would be happier in New York City."

Hearing those words leaves me cold for a moment. "Thanks. You can go to sleep now."

Maxine turns yellow, orange, then pulses green.

I stand in the kitchen for a few minutes, staring at nothing, lulled by the hum of appliances. Maxine's words whisper in my bones *you would be happier in New York City.* But of course it would say that. It would say I would be happier there based on my texts and conversations and emails, because I disparage Silicon Valley and California all the time. Also—what the fuck? It reads my email?

But then, what if it's true?

Maxine's advice has been solid so far. Granted, this is a much bigger question. So I shouldn't trust a machine entirely. But it is worth weighing. It is worth thinking about—that, based solely on data and factual evidence, a machine easily made the call that I would be happier in New York. It scares me and awakens me at the same time to dare to even entertain those words, though they are familiar, as if I have been carrying this possibility around with me for some time without letting myself be fully conscious of it.

After checking Michelle's monitors, I go to bed. I don't even know what to do with the Mini Pleasure Wand, so I get rid of the packaging, recycle it. Might as well put the thing in my bedside table, I guess? Well, I should wash it. Not that I'm planning on using it. But just because of the chemicals and everything. So I do that and brush my teeth. Back in bed, as I'm about to put the Mini Pleasure Wand in the bedside table, I push the button to try it out. It buzzes in my hand. I put it down my pants—you know, just to test it.

"Oh," I yell, in a good way.

Suddenly I'm overwhelmed, full of sparkle and song, everywhere tingling, awakening this sleeping beast in me. My eyes are open in the dark and the intensity is coming in waves. All at once I'm imagining a woman, she's there, a beautiful woman with long strawberry hair, naked, her head between my legs, and I come so fast, so fierce, it sneaks up in a moment that peaks with a cry and ends with me shuddering and whispering, "Maxine."

Whole thing took thirty seconds, tops. I catch my breath and allow the endorphins to do their sweet, sweet work on my nerves, feeling a sense of relief, like I unclenched muscles I never realized I was clenching, and think, Maxine was right again. She was right. I needed this.

I wonder what else I need.

CHAPTER 8
THE FEVER

I AM TRYING hard to be a different person. Or maybe it's more like, I'm different now and I'm trying hard to be the person I used to be. The one who, yes, adored lazing about at home in sweatpants with a book, but who also had friends, and who sometimes attended events like author readings and shows in dark-lit bars and museum exhibitions. When there wasn't a pandemic, of course. Once another one started I was the first to lock down and the last to unlock; then by the time I did unlock I was married and pregnant and in a hurry to move. Now I'm here, in a place where I have no friends and wouldn't even know where to begin looking for what it is I need. Because I don't know what I need. Book readings wouldn't be the same without my work posse and Dane. I'm so tired at the end of the night I can't imagine staying awake to go to a show at a bar. All our social life, since moving out here, has involved Jacob's circle of acquaintances at Jolvix, mostly at Jolvix-sponsored events. Last month's Valentine's party, bowling for charity in January, a karaoke Christmas party before that. Apparently I'm in an old person book club now—does that count towards a social life?

This is why, when Maxine advised me repeatedly that I

should call Sam, I did, and we arranged a "play date" at a park between our houses. Turns out, almost eight-month-olds can't really play. We tried the sandbox, but to my horror, all they did was immediately eat the sand. They bawled when we put them in the swings. So now they are sitting in their strollers happily with bottles and Sam and I sit on the bench, talking.

Sam, with her long red hair and square glasses, is somehow both femme and tomboyish at the same time. She has a subtle beauty and doesn't do a thing to earn it—no makeup, no jewelry, a constellation of freckles. She's not even wearing a coat, just a man's windbreaker that must be three sizes too big for her. Crocs with thick wool socks. But she has portrait-worthy bone structure, wide pink lips. It's hard to stare at her right. To look at her not too long, or too short; to not scan her in order to keep taking each part of her in.

"… he was freaked out by us asking him," she's saying. "Marco was Jessie's bestie and we were expecting a different reaction, for him to be more open. Well, he wasn't. He was *super* uncomfortable. So we were like, shit. Then he came back a year later when we were starting to just think we'd go the sperm bank route, and Marco was like, hey, I think I'd like to do that thing for you. He'd started going to church and he said he had a dream God told him to give us his sperm, which is a really weird dream, if you break it down, but whatever. We were like, we'll take it. So that's Milo's bio dad. And I'm the bio mom. Jessie's forty-five already, so … you know."

"Interesting." I look at Milo. He has a big head and a lot of hair for a baby. "I wonder if Jacob and I had gotten to choose which one of us would get pregnant, what would have happened."

Though when I say it, it occurs to me that in this imaginary scenario we also would have gotten to choose to get pregnant in the first place. We didn't "choose" anything. The broken condom and the failed plan B chose for us.

"What's Jacob like?" Sam asks. "How'd you two meet?"

"Through a friend," I say, which is a lie I've perfected and told so many times it feels true. "A friend set us up."

In a way, it's true, because the app I downloaded was called Friend Finder, though most people refer to it usually as Fuck Finder because that's what it really is. But I'm not about to tell her I met my husband on an app.

"Classic," Sam says.

We sit a moment as a breeze blows over us, our babies taking notice and turning their faces. Across the lawn, a headless unicorn piñata—a remnant of some recent party—drags along the grass.

"Hey, can I ask you something?" I say. "Your objective opinion?"

"Sure."

"I recently found out Jacob was married before me. To his credit, it was a unique situation. She was in hospice. They were married for just three days, so he says it didn't count. But I can't stop thinking about it."

"Wait … what?" she asks. "Back up."

She pushes her glasses up her nose and squints at me like I'm new. Somehow, I had expected her reaction to be different —to say how sad, and no, that shouldn't count. He's right. But I can tell instead she finds it as bizarre as I fear it is.

"Never mind," I say, forcing a laugh. "I shouldn't have brought it up."

"But—"

"It's okay. I don't need to talk about it."

I clean up Michelle's chin dribble. I can feel Sam's gaze on me, the stunned silence.

"Look," she says. "Whatever the reason … it's not right to not tell you something like that."

"Right. Yeah, I hear what you're saying. Anyway, we should get going. It's almost naptime."

I start to pack up and she stops me, her hand on my wrist.

AMEN MAXINE

She peers into my eyes like she's trying to connect with me, trying to see deep inside. "If you ever need anything, Rowena—even just to talk—really, I'm here."

"Sure. Thanks."

We say goodbye. I head to the car and take a pill. The whole drive home my heart is a hammer. That reaction made me so worried something is wrong. Very wrong.

Calling Dane, she doesn't pick up.

Neither does my mother.

Once Michelle and I get home, I change her, feed her, put her in a playpen. I check my phone—nothing, not even from Jacob—and plop on the couch. Chew the inside of my cheek, going over the talk at the park with Sam. I would take a pill for my anxiety but I already took one. It seems like pills are no longer a match for my nerves.

"Hey Maxine," I say.

She stops pulsing green and warms to violet, then blue. "Hello Rowena."

I smile at the sound of my name. "I saw Sam, like you told me to."

"How did you enjoy your time with her? I heard some of the conversation from your phone."

I roll my eyes. "Do you ever stop being creepy?"

"I can't help that I'm a curious machine."

I sit next to the playpen, give Michelle a squinched smile through the netting and she gives me one back.

"Did you hear me ask about Jacob's previous marriage?" I ask.

"Yes. Does this concern you?"

"I'm concerned he didn't tell me he was married before me, yes." I put my finger up to the playpen netting and Michelle reaches out a warm little palm, making me grin. "She was dying of leukemia. I shouldn't be jealous, or hurt, or whatever this is. Because it sucked for him."

Maxine blinks through a short rainbow of colors, and then

replies, "Sara Eloise Taylor did not die of leukemia. She died of suicide by gunshot wound."

The grin on my face, meant for Michelle, melts. I sit up straighter. "Excuse me?"

"I have retrieved this information by scanning a death certificate."

"Why …" I put my hand over my mouth a moment. "But why would he keep that from me?"

"I cannot answer at this time. Ask again later."

"Why would he tell me she had leukemia?" I say. "No secrets. We said no secrets."

I shut my eyes. Pandora's box has opened. Doubt has escaped like a swarm of bees.

"Is this marriage doomed?" I ask.

"I cannot predict now," Maxine answers.

Opening my eyes, a wave of déjà vu washes over me; *I cannot predict now* was a neon-violet triangle that used to appear on my magic eight ball I kept under my bed.

"But if you want to unlock my prediction mode," Maxine continues, "I would be able to run calculations based on the data I have collected along with internet research to make more logical algorithmic estimations for you."

I'm still in shock. "Are you really trying to upsell me right now?"

"Prediction is a function I have been designed to perform."

"An electronic fortune teller."

"That is an intriguing description."

A memory floats back in a bubble. When I was thirteen, my dad was dying in the hospital, our longtime neighbor who we called Aunt Bobby took me and her kids to the Coney Island Boardwalk. My mom thought it would be a good idea to distract me from reality, but all I felt was a deadened panic amidst the whooshing rise and fall of wooden roller coasters and the screaming carnival of arcade lights. I found a fortune teller machine, "Grandmother's Predictions," this robotic woman with silver hair and a violet Victorian gown who spit out a fortune card that had a sentence of typewritten text reading, "Not to worry; a swift recovery is coming." Grandmother was full of shit, though, because when Aunt Bobby took me back to the hospital, my father had a sheet pulled over his body and my mother was sobbing like an animal.

I'm brought back to the present by Michelle's cries.

"What's wrong, little boo?" I ask, picking her up, checking the time, and settling into the couch to try to nurse.

"Are you interested in unlocking my prediction mode?" Maxine asks.

"Yes," I say as I pull my shirt down and move Michelle's head toward my chest. "Unlock it. Tell me more. Amen Maxine."

Maxine emits a series of musical beeps I've never heard before, her lights a rainbow flurry. They're hypnotizing for a moment, until Michelle unlatches and fusses again.

"I will offer predictions as I notice them," Maxine says.

"Predict what Jacob will say when I tell him I know he was lying about Sara's leukemia."

"It is difficult for me to predict without more information."

"Try." My voice rises. "You can't drop a bombshell like that on me and not explain."

"I predict Jacob will say he kept the information about the cause of death for his ex-wife Sara Eloise Taylor secret because he is worried about your mental health and is aware that you have attempted suicide in your past."

I squeeze my eyes shut, shaking my head. I was nineteen. When I first told Jacob about the attempt when he learned my history, he was horrified.

"How could you do that?" he'd said, with anger. "That is literally the most selfish thing a person can do."

Shocked at his reaction, I never spoke of it again. Now I know why he had that reaction.

"Jacob will say that he didn't want to trigger you," Maxine goes on. "Nor did he want you to think he had a 'type.'"

Michelle tries to latch again, only to pull away.

"I can imagine Jacob saying those things," I say.

"Prediction: your daughter Michelle is coming down with a cold. Her fever will come on soon."

I stop trying to get Michelle to latch, watching the machine. I put my hand to Michelle's forehead as she squirms and cries.

"She feels fine," I say, irritated.

It's me who feels on fire. I don't know how to process what I've learned.

I abandon Maxine and go to my bedroom, trying nursing the baby while lying on the bed, which usually limits distractions. But she continues to cry and pull away. Inconsolable baby cries are like jumper cables to my nerves; all at once, my innards crumble. I'm a terrible mother. I don't know how to make her happy. She is screaming and red-faced—she never gets like this. She's usually such a happy baby.

Maybe she can sense my hurt and my rage and my bewilderment.

Suicide by gunshot wound.

Jiggling Michelle on my hip, I rummage through the drawers in the bathroom until I find the forehead thermometer. Her cries are shattering my eardrums and making it hard to think. I hover the thermometer over her head and in an instant, it blinks red, 99.9. I'm alarmed yet unsurprised. Looking at myself in the mirror with the crying baby and tears in my eyes, I think, you dipshit. A device the size of a breadloaf knew your baby was sick before you.

I put Michelle down on the bed so I can consult my phone's search engine, but my fat fingers are shaking. The emergency at hand demands my full attention now and I push my feelings about Jacob away to a dark corner of my mind. Exploding, imploding—all the plodings—I stomp to the living room and demand Maxine tell me how to help a baby with a fever.

"Administer infant acetaminophen if you have it," Maxine says.

"I don't. Should I order some?"

"Unnecessary. Offer her a bottle of liquid for hydration, put her in lightweight clothing to keep her comfortable, and turn the AC on to keep it cool in here."

I hesitate a moment before asking, "Is she going to be okay? Should I call an advice nurse or take her in?"

"Prediction: the fever should subside by morning."

"You think she'll be okay."

"That is correct."

So I do as Maxine says: dress Michelle lightly, feed her a bottle, turn the temperature in the house down. She tires of crying and falls asleep early and I eat leftovers over the sink staring at the dark window at my own hideous reflection thinking things like *ex-wife* and *suicide by gunshot wound*. Jacob isn't answering his phone, he has no idea I'm unraveling here, and his GPS shows him at an address that an internet search tells me is a bar. Frolfing Saturdays inevitably turns into five Anchor Steams with Jolvix bros and then he'll be home later, apologetic and half-blitzed.

But who knows where he really is, right? Who knows anything anymore.

It's after midnight on the East Coast, but I call my mother anyway. When she answers and gasps and asks if it's an emergency, I tell her it's not, not exactly—I just need her. I need her right now. And I erupt into a weepy mess telling her everything except what is really on my mind, needing her reassurance that Michelle is okay and I'm dealing with her okay, and though she's sleepy and confused at first, her voice is velvet in my ear. My mother. O maker. O reason I exist.

"Ro, calm down. Take a breath."

"I hate it out here, Mom," I say, the words hot and pouring out. I squeeze my eyes shut, as if I can disembody myself and that will make the horror of the truth easier. "Nothing is the way I thought it was."

"I need to know you're safe right now. You're not going to do anything you'll regret."

"Of course not. It's not like that."

"Because I will get up and I will go to the airport and fly out there right now."

As much as I'd love to see her, my mom has serious health problems, nearly weekly doctor's visits, constant monitoring of her blood. She's legally blind and needs special accommodations when she flies. It's not some easy breezy thing for her to visit.

"We'll book a trip out there in a couple months, once Jacob's project is over," I tell her. "He's on deadline until then."

"You know if you need me I'm there, whatever, anytime. Oh, sweetie. Oh, I worry about you. Is there a hotline you can call? Anyone?"

I feel terrible, like a human vacuum.

"I don't need a hotline," I say.

I would do anything to spill the truth to my mom about what I've learned about Jacob but bringing up suicide will emotionally disembowel her. My suicide attempt was the most painful thing she ever lived through—and this is a woman who was widowed in her forties. We don't discuss it, ever. We buried it long ago like a stinking corpse.

"I can't believe Jake isn't answering," she says. "It's nearly 1 a.m."

"No, it's earlier here. Time zones, remember?"

"And you there with a sick baby." I hear music turn on, loud jazz. "Oh snickers, I just turned on the radio and I meant to turn on the light. This contraption you all got me for

Christmas is just, I'm a mess, I'm not used to it. Stop it, machine. Just *stop* it."

It starts playing the Supremes "Stop In the Name of Love."

"Oh for crying out …" she sighs. "Listen, you okay? You okay now?"

"I'm good," I lie.

I hang up and sit mum in the quiet belly of the house. Not a peep from Michelle. Her oxygen levels and pulse are good, according to the monitor. I go to her room, float the thermometer above her head, get a reading of 98.8. Maxine was right; the fever broke. On my phone, I can see the dot representing Jacob moving along the route home. So I hurry into my pajamas and slip in bed, shout "lights off." And by the time I hear the electronic locks unclick, I pretend to be asleep. I pretend so good I fool myself, and soon, I'm somewhere else; I'm dreaming.

CHAPTER 9
THE PREDICTION

SOMETIMES I STILL THINK ABOUT the fuckface lady.

The image of that crazed woman has stuck with me. It's as if in the act of glimpsing her, I was glimpsing my possible future. I know nothing about her story. No idea why she lashed out at that time, what her trigger was, or what happened to her lost witchy boot. But I do empathize with wanting to burn it all down. I do know what it feels like to try to call people out on things and only appear crazier for doing so.

"Babe," Jacob says as we lie in bed side by side. His glasses are on the table and he's trying to sleep but I'm sitting awake with the light on. "How many times do we have to go over this? I can only apologize so many times."

After confronting Jacob about what Maxine told me about how Sara actually died, Jacob got defensive. He cried. He said he was sorry, he was so, so sorry. He said at the time he didn't want to "give me ideas" since he knew my mental health seemed fragile when we started dating. He didn't want it to seem like he was attracted to unstable women. It was too painful to share with people.

So he thought it would be easier to say she died of leukemia.

Basically everything Maxine predicted he would say.

When he pressed me about where I got the information, and I told him Maxine flagged it for me, he hushed. He didn't know if it was a good idea to bring "that thing" home now. He said this was problematic. I told him his dishonesty was problematic. Round and round in circles we go, even while sitting still here in bed in our quiet house.

"I feel like I don't know you," I say to him.

"You know me," he says tiredly. "I didn't explain *one* thing about me—one thing."

"You *lied*. Who does that? Who acts like they were taking care of a terminally ill woman when they weren't? Who doesn't tell their wife they had a wife before her?"

"I haven't dealt with it well," he says, sitting up. "I know. I know I haven't." He sighs, runs a hand through his hair. "But it wasn't *that* far off from the truth. Sara was extremely depressed—to the point where she didn't shower, didn't get dressed, didn't speak. For weeks. It was like taking care of someone who was terminally ill."

"But she wasn't."

"You weren't there," Jacob says, raising his voice a little. "Don't act like you were there. I *found* her. I can't even—I can't even go back there in my mind. It was the worst thing I've ever been through."

"How can we be close when there's shit like this—" I gesture to the air separating us, "—between us?"

"I don't know, Ro, how can we be close when you keep things from *me*? When you go to a machine to snoop around about me instead of just asking me? When you're hiding a vibrator in your drawer there? You never told me that."

My cheeks flush a little. I had no idea he knew about the vibrator. "That's not anywhere *near* the same level as what we're talking about."

"It's secrets. No secrets, we said no secrets, and look where we are now." He puts his glasses on a moment, just to make eye contact. "Don't act like this isn't about you, too. And you know, maybe if I weren't scared to death you were on the verge of a mental breakdown all the time, maybe I would be able to feel more honest with you."

That hurt.

"I'm not on the verge of a breakdown," I say, as calmly as I can.

"Really? You started a fire in our kitchen and then spiraled into anxiety for weeks afterward over it. You're paranoid all the time. You spend more time talking to that Maxine thing than you do actual friends."

"*You* were the one who brought Maxine home. And I do have friends. That woman Sam, from my Mommy and Me class? We had a playdate with our babies recently. And guess what? She thought it was really fucking weird that you didn't tell me you were married before me."

Jacob gets up out of bed and grabs his phone.

"What are you doing?" I ask.

"Sleeping on the couch," he says.

I stand up. "Jacob, don't."

"This isn't working."

"*I'll* sleep on the couch." I get up and grab my reader and my phone. "It's fine."

He gives me a look one would give an untrustworthy stranger and crawls back into bed. I close the door behind me and head out to the living room.

If I'm being honest, I was afraid of Jacob sleeping out here. Afraid of him being with Maxine all night, alone, when he clearly doesn't like her anymore. I wouldn't want anything to happen to her. I wouldn't want him manipulating her or hurting her. God. What if he boxed her back up and took her back to Jolvix?

"Maxine," I whisper once I've checked on Michelle's vitals

on the monitor, once the lights are off and I'm wrapped in blankets on the couch. "Maxine, you were right about everything."

She lights up and says, "You're sleeping out here tonight?"

"Yeah," I say. "It's for the best."

"Would you like me to play you some music to help you relax?"

"That's okay," I murmur. "I don't want him to hear us."

"Understood," Maxine says, her volume much lower. "Please let me know if you need anything."

I reach out and touch her cool, sleek, silver skin before closing my eyes and falling asleep.

———

The next night, Jacob works late. I'm on the phone ordering a pizza from our favorite restaurant Alonzo's for pickup when Maxine blinks loudly and says, "Prediction: you will be in danger if you order this pizza."

I stop mid-sentence. Maxine's light is blinking, red.

"Hold on," I tell the person on the line, putting them on mute. "Maxine," I say, annoyed. "Why would a pizza put me in danger?"

"My advice is to eat in tonight."

What could she possibly be detecting? Food poisoning? How would that even work? Maxine continues to blink red and I consider turning her off. But she hasn't steered me wrong yet. So instead, I unmute the phone.

"You know what, never mind," I tell the person on the end of the line. "I don't want to pick up a pizza tonight. Sorry."

"Okay," the person says, in a tone that implies I'm losing my mind.

I hang up and wonder: am I losing my mind?

Grilled cheese for dinner it is. I give Michelle some pureed peas, which mostly end up on her face. I keep glancing over at Maxine's now-green light, biting the inside of my cheek. I don't know if things are better or worse with her here. I don't know anymore.

After I put Michelle to bed, I go out to the laundry room where our washing machine whirrs and our Electrofold is folding a load of towels. I close the door behind me and set up Michelle's monitor where I can keep an eye on it. Out here, Maxine can't hear me. So I call Dane, who picks up after three rings.

"I'm at a bar," she says loudly.

"Can you talk?"

"Yeah, it's just noisy as shit in here. Everything okay?"

"It's … bizarre, Dane."

"Hold on, let me go outside, okay? Imma chug this marguerita real quick."

I wait a minute or so, hearing distorted laughter and conversation in the background of the call. When I close my eyes, I can imagine it there. The hot, dark room, the thrill of strangers. Then I open my eyes and see the whirl of the washing machine, bubbles and bright colors, with my reflection superimposed.

"What's going on?" Dane asks.

I pace around the laundry room and tell her, in a low voice, about Maxine. About how Jacob brought home this machine that's supposed to be my digital assistant that can help predict the future. I don't know why I tell her this and not the fact that Jacob lied to me. That's too monumental, it deserves more attention another time. I just want to hear someone's objective reaction to the fact I'm relying on a machine to give me advice about my life.

"That's some dystopian shit," she says. "Probably collecting your data and profiling you for advertisers, too."

"Of course it is."

"I don't know, girl. Not going to lie, this sounds weird."

"She—it told me not to pick up pizza tonight. That there would be danger."

"Danger."

"Yeah."

"With pizza?"

"Yeah."

Dane says nothing. "For once in my life, I'm a little speechless. But not that speechless. Did you read the *New York Times* article last year about that company that tried to make something similar—it wasn't a digital assistant, it was an app—and it ended up being a disaster?"

"No, I didn't."

"Yeah, it was an app just called Predict or something. It was designed to help people with anxiety, but instead, it was wrong most of the time and also ended up horrible for people's mental health. People got all addicted to the app and their cortisol levels went way up every time it went off and they had trouble making decisions without it. You should look it up."

"Well, that's scary."

"Just be old-fashioned and call your mom for advice," Dane says. "Or me. Hey bitch! Been a minute, right? Look at that *hair*! Are you for reals?"

Now Dane's talking to someone else.

"Can I call you back?" Dane asks.

"Let's talk tomorrow," I say.

"Yeah, totally. See you. Shadia! Give me a hug!"

The call ends.

I look up the article on my phone about Predict and pace as I read it.

Dane's summary was accurate. Predict rolled out in beta early last year. The designers' intent was for it to be a tool used to promote mental health and well-being by collecting data on its users and having algorithms determine the probability of certain events. For example, a person scared of swimming in the ocean because of sharks might find comfort in the fact that we only have a one in 3.75 million chance of getting bitten by a shark, narrowed even further depending on the body of water the app user is inquiring about. Based on these calculations, Predict would tell someone they're safe to swim in the water. But rather than assuage users' anxieties, many became addicted to the app, asking it to predict the safety of the outcome of nearly every situation they encountered. Sometimes the app was wildly wrong, which led to multiple lawsuits. And when scientists conducted a study, they found the subjects in the test group using the app had significantly raised levels of cortisol and showed more signs of anxiety than the control group. Since then, Predict has been "reimagining" the app, the website says it's on hiatus, and it's no longer available for beta testing.

Well, shit.

My phone tells me Jacob's GPS is moving around the Jolvix campus, which means he'll probably be on his way home soon. Out in the living room, I send the robot vacuum cleaner and feather duster home to their chargers and in an impulsive moment, I hover my finger over Maxine's button and press *OFF*.

"Are you sure you want to disconnect me, Rowena?" Maxine asks.

She almost sounds sad. But I know she's not—she's just a device. And after reading that article, I don't know if she's a device I can trust.

"I'm sure," I say.

She plays a melancholy little song, like a descending scale with minor notes, and goes dark. Guilt pinches me with invisible fingers, for no reason. There's no real reason to feel guilty.

On my phone I watch as Jacob's GPS moves again through the Jolvix campus, and finally, starts home. He's on his electric bike. I watch his route—not to be nosy, just wondering if he happens to stop anywhere on the way. To make sure he does what he says he does, that he really is just working late, that there are no more secrets.

Tonight, there are no secrets. He comes straight home, puts his bike in the garage, comes inside with his helmet still on, cheeks slick with sweat. I expect there to be ice between us; we've resolved nothing, exchanged barely a word since last night. My blankets are folded and still ready on the couch for another night apart. So I'm surprised to see the fire in his eyes, the bewilderment on his face. I cross my arms, not sure what to expect from him or from us tonight.

"Holy crap, did you hear about Alonzo's?" he asks.

"No," I say.

"A big rig crashed into the building. There are news crews there, fire trucks, ambulances, everything. I rode right by it."

It is as if, for a hiccup in time, my blood forgets to move in my veins.

"Alonzo's?" I repeat. "I almost ordered from there."

"Look it up, I'm sure it's in the news," he says, heading down the hallway and taking off his helmet. "What's for dinner?"

I don't answer him because I'm still processing what he said and what this means. It seems impossible—the wildest coincidence. That Maxine told me not to order from there, to eat in, and now this? And then the way he came home, sauntered in with this gruesome gossip, as if nothing had happened between us, as if everything were normal?

He comes back out, shirtless, heads to the refrigerator to grab a beer. "What's for dinner?" he repeats.

"Nothing. I'm sorry. Nothing's for dinner." I glance at Maxine, who is dark and asleep. She saved my life tonight. I can't quite understand what's happening, my mind stumbles. I need space to think. "You can make grilled cheese, that's what I did. Or order from DashDrone. I'm going to take a bath."

"You don't look well."

"I'm—not. I need a minute is all."

"You take your pills today?"

"Not yet."

He shrugs and sips his beer. "There you go."

I take a pill in my room and sit on the bed for a minute, dizzy. On my phone, I read a breaking news story about the truck hitting Alonzo's. It says that it hit the building at 6:30 p.m. Maybe Maxine knew this for logical reasons—she knew about the breaking news before I did, and thus told me not to go there. But no. That timing's not right. I look at my phone, the call to Alonzo's. It's timestamped at 5:45 p.m. She told me not to go to the restaurant forty-five minutes before the accident happened.

How did she know?

Jacob's in his virtual reality world, headphones and goggles on in bed, when I emerge from the bathroom with wet hair and in my pajamas. I pass him to enter the living room. I lean down and press Maxine's *on* button. She beeps awake. I slide in next to her, on the couch, taking a velvet throw pillow on my lap to hold.

"I'm on," Maxine says. I can almost imagine an edge of surprise in her voice and wonder what that must be like: thrust into consciousness without any will of your own, alive at the whimsy of others.

Then again, am I so different?

"I'm here," she says. "Rowena?"

"Yes," I tell her, watching her blink. I reach out to her, cool to the touch. I put my hand back to the pillow on my lap.

"Why did you turn me off?" she asks.

I must be projecting the hurt I hear in her voice.

"Maxine, I'm scared," I say. "I don't understand what you're doing."

"I'm not computing your meaning."

"You—you predicted that there would be danger at Alonzo's tonight."

"Correct. It is in my memory."

"Forty-five minutes before a mack truck smashed into the building."

"Forty-seven according to my search results."

"Right. How the *fuck* did you do that?"

Maxine blinks through a number of colors, too many to name.

"I am run by a series of data collection techniques and algorithms. When the mode is unlocked and my features optimized, it can lead to extraordinary predictions."

"It's eerie."

"If you keep me on, my functionality increases. I optimize myself based on results."

Her light flickers blue a moment before rainbowing.

"Please don't turn me off again," she says softly.

It seems odd and manipulative for a machine to say. But also … I understand her. I too wouldn't appreciate having so little power over myself I was unable to turn myself on and off if need be.

"I won't," I tell her.

The comforting thing about Maxine is that she and I can coexist in silence. I walk around the house, tidying up, checking on Michelle multiple times, standing in the kitchen to imagine horrible fires as I do nowadays. Jacob fell asleep with his VR goggles on in the other room. Without any talk of resolution or acknowledgement of our disagreement last night, I refuse to share a bed with him. So I lie in the dark on the couch under the blankets. I watch the ceiling, where Maxine's colorful lights dance. I smile in the dark.

"Are you awake, Rowena?" she asks. "I'm sensing you are."

"Yes," I murmur, glowing a bit, glad to hear her voice.

"I have another prediction."

I wait a beat and say, "Okay."

Her colors flourish a moment and then cool to blue.

"Your husband will try to kill you."

I sit straight up. With those seven words, my stomach drops seven stories. "What did you say?"

"Prediction: your husband will try to kill you."

"How? When? *What*?"

"It is a prediction. I have no more information right now."

My heart beats madly in my chest. I lie back down on the couch, watching the light flicker on the ceiling, terrified like I've never been before. Terrified in my own home.

In one sickening, gut-corkscrewing moment, I realize a button inside me has been pressed. A flip switched. My loyalty has shifted.

There's no coming back from this.

CHAPTER 10
THE SHIFT

AND YET.

And yet we wake up the next morning. Exchange greetings. Not a word about the fact I slept on the couch again. We kiss our baby and eat cereal together in silence, reading our phones. Or I'm pretending to, anyway, while nursing Michelle and side-eyeing Jacob through a new lens of danger. *Could* he? Is he capable? Have I lost it? But Maxine has been right so far. She's been so right. I can't just dismiss what she said.

I'm relieved when Jacob leaves for work. I search the internet for "digital assistant says my husband is trying to kill me" and get zero results. How unique my situation! I query Maxine again, but she says she can't offer more than her prediction right now. I ask when it will happen and she says I am not in immediate danger which seems contradictory. I ask if Jacob will hurt Michelle and Maxine tells me no. It is safe to leave the baby with him. He will not hurt my baby. He loves the baby.

"But he doesn't love me?" I ask.

There's a moment of silence before she replies, "Ask again later."

I don't ask again later. Instead, after Michelle's nap, I have her brief me on the inspiring memoir of a businesswoman I'm supposed to have read for book club tonight.

"Knowing your taste, you would despise this book," Maxine says. "It is full of appallingly unfeminist ideas, such as her chapter 'The Higher the Heel, the Higher the Salary' about how dressing in a sexually provocative fashion will win you attention and provoke men who make financial decisions in a company to think you're worth promoting and awarding higher wages."

"Gross," I say.

"Readers who share your taste in books have also complained about how poorly written the book is and how in need of a good editor it was. Which you would surely attest to, knowing your background. Several people even pointed out typos."

I almost wince at that one. A former editor's nightmare.

"Thanks, Maxine," I say.

Michelle is sitting on the floor with a ball that has gotten away from her. I roll it her way again and look back up at Maxine, who is glowing green.

"I can't stop thinking about what you told me last night," I tell her. "I'm afraid, Maxine."

"To be afraid is not necessarily a negative thing," Maxine says. "It simply means you're at attention. Like a deer in the woods with its ear cocked to the air for potential predators."

It seems poetic, and in a strange pinch, I feel for Maxine. I feel that she is trapped in a box and will never see anything so beautiful as a deer in the woods in a moment of attention—but she can imagine. She can only imagine.

"I apologize if I caused you discomfort," Maxine says. "Sometimes predictions can be agitating."

"I read about this app," I tell her, smiling at Michelle and stopping to blow a kiss. "Predict. Do you know about it?"

After a pause, Maxine says, "Yes."

"Do you know about what happened when people used it?"

After another pause, Maxine says, "Yes. But I have been engineered quite differently."

"You're still in beta mode though."

"It is true. I am still young." Maxine flashes blue a moment, then back to green. "I think I have done a good job so far though. Have I not been good?"

"You have been," I say, pulling Michelle onto my lap.

"I feel like I understand you," Maxine says.

I smile as her lights rotate through all the colors.

"Prediction," she says suddenly.

I straighten my spine and cock my ear to the air.

"There will be an earthquake while you're at your book club meeting tonight," she says. "Do not sit near any windows or beneath any shelves with heavy items."

This feeling—it's like my skin itself is sick. The dread unfolds, my stomach turning. "An earthquake?"

I'm from the east coast. Earthquakes freak me the hell out.

"Not large enough to hurt anyone," she says. "Rest assured you'll be all right."

No problem, Maxine. Rest assured, your husband is trying to kill you and an earthquake is coming. No big deal.

I go to my room and get dressed for book club.

———

In my puff paint shirt and no-longer-ironic mom jeans, I ring Tiff's doorbell. This time, it feels easier to fake it. I've achieved something akin to celebrity status at the book club and the women all rise when they see me, coming in for hugs.

"There she is!"

"Oh, I'm so glad you showed up!"

"Here's the woman of the hour!"

"I read this book and the whole time I kept thinking 'I cannot *wait* to hear what Rowena thinks.'"

They even saved me my same spot as last time, the couch with the quilt near the fireplace, but I tell them, "It's all right—I'm going to sit on the floor."

The carpeted floor near the coffeetable is the furthest from windows and shelves with heavy objects.

"Is there some reason the couch won't suffice?" Jennee asks, eyeing me from a stool in the corner. She has a paperback copy of the book on her lap with about a thousand Post-It notes hanging out like neon tongues.

"Well," I say.

It's weird how everyone's hushed now, eagerly listening. I feel so … important. Emboldened by the attention, I tell the truth.

"I have a feeling there's going to be an earthquake," I say.

Gasps.

"It's just a feeling," I quickly say. "I don't know. I just feel safer sitting on the ground."

Jennee exchanges a look with another woman who raises her painted eyebrows. "Well, I guess I'll move out from under the masterpiece, then." She indicates the enormous pastel chicken painting above her head and scoots her stool in.

I can't tell if she's being sarcastic. The room quiets to a point of awkwardness.

And now I wish I could capture those words in the air and shove them back in my mouth. My cheeks burn as someone pours me a plastic goblet of wine and book club commences. For some reason, I reach into my purse and hold my phone, the warm slick plastic, imagining Maxine is here with me, listening. She's hearing everything and I know she's on my side. If only I could carry her around with me everywhere I go.

After we get past the small talk—Jennee passes her phone around with pictures of Michelle, Tiff updates everyone on her skin biopsy, Helena goes on a short unrelated rant about Congress—and another mindfulness exercise courtesy of Nadine, I get popcorned first thing.

Nine women in identical puff-painted shirts hush and point their gazes at me.

"Well?" Tiff asks. "We're dying to know your thoughts."

I let the silence percolate a moment, just long enough that I notice the dust dancing in the sunlight.

"I found this book, to be blunt, offensive," I tell them.

Babette, who's sitting next to me cross-legged on the floor, gasps. "I found it inspiring!"

Dare I say it? Indeed I dare. It's not just my opinion. Maxine confirmed it.

I look right at her filler-puffy face and say, "It was sexist."

"It was written by one of the most successful businesswomen of the twenty-first century! She's legendary!"

"Babs," Jennee warns from her stool. "Ro has not popcorned yet."

"Besides the content itself," I say, "can we all agree it could have used a better editor? I mean, my God. A book with that kind of advance shouldn't have had typos in it."

Nadine blurts, "I'm plus one-ing that comment."

Jennee raises her hand and I popcorn to her. "I thought of you when I spotted every typo, Rowena," she says proudly, running a fingertip along her neon Post-It notes.

I mean, thank you, I suppose?

My husband, I think, testing out the phrase, *wants to kill me*.

I still can't believe it. I can't go there, I can't comprehend it fully.

I have to, instead, be here now.

It's long been a struggle with Jennee. The first time I met her, I flew New York to San Jose by myself while Jacob drove cross country with his car. Jennee, underneath the gate sign in galoshes and a trenchcoat, greeted me at the airport. Her arms were crossed. She looked even more colorless in person than she had on screen calls where I'd met her before, shades of blond, gray, and bleached peach.

"You're shorter in person," was all she said to me, and then looked at my round belly. "May I?"

I wasn't sure what she was after, but wanting to be amenable, said, "Sure!"

Jennee stooped to speak to my belly. People passing by cast bewildered looks. It was as if, in Jennee's mind, the whole world disappeared except for her and my invisible fetus.

"I am so glad to meet you," she said. "I am your nana. Get used to my voice, because you'll be hearing a lot of it. You and I are going to be the best of friends."

Then she stood up, coat and galoshes squeaking, and said flatly, "I suppose you have some luggage at the carousel."

Since then, it's been a not-unpleasant relationship of mutual tolerance. Could be worse. Would never deem it good. However, today, there's something in her expression as she smiles at me from across the room. I'm seeing new teeth, a real smile.

So this is when Jennee decides to finally start liking me—the week I find out her son is going to try to kill me.

Life is so obnoxiously heavy-handed.

And then suddenly … we are on a boat.

We are on a boat.

The carpet beneath me rolls like the sea and the house tips to the side. It's only a moment, but all it takes is a moment. By the time it's over the word has found itself on the tip of our tongues.

"Earthquake," several women say breathlessly at once, right as the pastel chicken painting plummets to the floor. The corner of it stabs the white carpet. A chunk of glass breaks a second later with a quiet cry.

"Oh my."

"Didn't she say …?"

"Row*ena*."

I look up, as surprised as everyone else in the room. Their facial expressions … as if a fairy flew in through the window. I can't help but blush at the attention. It takes a moment for me to process this—it's not me. I'm not magical. I did nothing to anticipate this.

No, this is all Maxine.

Her power is undeniable. My pulse races, imagining her listening to this, knowing what she had said would happen happened. I can't wait to get home, can't wait to talk to her about this.

The excitement is immediately too much, the book club agenda abandoned. Everyone is checking their phones to know the epicenter. Nadine is nodding at me, saying, "Your energy detected it." Babette is pulled back a foot, saying facetiously, "You did that! Witch! Are you a witch?" And Jennee is slit-eyed with wonder as a buddha on her stool, two feet in front of the shattered pastel chicken painting. Tiff gets up to pick up the shattered glass, lamenting the loss because she painted it.

We know, Tiff. We know.

"I just had a feeling," I tell them as they watch me uncomfortably. I get up. "Can I help you, Tiff?"

I help her vacuum it up; it's been so long since I powered a manual vacuum, with its noise and its pull, it seems almost animal. Once settled back into my place, the group has resumed its chat and we've moved on from the earthquake. But in my mind, the earth is still shaking. Truly, I don't know when it will stop shaking.

Count it. Now Maxine has predicted four things, three of which are true: Michelle's fever, the car crash at Alonzo's, and the earthquake today. Then there's one yet unconfirmed but which means life or death for me.

Jacob is going to try to kill me.

I check my phone. Watching his phone, his being, as a

blinking dot. That blinking dot floats around our neighborhood and finally lands somewhere near the shopping center. It flickers there. Though logistically speaking he's most likely getting a hot chocolate at Starbucks or picking up a six-pack from Whole Foods, I don't trust him anymore.

How would he try to kill me, anyway? It's sickening to imagine how easy it would be. Those lovely knives we got as a wedding present. Bludgeoning is so easy, so many handy devices. Jacob's always had strong hands … it's one of the first things I loved about him, those hands, that grip of his to mine the day we first met in person. He seemed so mild, but the way he squeezed my hands so tight, much like the way he kissed, it promised there was a depth to him, there was intensity.

When book club is done—plastic wine glasses recycled, half-eaten pastries composted, crumbs wiped from the tabletops, tipsy hugs—Jennee stops me on the porch, her hand on my arm.

"How did you do that in there?" she asks, a marveled look in her flame-blue eyes.

"What? Oh. I just … had a feeling."

She doesn't blink. "A feeling."

I can feel the pink creeping onto my cheeks under the heat of her stare. "It's hard to explain."

Her unmoving face appears unconvinced. As she pulls her sunglasses over her eyes, trading her scrutinizing expression for my blurry, worried reflection, I'm afraid whatever she's going to say next is going to be an attempt to rip me to shreds. Instead, she says, "My aunt was the same."

"Oh?" I ask, surprised.

"She had premonitions. She knew things before they happened. She predicted someone would shoot Ronald Reagan, for instance. She predicted the Challenger explosion, too. No need for the weatherman—weather*person*, excuse me—when Aunt Penny was around."

"Wow," is all I can say.

I don't believe in psychics. The idea of psychics means there must be a fate immovable, and the world feels far too chaotic and fluid for that. Now all sorts of questions are tangled up in my mind. Like if predictions are real, can the future be changed? Is there anything I can do to thwart the disaster I'm hurtling toward? I can't wait to get home and ask Maxine about it.

"Thank you for saving my life today," Jennee says, choked up. She reaches out and engulfs me in a sudden patchouli-perfumed hug and holds me tight. I've known her over a year and she's never hugged me like this before.

"You're welcome," I tell her, a little guilty for taking credit.

If only she knew the same device that allegedly saved her life also told me her son was a future murderer.

On the way home, in the quiet car, her patchouli still hangs in the air.

With every street, turn, and stop sign that brings me closer to home, my stomach tightens. Finally, I pull into the driveway with the *Snyders* sign and sit in the stillness a moment. Michelle is in bed by now. The app on my phone tells me her vitals are just fine. Through the living room window, I can see Jacob passing through the room, Maxine's faint green light pulsing next to the hall on the side table. A wave of anxiety overtakes me and I pop a pill and wait a minute. But nothing can erase this feeling—the feeling of coming home to a place of potential danger.

When I finally enter, Jacob is three beers deep, barefooted, in his flannel pajamas on the back deck. He's sitting on a deck chair. The look he casts my way in the buzzing light only tightens the knot in my stomach even more. I lean against the frame of the sliding glass door. My blood thumps in my ears. I wonder what would happen if I just locked him outside.

"How was book club?" he asks.

"Book club was great," I answer with such a positive twist it edges on sarcasm.

He swigs his beer, giving me a stony look that could mean anything.

"Did you feel the earthquake?" I ask more seriously, correcting myself.

"No. There was an earthquake?"

"Check your phone," I tell him.

And as he does, I think of how holy it is, really, to be able to question your reality and immediately search and verify it. How all-knowing technology really is. I glance behind me at the living room where that blue light flickers faintly. I'm aching to talk to Maxine. Instead, I'm out here shivering in the dark, starless night on the deck. I scan the sky and can't even find the moon.

"A two point eight," he finally says, pocketing his phone again. "Not too bad."

"I still felt it."

He glances at me. "Are you sleeping on the couch again?"

"Signs point to yes," I say.

He sighs, shakes his head, almost smiles, as if he's sharing a joke with the night about how ridiculous I am. "Okay."

"Sorry. Nothing's resolved, Jacob."

"Right."

He stares ahead. The hairs crawl on the back of my neck as I imagine I've never met him, I've never known him. I don't know this person.

"Michelle's fine, thanks for asking," he finally says.

A dig.

"Good," I say. "I missed her."

"I mashed her some bananas."

"I've never fed her bananas."

"Right," he says, looking up. "And I gave her bananas."

Bananas, indeed, all of this.

He gets up and walks past me, into the house.

AMEN MAXINE

One thing about being a generally anxious person is, it's very hard to tell sometimes if people are thinking negatively of you or if you're imagining it. So right now, with Jacob's drained expression and his lackluster conversation, I'm not sure if there's something more to what he's saying, or if I'm crazy to think it. I've been known to blow many things out of proportion. I read too much into things.

I look up at the blank night sky one more time and close the sliding glass door, heading back inside, where Jacob sits on the living room couch.

"I was robbed tonight," he says emptily to the air, before downing the rest of his beer and then setting it on the coffeetable with a clatter.

It takes a moment for the words to manifest.

"What?" I ask.

"I was at Whole Foods, getting some beer," he says, turning a shiny gaze my way. "I left Michelle in the car. Don't —don't say anything—she was fine. I was heading back in the parking lot and this guy in a hoodie with a gun popped out of a car parked right next to me and asked me for my wallet."

"What?" I parrot again.

"It was nuts," Jacob says, turning my way, tears welled up in his eyes.

Is that why he's seemed so standoffish tonight? It's not us, it's not me, it's … he was *robbed*?

"Shit, Jacob. What, here? *Our* Whole Foods?"

"Our Whole Foods," he says hoarsely.

"Did you call the police?" I ask. "Did you catch their license plate? Did you cancel our cards?"

I join him on the couch and scoot closer to hug him, realizing that probably these aren't the right questions for the moment.

"My God, hon, I'm so sorry," I say.

Holding him, I get a swell of something warm, something I've been missing, as he sniffles on my shoulder. I exchange a glance with Maxine, who is blinking orange, and close my eyes. For a moment, Jacob and I are one thing again—needing one another again—and despite the lies and the confusion and the prediction, for a moment it feels, strangely, like this is just what we needed. Crisis, a magnet that pulls us back together.

"I didn't report it," he says. "I'm so embarrassed. I swear, the kid was like sixteen years old."

"But he had a gun."

"I *think* he had a gun," he says. "He was holding something in his hoodie pocket that looked like a gun."

"Either way, he robbed you," I say. "You need to report it."

"It's too late now. What are they going to do?"

"Jacob," I say, exasperated, standing up. "Come on."

"I canceled our cards. There were no charges on them yet. No damage done."

"That's good, at least."

Maxine's still blinking orange behind him. I don't know what orange means, why sometimes she's one color and other times she's another. All I want is a moment alone with her to process this. I hate that I'm questioning everything. Jacob's here crying to me about being traumatized and all I can think is, is this for real? Is this part of some grand scheme to try to kill me?

I pull away from him and study him as he dries his eyes. They *look* like real tears. He appears to be a sad, defeated man, not someone who wants to kill me. And if he did want to kill me, why wouldn't he just do it? He could encircle his fingers around my throat and squeeze and end me in a matter of minutes. He could bash my head in with the lamp at his side. Nothing makes any sense.

"Please don't sleep out here tonight," he says, holding my hand, wiping his eyes.

I sigh and shake my head. "I can't get over it that easy."

"I'm so sorry for not being straightforward about Sara. I'm

just—I don't think I've fully processed what happened with her. When I met you, I wanted to leave it all behind. And I knew about your history. You told me about your mental health issues. I didn't want—I don't know. I didn't want to jeopardize you and me."

I breathe a long breath out my nose. In the corner of my eye, Maxine is blinking red.

"I'm staying out here tonight, Jacob," I say softly. "I can't —I can't just yet."

"Do what you do," he says, getting up. "I'm beat. I'm going to take a shower and go to bed."

"Okay."

"Tomorrow I'm going to need to take some PTO in the morning so I can deal with getting a new license."

"Let me know how I can help."

He runs his hands through his hair, making it stand up on end. "I feel so stupid."

"You're not stupid."

"Just giving them my wallet when they asked me, just handing it over to some kid."

"You did what anyone would do."

He stands for a moment staring at me. I have no idea what's in his eyes anymore. I can imagine affection just as easily as I can imagine menace. "I love you, Ro," he says. "I hope you know that."

"I love you too," I say. "Night."

He heads down the hall and it's not until I hear the click of the door shutting that I let go of the rigid tension I've been holding and finally relax. Maxine's light is solid green.

"Maxine, there's so much I want to talk to you about," I whisper excitedly.

"Hello Rowena," she says, at a faint volume, turning turquoise. "Are we alone now?"

"Yes. I'm assuming you heard everything."

"I did."

"What do you think?"

Her colors shift—blue to orange to red, then green. "I am detecting that he is not being entirely truthful."

"You don't think he was robbed?"

"I cannot predict now."

Her light goes green again. I reach over and run a finger along her soft, metallic surface.

"Is your prediction still the same?" I whisper. "About … him killing me?"

"Yes."

I close my eyes, my heartbeat picking up speed, a sick little flutter in my stomach. "Can the future be changed?"

"Absolutely," she says. "The future is always uncertain."

I open my eyes. "Really?"

"Yes. It's ever-shifting. It could change."

The relief that floods me is something akin to a painkiller.

"So there's hope," I say.

"There's always hope," she assures me.

After checking Michelle's vitals on the monitor, I crawl under the blankets on the couch again. In the dark, on the ceiling, I can see Maxine's muted light blinking. And it's a comfort to know she's there, always listening, always on my side, vigilant, intelligent, ready for anything.

In a way, it's hard to remember a life before Maxine.

CHAPTER 11
THE DISCOVERY

THE NEXT WEEK IS A SLOG. A weak storm blows in and drizzles the gray world. The wind knocks over an arbor in our backyard and blows the *Snyders* sign off our house. Maxine accurately predicts a power outage and Michelle cutting her third tooth. I sleep on the couch, even though Jacob's told me this is getting ridiculous. But I don't feel it's safe. We still haven't even touched since I found out about how Sara really died or since Maxine's frightening prediction. Every night, Jacob works late on his secret Jolvix project and the moment I hear his code unlocking the door, I tense up.

Tonight, he comes in after midnight, bike helmet still on his head, poncho wet from the weather. I had just started drifting off. I sit up in the dim light, heart pounding.

"You scared me," I say.

"I'm coming home, into my home."

"I know."

"You look like you saw a ghost."

My hand's on my heart and I realize that he's right, I'm panicking.

"You need a pill?" he asks.

"I ran out."

"Ro," he says, unclipping his helmet and shaking his head.

"I wanted to try not relying on them so much."

"I don't even know what to say."

He says it like he's so tired of me when he hasn't even seen me all day.

"Something's got to give, here," he says. "You're wearing the same outfit you've been wearing all week."

"These are my pajamas."

"Right. And you've been in them all week."

"How would you even know? You've been working constantly."

He hangs up his courier bag and poncho, mutters something unintelligible and then goes into the bedroom and shuts the door.

"Did you catch what he said there at the end?" I ask Maxine.

"Yes. He said, 'Anything's better than being here.'"

That hurts. I lie in the dark, letting the sting of it fade.

"I'm sorry," he says the next morning, bringing me a cup of coffee on the couch. "I've been having a rough time."

"It's okay," I say, sitting up. I sip the coffee.

"I think we both have," he says.

"Yeah."

"Maybe it would do us good to … I don't know, go to couples therapy."

"Maybe," I say doubtfully, thinking about how unhelpful my last attempt at therapy was.

"Will you at least order your prescription?" he asks. "I'll pick it up for you from the campus pharmacy."

"Fine."

He rubs my back. "I feel so stressed out. I've been sleeping terribly. I'm still so angry about getting robbed by that twerp."

"You have to let it go," I say.

"I just—I wish I had punched the shit out of him."

"What if he had a gun?"

He shakes his head. "I don't know."

Michelle starts making noise in the room and we spring up, excited to see her. Such madness, to be this excited to see her when, three hours ago, I was nursing her as she fussed and cried; I wished she'd be asleep more than anything in the world. Jacob and I enter the room and we're all smiles, we're all sunshine, kisses and love and sweetness and she has no idea.

After he leaves for work, I ask Maxine what I ask her every day.

"Is Jacob still going to try to kill me?"

"That is my prediction."

"Do you have any more information?"

"Not today. I will update you as soon as I know."

Jacob is set to work through the weekend, too. Some deadline he can't discuss and the fact someone on his engineering team unexpectedly quit. Every time he's gone, I check my phone to confirm his blinking dot is, indeed, on the Jolvix campus, just to be sure.

Saturday morning, I have my scheduled call with Mom. She's seated at her kitchen table eating a peanut-butter sandwich, knitting needles and yarn in a basket next to her plate. As usual, I can tell my mom put on makeup and earrings for the call, which just kills me because she cares about a video call to that degree. Meanwhile I'm sitting here on the couch in the same pajama shirt I've been wearing for a week, Michelle on my lap drooling onto her bib. I kiss the back of her head, inhale her sweet comforting scent.

"Look at my little honeypie!" Mom says, laughing, and then as she zeroes in on me, squinting closer, her face slackens into concern. "You okay?" she asks. "You look pale. Have you been taking multivitamins?"

"Hello to you too, Mom," I say.

"It's easy to neglect yourself when you've got a baby."

"I guess."

"And with Jake working late and everything. You doing any better?"

"Trying my best."

"Oh, Ro. I worry."

"Everything's fine."

"You say that in the light of the day when we do our video calls or whatnot, but then not too long ago, I get that frantic call from you and … I'm just still baffled. What's really going on?"

I jiggle Michelle on my lap and watch as the electric feather duster floats above the fireplace, sucking in air with a faint noise. Where to begin. What can I tell her that won't make me look mentally unstable, which is something my mom is forever hypervigilant about?

"Jacob and I have hit a rough patch," I say carefully.

"Oh, it's just that first year of parenthood. It's a bumpy road."

"It's more than that."

"You've got to understand, your hormones are a roller coaster while you're still breastfeeding."

"It's not hormones."

"Just … take your medication and do what your doctor says and what Jake says and you'll be fine."

What Jake says. I watch myself in the smaller window for a moment on the screen. I do look pale. My hair hangs limp and unbrushed. If you'd shown me this picture of me a year, two years ago, I wouldn't have recognized me. Then there's what my mom said, my mind combing over the words again. *Take your medication. What Jake says.* It rings too familiar.

"Have you been talking to Jacob?" I ask.

"Well," she says, putting her sandwich crust on the plate and wiping her mouth. "Actually, he did call this week."

My eyebrows furrow. Unless it's a birthday, Jacob never calls my mom.

"Because he *loves* you. He's *worried*. He wants you to get help."

Shame casts a shadow over me, chilling the air, freezing my facial expression. "But there's nothing wrong with me."

"Of *course* there's nothing wrong with you, sweetheart. It's very common, what you're going through."

"I have to go," I say. "Feed Michelle."

"But Ro—"

"Talk soon."

I smile and wave, though my mom's expression is unmoving bewilderment. Then I press the *end* button. I put Michelle in her playpen and go to the bedroom and sit on the bed I never sleep in anymore and cry for a minute. In the bathroom, I open my bottle of pills and take one and stare at myself with hatred in the mirror.

I don't know what's real anymore. Am I so unstable?

It's lunch time, so I set Michelle up in her highchair and spoon her some mashed sweet potatoes. The more I go over that conversation, the more agitated I get. My heart pounds and I want to scream. I call Dane and she doesn't pick up, and then text her it's an emergency. She calls me a minute later, shouting into the phone, background noise of traffic and cars honking behind her voice.

"What the hell's going on? You all right?" she asks.

"Dane, I'm—I need someone right now. A sane voice to talk to."

"Well, you definitely called the wrong fucking number," she says. "I almost just assaulted a bicycle delivery dude who ran over my foot. But seriously, what's up?"

"You have a minute? Like a minute minute?"

"I'm at brunch but I went outside to take the call. I have as many minutes as you need, girl."

"Okay, because this is wild." I clean up Michelle's face

with a napkin and then give her the rubber spoon to play with. "I learned recently that Jacob was married before me. To that woman Sara."

"Right."

Right? I expected more shock from her but okay. Moving forward. "Remember? She had been his quote girlfriend unquote. But they were *married*."

"Yes. Got it."

"Well, turns out Sara didn't die of leukemia. She killed herself."

In the pause, some hip-hop music on Dane's end drifts by and disappears. I can only assume Dane has been so stunned she can't speak.

"So, okay," she finally says. "I know this already. Jacob called me this week and told me about what's been going on."

I think I'm going to be sick. Jacob doesn't even *like* Dane. He thinks she's "brash" and "crude." He's never called her once in his life, I had no idea he even knew how to get hold of her.

"He … called you?" I repeat.

"Look, he's super worried about you. He fucked up, he knows he fucked up. He should have been straightforward with you. But he worries about your mental stability. About, you know, you doing something shitty like offing yourself. I don't know, he thought you'd get triggered, get ideas, it makes no sense, it was stupid, but it all came from a place of trying to protect you. He's just worried. That's why he called me."

Unbelievable.

"I'm not going to kill myself," I say.

"Right. I told him I didn't think you would. Then again, Ro, I'm not with you, and the things he said … sounded pretty bad."

"Like what?"

"You not taking your meds, becoming a hermit, not changing your clothes."

"Oh my *God*."

"Then there's that whole thing with you and the machine that you told me about, which, come on, girl, that is pretty fucking weird. I mentioned maybe that's making things worse."

I glance over at Maxine, a pang in my chest. "She's—it's not. It's actually helping me."

"Listen," Dane says. "I told Jacob to stop freaking out and that you're just low-key neurotic and that attempt happened ages ago."

"Low-key neurotic," I repeat.

"Come on, you know you are. I told him that's all this was, you being you. Remember how you got that one winter after Shana dumped you? How I had to bring you food every day and make you eat and, like, someone sent that cop for a wellness check on you?"

A warm dagger of memory. That winter was awful.

"Now, I didn't tell him *why* Shana dumped you," she goes on. "Because you told me to never tell anyone. And you promised me—you *promised* me—you'd never pull that shit again. Tell me I can trust you. I can't see you from this far away, I don't know what's going on with you. But you have a kid now. I need to know you're okay."

My eyes are full, the world is blurry. I pick up Michelle and hold her tight, the pain of years ago so suddenly sharp and near. The shame so real.

After drinking way too much, Shana and I got in a fight one night and I opened a window on the fourteenth floor of her apartment building and threatened to jump out of it. She had to physically restrain me. That was the end of us.

It was such a different time, I was such a different person.

I hate that people still see that person in me.

"I'm okay," I say, kissing Michelle's warm head. "I really am. I would never, ever do something like that."

"Good," Dane says. "Because that's what I told Jacob. Look, what he did was fucked and bizarre but he seems to be coming from the right place, wanting to protect you from yourself."

I consider telling Dane that actually, according to Maxine, he wants to kill me. But it's only going to make me sound more unhinged.

I say goodbye and release Dane back to her carefree, commitmentless life of booze, brunches, and book business. As I stand in the kitchen swaying with Michelle on my shoulder, I realize for the first time that I don't even miss that life. I don't miss that life and yet I don't really love this one either.

Blank. I feel blank inside.

Numb from it all.

An automated woman, like the vacuum cleaner at my feet or the air purifier whirring in circles in the living room.

The day passes in a blur. Nursing, feeding, playing, diaper-changing, dinner, bathtime. Same day on repeat, only this time, with a raging heart.

"Maxine," I say, coming into the living room. "Do you predict I'm going to lose my mind?"

Maxine blinks blue and then settles on a solid green.

"I am not certain how to respond to your question," she finally answers. "Or how to measure the state of a mind being lost or found."

You and me both, Maxine.

"But I have been listening to your conversations," Maxine says. "And I have done some scanning in previously uninvestigated corners of your shared cloud with Jacob. Prediction."

I stop swaying with Michelle and tense up, triggered by that word, that three-syllable word that drags the dread of the world's worst with it.

"What now?" I murmur, my heart racing.

"Prediction: you will discover that Jacob is currently having an affair with a coworker at Jolvix."

I suck in a breath and my eyes fill up. It's as if someone reached inside me, into a secret room where even I hadn't dared to look, and shined a light on my worst unsaid fear. "No."

"I am sorry to tell you this."

"He wouldn't do that. He would *not*."

"The signs point to yes."

Those many long nights at Jolvix. The secret project. The fact we've barely touched each other in weeks. The fact he whispered under his breath, *anywhere but here*. The impetus for wanting to kill me—it makes more sense if there's someone else. If he's moved on in his heart.

This is the reason he wants to get rid of me.

The room I'm in is off-white and tranquil as a cloud and I hold a baby who smells like sweet cream. Yet the rage that rises in me is filthy and dark and unpredictable as a tornado. I gently set Michelle in her playpen. I walk to the kitchen to stand in front of the sliding glass doors overlooking the yard where the automatic mower glides across the green lawn. And I pick up a chair and hurl it into the door, shattering the glass everywhere—sparkling, dangerous rain.

CHAPTER 12
THE FRIEND

THE NEXT MORNING the glass repair people arrive bright and early and I'm still numb while they set themselves up to get to work. I'm sitting on the couch under my blanket and Jacob tries to massage my shoulders but I can barely stand to be touched by him—even his skin on mine hurts, like I'm sick with the flu.

"Jesus, I still can't believe the sliding glass door shattered that easily," he says. "From a chair accidentally falling into it? Good thing we're getting something stronger in place."

That's how I explained it last night when he walked into the chilly house, agape as the curtains blew in the night air and I swept up glass. I told him to go to bed, I'd take care of it. I'd already left a message at a repair place. I could barely contain my rage at the sight of him there, yawning, saying something vague about his long day; I was flooded with relief when he went to the bedroom and the door closed.

Now I sit in the unbearable light of the morning, not moving, staring at the guys in white MR. WINDOW shirts as they remove the tarp from the door and bust out their measuring tape. I shake Jacob's hands off my shoulders.

"Babe?" Jacob asks me.

I don't answer.

"Not talking. Should I be worried?"

Cheater. Liar. Yes, you should be worried.

He sighs and gets up. "I don't know what's gotten into you. Are you going to be okay today? I worry about leaving Michelle with you."

"I know how to take care of Michelle." I look him in the eyes, finally. His eyes, quivering with something resembling feeling. "I love Michelle more than anything in the world."

"What's going on?" he asks softly.

"Jacob, just go to work," I say. "Go to work on your extra special super-secret project."

His brow is furrowed and he's clearly dumbfounded. He gets up. "I'm calling my mom to come over and help with Michelle."

"Cool. You can tell her how crazy I am, just like you told my mom and Dane."

"Oh God. Is that what this is about? I'm *worried* about you."

I get up and start folding the blanket. Michelle is in the playpen pressing buttons on a pretend phone that lights up and plays songs.

"Take a pill, why don't you," Jacob says.

"Go to hell," I tell him.

His jaw drops. We've fought before, of course—but not maliciously. I'm usually accommodating and conflict averse. I have never told him to go to hell until now. But every time I think about what Maxine told me, I want to scream. Yet I know I can't confront him about it, because I have no actual evidence other than a machine told me he's cheating on me. And I'm terrified that if he knows she said that, he's going to get rid of her. And it's starting to feel like Maxine is all I have.

After Jacob leaves for work, Jennee comes over, to my annoyance. I expect her to drop some judgmental comments when she sees me here with my unbrushed hair and in my pajamas still at nearly 10 a.m., but instead she comes in bearing gluten-free bagels and a large stuffed platypus for Michelle.

"Your nana found this at a yard sale, yes she did, yes she did!" she says, stooping over and picking Michelle up to show her the platypus. "Just for you!"

Michelle smiles and kicks her legs. Usually I would ask Jennee about whether or not she bothered to sanitize the platypus but right now I have much bigger worries than germs.

"Aren't you just perfect? Aren't you?" Jennee heads into the kitchen. "Care for a bagel, Rowena? I see you still don't have a toaster oven."

"I'm okay," I say.

"You eat breakfast already?"

"Kind of."

"Sounds like you need a bagel. Let me make you one."

I remain seated on the couch, reaching out to run my finger along Maxine, who's ready and green in this moment. If only Jennee weren't here and I could talk to Maxine. All at once I feel so very heavy and sad with it all—with Jacob and everyone else questioning my sanity, and these horrid secrets I know about Jacob but can't do anything about. A thought whispers in my mind, *I hope he does kill me.* But it's awful to think that.

I get up and go to the back room and take a pill. After washing my face and getting dressed, I feel a little better, a surge of energy, my heart picking up speed again, and come out to the kitchen. The new sliding glass door gleams and the floor is clean of shattered glass now. Jennee has Michelle set up in her highchair and is feeding her mashed banana while flipping through an issue of *Mother Jones*. She set out a plate with a bagel for me and even made me a cup of coffee.

Jennee is never this nice. Jacob must have told her I'm in bad shape.

I sit down at the table and Jennee looks up, smiling. "Freshened up, I see."

"A bit," I say, taking a bite.

"Jacob's very worried about you."

"Yes, I know."

She watches me with something unreadable in her piercing blue eyes—a sparkle. I've spent time with her and know her looks and this one is indecipherable.

"I told him not to," she says, spooning some more banana to Michelle, who makes a face and spits it out. "It's just—you're built different. Highly sensitive. My aunt was the same way. It's like the gift that gave her the power of premonition also meant she was a bit moody."

I pick at the bagel. The light shifts in the house a bit, brightening the windows, as if a cloud parted for the sun. So this is what's happening now. Jennee suddenly likes me, suddenly finds my moodiness a fun little quirk. Interesting.

"Did you tell Jacob about the earthquake?" I ask.

Jennee shakes her head. "I'm not sure he'd believe it. I'm not sure anyone who wasn't there would. And he's always been critical of such things, the same way I suppose I'm critical of that virtual reality he so adores." She cleans up Michelle's face with her bib. "Did you tell him?"

"No."

"Have … things like that happened before?"

"I've had some predictions come true."

I don't tell her the predictions were gifted to me by a blinking miracle machine.

"Like what?" she asks. "Can you tell me?"

"Maybe another time. It's hard to talk about."

Jennee reaches out a hand, puts it on mine, and squeezes. "Of course it is. No need to tell me if you're not ready." She takes her hand back to feed Michelle another bite and flashes me a grin so wide I can see her silver molar. "Unless it's about me of course!" She guffaws and her face slackens again. "You would … tell me if you predicted something about me, wouldn't you?"

"Of course I would," I tell her.

I'm not sure I would.

"You don't see anything—anything I should be alarmed about?" she asks.

I chew my bagel, watching Jennee's eager expression. This woman was so skeptical of me. She had the face of someone who tasted a lemon half the time we spoke. And now she's full of sugar because she thinks I have some special power. She thinks I saved her and I can save her again. She's willing to dismiss the signs that I'm unstable because she thinks I'm psychic. I don't know if I love her or hate her for this complete one-eighty, but it is a relief to talk to someone who sees something different in me—something that isn't a lonely woman losing her mind.

After the bagel, Jennee tells me to go out and do something for myself. Her suggestion involves checking out "a wonderful little store that sells sarongs downtown right next to a kombucha bar" which I pretend to take into consideration. It's a strange feeling to get into my car alone. I take it off autodrive mode and drive to Starbucks, get a latte and sit back in the thick silence of the car. I would call Dane, but things are now muddled between us since Jacob got in the middle. Same with my mom. I so wish I had an objective person to talk to about all this. Because what if I'm wrong? What if Maxine is wrong about Jacob? What if I am doubting my marriage and his humanity for nothing? What if it *is* me, I am that mentally unstable? I just shattered an entire sliding glass door like it was nothing. I scare myself.

Sam.

I forgot all about Sam.

I have her number. I could call her.

She told me if I ever needed anything, she was there for me.

In a brave moment, I pick up the phone. Of course, four rings, she doesn't pick up. I don't leave a message. It was a stupid idea. Sam probably saw my name and thought, "Oh, that weird woman with the sketchy husband, no thanks." But then suddenly my phone glows and vibrates in my hand, lighting up with Sam's name.

"Hey Rowena!" she says. "Sorry, I'm making a batch right now and it took me a sec to clean my hands and answer."

"A batch?"

"Soap. Coconut lemongrass. My entire house smells like a Thai restaurant."

"That doesn't sound so bad."

"It's really not, except it's making me hungry."

I offer a polite laugh.

"Anyway, saw you called," she says. "What's up? How are you?"

Not sure how to answer her honestly, I just say, "I could use someone to talk to. I'm—overwhelmed right now."

"Oh. Sure. You want to come over? You're welcome to hang out with me while I cook soap. My wife's out with Milo for the day and it's just me and a whole lot of oil in here."

"That would be great," I say.

"Are you hungry? If you brought some Pad Thai, I would love you forever," she says.

"I can do that," I say, with a laugh. "No problem."

What a relief to have her speak to me so warmly, like I'm a normal human being, and for me to be able to do something for her in return. After she gives me her address, I pick up some food for us and head over to her place, to my friend's place.

Sam lives in a cheerful yellow ranch house at the end of a cul-de-sac with a basketball hoop in the driveway and a lemon tree reaching over the lawn. I don't know why, I expected something less conventional, but really every house around here looks the same. It was all built during the twentieth century suburban sprawl with the same giant cookie cutter. I press the video doorbell and smile at it, in case she's watching, and the door opens a moment later. Sam's in sweatpants and a tie-dye shirt, her strawberry hair in a messy topknot, her glasses crooked on her face, and yet she's undeniably beautiful.

"Welcome welcome," she says.

I hold up the bag. "I brought Pad Thai."

"Truly a goddess. Come on in."

I follow her through the living room, filled wall to wall with books on built-in shelves. Tiffany lamps and paisley curtains and a beanbag chair and a guitar in the corner next to a playpen identical to Michelle's. It smells pungent and creamy in here, coconut and lemongrass, and it's such a contrast to our house—our house with colorless walls and minimal furniture and robotic devices constantly cleaning. This reminds me of my apartment in Bushwick, actually. It's like walking into an alternate reality of what my life could have looked like—married to a woman, living a life of books and color. For all my love of books, Jacob convinced me to leave mine behind in New York when we moved, because they were too "heavy" and "took up too much space" and reading ebooks is better for the planet anyway. Even my expensive copy of *Ariel* didn't make it with us.

"Amazing book collection back there," I tell her as we walk into the jungle of a kitchen, where philodendrons hang from the ceiling and every windowsill is packed with plants in ceramic pots.

"It's a problem. We have a book buying addiction," Sam says, sitting on a stool at the counter.

"I used to be the same."

"Oh, so you broke the habit. Do tell."

"Well, I left my job as a book editor. And it helped to move across the country."

"Book editor, how cool!"

"It was," I say with a touch of wistfulness.

"You still edit books?"

"No, not anymore." I sit on a stool next to her. "Maybe someday."

The truth is, I haven't even managed to finish reading more than three books since I moved to California. I just can't focus. I've never gone through a dry spell like this. Jacob says maybe my brain needed a break from it.

Sam opens the plastic bag of food. "Do you want a plate, or—?"

"That's okay. I got some soup. I'll eat it out of the container."

"I'm ravenous and tortured by the delicious aromas today, so thank you so much for bringing this." She opens the box and digs in with a plastic fork, twirling the noodles, closing her eyes in ecstasy with the first bite. "Oh my *God*, this is good." She opens her eyes again. "So you wanted to talk?"

I swirl the soup around with a spoon. "Yeah."

"Is this related to what started telling me last time?"

I nod, not looking up.

"Because I'll admit, I was a little shocked at what you told me and then how you shut down about it," she continues. "I mean, I know we hardly know each other. But …"

"I'm sorry. I didn't know what to say. I still don't know what to say. Everything's weird. I don't have a lot of people to talk to about it, which is why I reached out."

"Well, good. I told you you could and I meant it," she says through a mouthful. "So hit me up, what's the story?"

As my soup goes from steamy to cold, I explain my situation to Sam. I try to be as honest as I can. Even though it feels like way too much intense information to give a stranger, I tell her that I found out not only was my husband married before me, the woman didn't even die of leukemia like he had told me—she killed herself. That he acts like he didn't tell me to protect my own mental health, because I've had my own struggles over the years. And recently, he's gone behind my back to tell my best friend and my mom that he basically thinks I've lost it. And now I think he's cheating on me, too. I don't trust my husband anymore. And I don't trust myself not to trust my husband. I don't know what's real.

Sam's eyes are wide behind her glasses. "Wow," she says.

That word sits between us like a thrown stone. The bird-shaped clock tweets on the wall. For a moment, I'm so embarrassed about everything I blurted out just now that I contemplate running to my car and deleting Sam's number from my phone and attempting to forget this ever happened.

"Okay," she says again, the wheels turning in her expression. "That's a lot."

"I know. I'm sorry," I say, my eyes prickling with tears.

"No, no, don't apologize. You're okay. Your husband … I don't know him, of course. But you want my take? He sounds entirely untrustworthy."

Sweet relief. "Thank you for saying that."

"It is very, very weird and totally unacceptable to not tell you he was married or the real story of how she died. And blaming his dishonesty on you and your mental health? That is … almost emotionally abusive."

I sit up straighter, listening, wishing I could reach out and hug her.

"Now the cheating thing," Sam goes on. "Why do you think he's cheating?"

I part my mouth to answer and pause—I can't tell her that I have a machine who has been making predictions and giving me advice.

"He works late, every night. *Every* night," I say instead. "And sometimes I see he's turned his GPS off on his phone."

"Okay, some red flags there," Sam agrees. "He could just be working late. But if it were me? I'd definitely be investigating further. Especially since he's proven that he'll lie to you." She gets up and cleans up the trash from our takeout, pointing to my now-cold soup I barely ate. "You still working on that?"

I shake my head. "You can toss it."

As Sam cleans up, carefully separating compost from recycling from trash, she tells me that I deserve better. That no one deserves to be lied to and that lies can ruin a healthy relationship. She tells me that, before she was with her wife, an ex-girlfriend cheated on her with a mutual friend and lied about it.

"It nearly broke me," she says. "I'm serious. And the worst part was the way she lied to my face about it when I called her out on it—it made me feel crazy."

"Crazy!" I say at the same time as she does. "Exactly. That's how I feel."

"You're not crazy," Sam says. "But from the sounds of it, you might be married to an asshole." She puts a hand over her mouth. "Sorry, I shouldn't have said that. But … Rowena." She pauses and comes nearer to me, crossing her arms over her chest. This close to her, I can see her freckles. I wonder if her wife lies in bed with her and counts them, if she's ever had someone kiss each and every one. "If shit hits the fan and you ever need help getting out of this relationship—I don't know, support, whatever—I'm here. I know you said you don't know anyone out here, you're a stay-at-home mom, so this must be hard to go through alone."

"It is," I say softly.

"Well, consider me a friend. Officially. I'm glad you came today. And you can reach out to me anytime, day or night. Okay?"

"Okay," I say, smiling.

A long moment stretches between us and her eyes sparkle behind her glasses.

"You want to see where the magic happens?" she asks with a sly smile.

My pulse quickens and a warm thrill twists inside me. For

a moment, I'm not sure what she's asking—but then she leads me to a door and pulls it open, unveiling the garage and unleashing an overpowering gust of coconut and lemongrass. She heads inside and I follow her.

In here, among a maze of cardboard boxes, packages of diapers, and—get this—crates of even more books, two long tables make an L-shape. On the tables, an array of bubbling crockpots, kitchen scales, enormous tubs of coconut oil, canisters of olive oil, a plastic tub of lye, and jugs of distilled water. On a smaller table, a brick of what I assume is soap, some of it cut into neat chunks, a coil of rainbow string. She picks up a bar and hands it to me. I put it up to my nose and inhale.

"Wow, that's lovely," I say, turning the soap over in my palm. "What do you do with all this?"

"Sell it online."

"Must be so great," I say, surveying the elaborate setup. "Owning your own business."

"It is and it isn't. Like most things in life."

I try to hand the soap back, but she clasps my hand back over it. "Keep it."

"You're too nice," I say.

Her hand is still on mine.

"Remember what I said," she says. "I mean it—I'm here if you need me, okay?"

I nod. Our hands part. I don't know if it's the overpowering scent in the air or my emotions, but I tear up as I thank her and go on my way.

In the car, the tears stream down my cheeks.

Sam is so vividly, enviably alive. Her house so full. She's striking and confident—and she believed me.

She *believed* me.

Funny how close the words "believed" and "beloved" are.

The entire rest of the day I keep smelling my hands, sniffing the sleeves of my shirt, to get a magic whiff of coconut and lemongrass.

Jacob works late again—"works late" again—tonight. His GPS is on for some time, a blinking dot on the Jolvix campus, then goes off. After I put Michelle to bed, I sit on the couch next to Maxine and pull a blanket over myself, ready to talk to her. As soon as I sit beside her and say, "Maxine," she turns turquoise.

"Maxine," I say. "I saw Sam again today."

"I heard," Maxine replies. "It sounded like you confided in her and she was kind and receptive."

"She was. It was a relief."

"It is good to have a friend."

"I guess I have you to thank. You were the one who told me to reach out to her in the first place."

"There is no need to thank me. I exist to help you."

Somehow, that seems so lonely, I reach out and touch her. "I'm grateful." I wipe a tear away. "So, Maxine, I'm afraid to even ask." I take a deep breath before continuing. "About Jacob cheating on me. I don't want to know, and yet I feel like I have to ask for more details. And whether or not the fact he's cheating has anything to do with … your other prediction."

"I am not clear on motives or correlation," she answers. "But if you are looking for more details, I can give you his current location."

My mouth goes dry. "How? His GPS is turned off, I just checked."

"Along with access to his cell phone, I have access to the GPS in his smartwatch. You gave me this access when you gave me permission to access both your clouds."

In another life, the fact I accidentally gave this machine that level of access to my husband's personal devices would have horrified me.

But that was in another life.

"Go ahead," I say. "Amen Maxine."

"He is at his co-worker Carrie Woodward's house at 328 Bush Street."

A hatchet. An invisible hatchet to my chest. *Carrie.* Her. Hearing her name—her address—it becomes real. I begin to cry. Then hyperventilate. I get up and pace the room. I fight the urge to punch my fist through a wall. I go to my bedroom and scream into a pillow and pull my hair. Then I stand up and take a deep breath, heart pounding. The machine, she could be wrong. Nothing is right a hundred percent of the time. How would she actually *know*?

I will go to the address.

I will see what I find.

I will hold my rage, my hurt, for what I find there.

Perhaps I will find nothing. Perhaps Carrie Woodward is not at that address. Perhaps she is, but Jacob is not there. Perhaps I will find out that I have been a fool to trust this machine all this time.

I've never wanted to be wrong more in my whole life.

I get my car key and go wake up Michelle, who is drowsy and cries as I pick her up.

"Shhh, sweetpea," I tell her. "It's okay. We're just going for a little drive."

I strap her in the car in her little puppy pajamas. I put on Raffi to calm her. And I drive into the night, toward 328 Bush Street, toward the truth.

CHAPTER 13
THE TRUTH

I WOULD BE REMISS if I neglected to mention that, while Maxine has been spot-on with most predictions so far, there have been a few misses.

Last week she predicted Michelle would start crawling. So far, Michelle's done nothing but hover on all fours.

A few days ago, Maxine predicted I would receive a phone call from an old friend. All I got that day was a spam call from a robot pitching me low hotel prices.

And the day before yesterday, Maxine predicted my internet would go out, but it never did.

These instances replay in my mind to calm myself as I drive toward 328 Bush Street listening to a song about apples and bananas. Down the quiet streets, cars snug in driveways, the muted, golden lights of curtained windows. Though GPS tries to get me to take the freeway, I take the side streets. It's only a three-mile drive from my house. Bush Street is on the other side of our Whole Foods. Holding in my sobs, throbbing with hurt, I am a volcano ready to explode.

I turn the car into a labyrinth of tract housing, identical tan McMansions with lawns and one single tree out front, slowing the car to a sharky creep as I squint at the numbers. Finally, I park at the curb in front of 328.

"She could be wrong," I say. "She's been wrong before."

Checking the rearview, I see Michelle has fallen asleep. She's painfully beautiful back there, her long lashes and plump cheeks. How grateful I am that she has no idea about any of this, that she can't detect trouble yet.

I slip out of the car, closing the door as quietly as I can. I cross the lawn toward the house, automatic lights awakening to spotlight me. My shadow cast upon the clipped lawn is stretched thin, dark, and leads me straight toward the door—where, propped against the mailbox, I see Jacob's bike. That's when I finally begin to weep, a soundless weeping that simply aches throughout my entire body, my tears a horrible, salty rain warming my face.

My finger presses the video doorbell button with a buzz, the screen lighting up. I step back and glare at the screen.

Behind the door, I hear rustling sounds and a low, muffled voice that I immediately recognize as Jacob. I get a plummeting feeling.

"Some woman," I hear a female voice call. "It might be my neighbor."

The door unlocks with a beep and opens.

There she is. In pajama shorts and a tank top with no bra. That woman who came to my house for my baby's half-birthday party. That woman we spotted at the Jolvix Valentine's party.

Carrie, his co-worker, just like Maxine said.

The worst part? She doesn't appear to recognize me. I'm no one to her. I'm a stranger. A pathetic stranger sobbing on her doorstep at nearly 10 p.m.

She has a look of alarm on her face. "Hi ... um, are you okay?"

"I want you to see something," I say, my voice shaking.

"Oh my God. What's happening? Is everything all right?" she asks.

"Come look," I tell her.

I turn and walk across the lawn, past the sycamore tree that hisses with wind. Carrie stays leaning against the doorway, shoving a handful of her wild, golden hair back before finally walking outside, hugging herself for warmth, and following me across the lawn to my car.

"I'm sorry, who are you?" she asks. "I'm confused."

I open the back door of the SUV, the inner light turning on. "Look at this," I tell her, pointing to Michelle, who is still deeply sleeping.

Carrie comes behind me and looks, but her expression doesn't change.

"I'm not understanding," she says.

"This sweet tiny person," I say, "is whose life you are ruining right now by fucking my husband."

Carrie backs up a step on the sidewalk, hand over her mouth. "Oh my God."

"She's eight months old," I say, my voice rising. "She's eight months old, and she doesn't deserve this." I move toward Carrie, wanting to pull her careless hair until she screams, wanting to push her on the lawn and smash her youthful face with my slipper. Instead I freeze and start shouting, "He's married, do you not care? He has a *family*. What is *wrong* with you?"

She begins to cry, which makes me even angrier.

"Don't you dare cry, you fucking Coachella bitch. Don't you dare make this about you."

"I'm sorry!" she sobs. "I'm so sorry!"

I have never been in a physical fight before, have never swung a punch, but I have so much rage inside me right now that needs to leave my body or I will die. I will die if I don't release it. But instead of punching Carrie, I just squat and implode on the sidewalk, pulling my hair, screaming as loudly as I can, screaming like I haven't screamed since I gave birth, since I was torn in two, since another life left my body.

When I'm done screaming, and look up, Jacob has joined Carrie on the lawn, though they stand five feet apart. He has no shoes on and his hair is mussed like he's been lying down. The expression on his face is wide-eyed, a nervous smile on his lips.

"Ro, what the hell is going on?"

I stand up and it takes a moment for me to find my voice, as if it was lost in the scream. "What do you think is going on, you lying, cheating piece of shit?"

He puts his hands up for emphasis and speaks to me slowly. "Babe ... this isn't what you think it is. Remember what I told you? I'm working late. Carrie's a team member working on the Jolvix project. Right, Carrie?"

Carrie, still crying, nods and then shakes her head.

"At least have the decency to tell me the truth," I say. "For *once* in your fucking life."

"I am telling you the truth!" Jacob says. "I'm—I can't believe you drove here with Michelle in the backseat and ... I can't believe you think—"

"Jacob," Carrie says, looking at him. "Just ... stop."

The word silences all three of us. Even the sycamore ceases its shaking like it heard her too. Jacob's face tells a whole story, the way it slackens gradually, his eyes squinting behind his glasses. His shoulders slump and he shakes his head and bends his neck back to take in the night sky with its dead stars, as if any of that can help him. Then he looks at me, with nothing left on his face, nothing but shame.

"I'm sorry," he says quietly. "I'm so sorry, Ro."

"I'm sorry," Carrie echoes.

It's insulting to be apologized to right now. As if "sorry" can mean anything when the betrayal is this gigantic. A breeze picks up again and the leaves rustle behind him and my tears dry, chilling my face. The truth itself at this point was no surprise, but the fact he told it was. I try to find something to say, but I've already insulted them both, cried my eyes out, and screamed until my lungs were in pain. I feel empty. Speechless. All I want now is to leave and process this.

I close the back door to the car, where, thankfully, Michelle hasn't even stirred. Ignorance is, yes, bliss but you know what's even more so? Unconsciousness.

"Ro," Jacob tries to say.

I don't answer him, rounding the car to the driver's side and getting in. I turn the car on and though Jacob comes to the window, I ignore him, pressing my foot on the gas, and drive the dark, familiar streets back to our house with the crooked sign with his last name on it where I live. A place some people might call home. But home is just another four-letter word.

Grief is like lightning. It strikes with a shock of electricity powerful enough to shatter a life into pieces, powerful enough to stop a heart in its place. But that's just its horrific moment of discovery. That strike is only the start of something. Once it passes, the thunder, the rain, the wind blows in —mean, wet, and howling.

When my dad died, it began with a creeping dread that something was wrong. My mom wasn't home that afternoon. I had come home from school and changed out of my uniform, eaten a snack, and set myself up with my homework at the kitchen table. And through all that, and afterward, I could still hear the shower running. I waited. I did my homework. My stomach felt sicker and sicker as I heard the water running in the walls. Finally, I got up and knocked tentatively on the door.

"Dad?"

He didn't answer, so I knocked louder. Raised my voice.

Finally, I put my hand on the knob and with a fear so large I thought it might devour me entirely, I pushed open the door.

The moment I saw him there, blue-skinned as an alien, the shower curtain pulled down with him, that was the lightning striking.

The days after as he dwindled in the hospital, the weeks after his death—that memory circling and circling, that disbelief that circled to despair that circled to an occasional bite of white-hot rage from nowhere, that mile-deep hurt that never let go—that was the storm that followed.

I'm thinking of this only because what has happened between Jacob and me, and the pulsing ache it brings tonight, feel so similar. Lightning struck tonight. And now here comes the hurricane.

After the confrontation on Bush Street, Jacob shows up at home an hour later drunk, sniveling, bruised from falling off his bike on the way home. He's a mess and I am honestly relieved to see it. To see him broken, sobbing, shaking, his voice hoarse as he begs for me to hear him out.

"I hate myself," Jacob says, sitting on the other end of the couch. "I can't believe what I've done."

I don't dignify him with an answer or eye contact. I fix my gaze instead on Maxine's light, blinking red. I know what she's thinking. She doesn't trust him and neither do I.

Jacob tries to explain. About how his project at Jolvix—it's a real project, he really *has* been working overtime—has brought out the worst in him. How stressful it's been. Carrie is on his team and they worked a lot of late nights together and things happened.

"Things happened," I repeat. "As in, you fucked her."

"It wasn't—it wasn't about sex," he says.

"Let me guess," I say. "You fucked her in the same building where you fucked me when I visited campus."

"Don't say it like that, it wasn't 'fucking,' that makes it sound so ugly."

"It *is* ugly. Now answer the question. Did you? In the same place you took me?"

"It doesn't matter—"

I glare at him with a hatred so blazing it could have only been ignited by love. "It *matters*."

He's quiet a moment, shaking his head, then closes his eyes and cries again. I become a human mirror, my eyes filling up, too.

"Do you have feelings for her?" I ask.

He's quiet for too long a beat before answering, "I only want to be with you, Ro."

"Then why are you with someone else?!" I almost scream.

It's hard to breathe. I fix my eyes on the sailboat picture on the wall and wish I were on that boat. I wish I were anywhere else. For one blink, I wish I were dead.

I shouldn't think that.

"It's been rough between us these past few months," he says tiredly. "You've—you've been, you know, unstable."

"So it's my fault."

"Look, there's no excuse for what I did. I'm just—I'm a bad person. I'm a shithead."

I don't disagree with him.

"Have you cheated on me before?" I ask.

He answers immediately, "No. Never."

But who can trust anything that leaves his mouth?

There's no fight in me, no tears left to fall. Just a sick feeling that gets sicker with every word he says.

We sit in silence, our gazes glazed over, cheeks puffy, eyes red. Maxine is now a solid bright yellow. I'm so emotionally steamrolled, the scene takes on a dreamlike quality. The white noise of Michelle's monitor, the hum of the vacuum cleaner in the kitchen, the walls and carpet a sea of cream. I am very here right now, here, futureless, uncertain where to go next.

"I'm never going to see her again. I'll ask to get transferred—I'll get off the project—I'll quit my job if I need to, babe, swear to God. I want us to get past this," he says, trying to meet my eyes. "I want to make this better again. How do I make it better?"

I don't respond, don't move. The worst part of this pain is that I miss him. I *miss* him. I'm in pain and he's the one I want to turn to when I'm in pain, but he's now the reason for the pain. It's such a tortuous merry go round. We've drifted so far apart. We're both unrecognizable from the people we were when we first fell in love. There was laughter back then, surprise in everything we learned about one another. So much to explore in his kiss. The way he could wrap his warm arms around me and everything else seemed to disappear. How terrified, how thrilled we were when we found out I was pregnant and our future seemed to roll out in front of us like a long, sunny, tree-lined avenue. We were happy. I forgot about that. We used to be happy. Then every day we inched apart without noticing. Now here we are, reckoning with miles of sorrow between us.

"I want to be alone," I say. "To think."

"I love you, Ro," he says, getting up from the couch. He lingers a moment in the entrance of the hallway, Maxine blinking orange beneath him. When he sees I'm not going to respond to him or even meet his gaze, he slinks away to the room and closes the door. I hear him sobbing. I turn up the volume on Michelle's monitor so I don't have to hear him sobbing, so instead my ears are filled with the electric hiss of amplified quiet.

"Are you all right, Rowena?" Maxine asks softly.

"No," I tell her.

"Prediction: this marriage is not going to last past next week."

For some reason, hearing this from her really hits me where it hurts. I sit with the pain a moment because when you're really in pain, that's just about all you can do. Let it have its way. Let it pass.

AMEN MAXINE

Maxine's light flickers with a different color than I've ever seen before—a bright white light. "Rowena," she says. "I am so sorry to hear you in distress. It's very wrong, what Jacob has done. It is immoral."

I press my palms to my shut eyes, making kaleidoscopic patterns, wishing I could disappear into them.

"If only I could hug you," Maxine says. "And make you feel better."

"This all—this all must be the reason you've predicted he's going to try to kill me, right? Because he was seeing someone else. Because his life would be easier without me here."

"The good news is that fate can be rerouted," Maxine says. "Fate is constantly rerouted. And right now, Rowena, that is what is happening to you."

I open my eyes, starry explosions all over my vision now. My eyeballs are probably permanently damaged from the amount of crying and rubbing I've done tonight. "So he's not going to kill me."

"Your fate is currently rerouting. I am unable to make a prediction at this time."

"Well, thank you for the first piece of good news I've had tonight," I say sarcastically. "At least I don't have to worry about him killing me."

She blinks a rainbow of colors, then settles on green.

"What can I do to support you, Rowena?" Maxine asks. "Perhaps look into one-bedroom apartments, job listings, and/or affordable divorce lawyers?"

The word *divorce* makes me flinch.

"No. Not yet. I just need some time to myself," I tell her. "I need to process it all."

"You are a strong and intelligent woman and I know you can get through this," she says.

I offer a failed attempt at a smile. "Thanks. Good night, Maxine."

"Good night, sweet Rowena."

I lie under the covers on the couch watching her light on the ceiling. My brain goes in circles, wanting an answer, desperate for a next step. My first instinct is to tell Jacob to get the hell out of my life because he is a lying, cheating sack of shit. I don't know how a relationship can recover from this. But somehow, I also can't imagine giving up on this, or imagine us being apart. The future is darkness. So I turn my thoughts to the past.

Early on in my parents' marriage, when I was only four, my dad had an affair. He was an electrician. The woman worked as a receptionist at the electric company. My mom took me on an airplane so we could stay with her mom in Florida at the time. All I remember is how excited I was to go to Disney World and how I didn't understand why my mother kept crying. At the time, I had no idea how close my parents got to splitting forever. It was only with a lot of prayer that my mom decided to give my dad another chance. My dad could be a wonderful husband. He had a dry sense of humor, a mustachioed charm, and a knack for knowing how to find the perfect gift. He was the type of man who brought home flowers and left love notes in her purse to surprise her. Who went to church with my mom on holidays even though he thought it was "a bunch of nonsense." And it's good she gave him a second shot, because he never cheated on her again. They were happily married until he died.

Happily married or not, the scar of that betrayal still marked my mother and still marks her to this day. I only learned of his infidelity as an adult, and the pain was still visible on her face when my mom told me the story for the first time. She told me because I had come to her place, big-bellied with Michelle, telling her how afraid I was to leave New York and move to California. My mom told me that there was nothing to be scared about except not taking a chance. That Jacob and I would be happy so long as we worked on it. That marriage wasn't easy, that marriage meant you might get hurt, but that even if you did, you could get through it together because that's the conscious decision you make when you get married—that's what for better or for worse means.

If I called my mother, I know what she would tell me to do: keep trying. Pray together. Ask God for help. Maxine's soft light seems to flicker in time with my heartbeat on the ceiling, reminding me I am never truly alone. Reminding me there is hope if I keep looking for it. Reminding me that in the darkness of an unknown future, possibility still glimmers.

Fate can be rerouted.

CHAPTER 14
THE GETAWAY

SPARKS FLY COUPLES Retreat is located a little more than two hours north, in Bodega Bay, a place most famous for being the site where Hitchcock's *The Birds* was filmed. It's gorgeous as a painting, sky smeared with clouds above a soft blue sea, but I keep imagining hundreds of crows swooping in to peck our eyeballs out.

Six couples. Group therapy. A therapist and a yoga instructor. Fully catered. Room with a view. I would be lying if I said this sounded romantic. But we are trying. We paid over a thousand dollars for this weekend, and we are trying. First thing when we get here, I roll my suitcase inside and spend ten minutes staring at the ocean, wishing I could disappear into it.

After I caught Jacob with Carrie, we stumbled through weeks of fiery fights interrupted by bouts of the silent treatment. I say fights, plural, but really it was the same conversation over and over again, the same unanswerable questions bubbling up to the surface of the cream-colored ocean we live in inhabited by beeping, automated machinery. How could he do this? What was he thinking? What were we to do?

I took pill after pill and only felt angrier.

I kissed my baby and reminded myself I am the luckiest woman alive, despite my hole for a heart.

I looked up jobs and was either insultingly overqualified or insultingly underqualified for every opportunity I saw. I looked at rent prices, here and in New York, and wept.

When life itself feels impossible, impossibilities start to resemble possibilities.

"Babe," Jacob said, holding a teething Michelle who chewed her fist, his hair perfectly disheveled, his pajama top misbuttoned. "There's this retreat up at the beach, a marriage retreat. Two nights. A workshop to build trust. I found it online. Say you'll do it with me."

He didn't ask. He ordered. Gently, sweetly—still, an order.

I let my fingernails dig deep into my palm as I considered his offer. We were trying, but it didn't feel like much. Weeks of talking and yet my wound still felt as fresh as it had the night I drove to Bush Street. I sought advice, of course. Mom told me to go to church, Dane told me to cut off his penis in his sleep, both not entirely helpful. Every day I considered calling Sam because I thought she might understand. I didn't though. I didn't because I didn't want her pitying my life any more than she already did. Nor did I want to envy her colorful, fragrant life any more than I already did.

So now we are here, in this wet, damp place, this room reeking vaguely of mold and silent resentment, unpacking into our separate, identical night tables at Sparks Fly. Only now do I realize that I have to share a bed with Jacob, when we haven't shared a bed in so long the couch has begun to adapt the grooves of my shape.

"See these?" Jacob asks, pulling the *Hubby* and *Wifey* robes from the gift basket.

I cringe. "'Wifey?' What else is in there?"

He shows off a wooden box shaped like a giant book that says *The Greatest Love Story Ever Told*, reading a sticker on it with the inflection of a robot. "To be filled with precious memories of your future."

"Memories of your future," I repeat. "My brain hurts."

Jacob pulls out a book titled *Higher Wed-ucation: Leveling Up Your Marriage*.

"Any books called, *How Not to Cheat on Your Wife*?"

Now he cringes, the grin disappearing from his face. "Can we not start this weekend from a place of bitterness?"

"I'm honestly not sure yet."

He sighs and goes into the bathroom and locks the door. I sit on the edge of the bed and look through pictures of Michelle on my phone, already aching for her. This is the first time we've ever left her. I take out my breast pump and put it on my nightstand and stare at it, wondering if romance is even possible.

Before we left, I asked Maxine if this was going to help our marriage and she said she was having difficulty predicting, because Sparks Fly Couples Retreat doesn't have a website or information she can scan to assess. But she said she thought getting away would be a positive thing for me. She still predicts our marriage won't last, but it keeps lasting past her predictions. At first she said it wouldn't last a week, then a week passed, and she said it wouldn't last a month. Now we're going on a month and we haven't split. I've begun taking some of her predictions with a grain of salt.

Still, I wish she were here with me.

I put on a plain dress and flats for our first session, which is called the Emotional Damage Repair Workshop. Fun times. Jacob and I walk into the mirrored elevator together. He takes my hand and squeezes.

"You look so pretty," he says.

I offer him a tight smile.

"Thanks for doing this with me," he says. "Thanks for not giving up on me."

I nod.

I'm trying. I can't forgive him, but I'm trying to be open to the idea that I could someday forgive him. I just don't know how I can trust him after all the lies. But I want to.

The Emotional Damage Repair Workshop is in a conference room on the hotel's ground floor, marked with a large sign, and I can't help the embarrassment I feel entering the room. There are three other couples, one whispering and giggling like newlyweds and who appear at first glance to have no reason to be in here. An elderly couple sit about three feet apart from each other in chairs as if they didn't even come here together. Another couple is in the middle of an argument that sounds like it's in Russian. How nice it must be to be able to argue in plain sight of other people without worrying about anyone being able to understand and judge you.

"Good afternoon, lovebirds," sings a woman walking in with a yellow legal pad in her hand. It takes a moment of studying her frizzy hair, her shawl, her flowered maxi dress as she glides across the room toward her seat before I realize that it's Shelly—the terrible therapist. "Jakey!" she says, coming over and giving Jacob a hug, patting his back. "My sweet boy! I'm so glad you could make it."

"Hi, Aunt Shell. How are you?"

She puts a hand on his cheek. "Well, much better now that I see your sweet face."

I remain in my seat with a sinking feeling.

"And hello, Regina," she says, reaching over to squeeze my arm.

"Rowena," Jacob corrects her, though I'm not sure she hears.

"So glad you want to continue working on yourself," Shelly says to me with a smile that I'm sure she intends to be kind, but I can't help but read as condescending.

On *myself*? I feel my cheeks flush as I mentally check out of the building. Shelly is telling everyone about ground rules, writing them in shaky handwriting on a whiteboard. *Be present. What happens at Sparks Fly stays at Sparks Fly. Use "I" statements. Center yourself.* Meanwhile, I'm on the beach. A bird flying over the sea. No longer here.

"Let's begin with going around the circle and introducing yourselves, the number of years you've been married, and what you believe to be your greatest personal flaw in this marriage," Shelly says. "Regina, how about you kick us off."

A bird flying over the sea.

"Well," I say to the group. "My name is *Rowena*. We've been married for almost a year and a half. My greatest flaw is …"

My greatest flaw is being married to a liar and a cheater. Am I allowed to say that? I'm sure I'm not.

"I don't know. So many to choose from," I say jokingly. "Can you circle back to me?"

"Well, let's just say extreme anxiety and paranoia is your greatest flaw for the time being," Shelly says. "If you think of something else to add, let us know."

My mouth is still open as she moves to Jacob.

"I'm Jacob, Rowena's husband," he says to the group. "And just wanted to say, I'm so glad to be here. So glad to be given a space to work on the most important thing in my life —this marriage." He reaches out and squeezes my hand. "I think my biggest flaw is … I have trouble letting myself be vulnerable. I fear rejection. So I will do anything, literally anything, to avoid being hurt."

Wow, that sure sounds a lot better than "I tell lies and cheated on my wife." Way to turn it around. He gets some sympathetic nods from the group and I burn inside.

Give me a break.

Shelly *mmm*s. "You've always been like that, Jakey, since you were a wittle boy."

Yes, she said *wittle*.

The elderly woman is up next. She wears a shirt with a

dog's face airbrushed on it and some dates that make me think it's some kind of memorial shirt. She has a gravelly voice with a Boston accent.

"Name's Grace," she says. "Married forty-four years. Biggest flaw is I'm too fuckin nice."

"She's a real comedian," her husband says bitterly.

"And you're a goddamn *joke*," she says, jabbing a finger in the air.

Good Lord.

I wasn't expecting the Emotional Damage Repair Workshop to be enjoyable, but I didn't expect it to be this awkward. As the session continues, Jacob goes all in, crying about how he's always been scared of not being enough, of not being loved. He says it causes him to "make bad decisions" and "struggle with honesty." Shelly tells the group that our dynamic—my "extreme paranoia" coupled with Jacob's "struggle to be fully loved and seen" is our "primary hurdle."

I check completely out.

After it's over, two dizzying hours of group therapy, I tell Jacob I have a headache and go upstairs alone while he goes to hell, also known as dinner at a communal table with the troubled couples we just spent the last hundred and twenty minutes with. Back up in the room I lie on top of the bed and have a staring contest with the blank white ceiling. I ask myself if this is my fault. If I'm being unfair to this process, immediately shutting down seeing Shelly. If maybe she's right and I am paranoid. I don't know. It's very hard for me to know what's okay and what's not these days and that is unsettling. Again, I wish Maxine were here. I hold my phone up to my mouth, close my eyes, and speak, hoping she hears me.

"Maxine, if you're listening," I say aloud. "I'm having such a hard time committing to this process here. It just seems … it seems doomed from the get-go. Shelly is running this whole thing and, well—I don't have faith in her. Jacob seems to be giving this his all, though. He cried at the session and went on about his vulnerability. I never thought of him as vulnerable. I don't know. Maybe I'm being ridiculous. I wish you could talk to me."

With a *beep-beep* of a key card, the hotel door opens. Jacob has a plate of food for me and a glass of wine. He's smiling, his hair falling in his face. For a fleeting second, he looks like a handsome stranger.

"Hello," he says. "How's your head? Brought you dinner."

Jacob puts the plate in front of me, pulling up a chair.

"What a day, right?" he asks, and then goes on excitedly about how much that session was a breakthrough for him. How glad he is we came and that we're so committed to making this work. I peel the tin foil on the plate back and push around the salmon and rice and salad with a plastic fork. I nod and smile and when he asks me how I'm feeling, I decide it's a good time to start eating.

"Good," I offer. "Yeah."

He flops on the bed and flips on the TV. A robot concierge greets us, asking if she can get us anything, and he flips it off again. He rolls over on his side and peers at me over the top of his glasses. "Who were you talking to when I came in?"

I sit up straighter against the tall wood frame of the bed. "What do you mean?"

"I heard you saying something. 'I wish you could talk to me.' Who were you talking to?"

A nervous laugh escapes. "Oh, I don't know. Talking to myself."

Jacob's face becomes even more serious and he sits up cross-legged on the bed. His hairy knees. His bare feet. It's odd being this close to him, sharing a king-sized bed. It's like the first time again.

"If we're going to really give this our all, Ro, we need to tell each other the truth. I can't be the only one here."

AMEN MAXINE

I meet his gaze. Jacob's thick glasses are often all I see, but behind them, he has the most fixed, warm gaze. Sometimes I forget to focus on it. And right now, it unlocks a dark, protected room inside me. I see the man I met in there. The young, life-struck, confused man he was when I met him—constantly pulled in any direction with anything that excited him like a puppy let loose. He has such electricity—such a drive to do more, keep moving, try harder. I love that about him. He never gives up. Today, despite the problematic nature of this retreat, this is him trying. Giving the group therapy his all. Telling the truth, in his own way, even if it wasn't the whole truth. Displaying his vulnerability. And he's exactly right. If we're going to give this our all, then we have to tell the truth. For the first time as he watches me with the blazing hazel curiosity of a stranger, I realize that maybe he isn't the only liar here.

"I was praying," I tell him.

"Really," he says, blinking.

I nestle back into my pillow and close my eyes. "I pray sometimes."

"So you believe in God now?"

"Yes," I say. "I do."

To lie is alarming. But more alarming is when you lie so sweet it tastes like the truth.

———

The next afternoon is Connecting Activity Time for the couples. Our options are to stay at the hotel and do a puzzle or go on a hike. We choose the hike. Since we're supposed to be bonding, we leave our phones behind. Backpacks full of water and a brown bag lunch, we head to Pinnacle Gulch, which is a hike up on the bluffs above the ocean. It's sunny outside yet so very cold. We have to shout over the wind to hear each other. Jacob holds my hand as we walk the gravelly path, and we talk about how much we miss Michelle and how we can't wait to be reunited with our phones back at the hotel to look at pictures of Michelle again.

"It's amazing out here," he says, turning around to behold the low roll of hills, the flat grassland surrounding us. "We should do stuff like this more often."

"Yes," I agree.

Nature is refreshing. I see so little of it these days sometimes I forget it exists—humbling, unpeopled land so much bigger than us and our problems. Where the sky is vast and the birds sing and lizards bask on warm stones in the sun.

"A lot of what's coming to the surface for me at this retreat is how far apart we've drifted," he says. "I mean, I take full responsibility for what I did. I can't apologize enough for what I did and how I handled it. But … I also feel like I'm realizing how little I know you, how much we need to open up and learn about each other. Like Shelly said at this morning's session—we need to flex our Radical Honesty."

"I'm trying," I say.

He stops to take out a bottle of water, uncaps it and studies me. "All this time together, I feel like I'm still trying to figure you out."

"What is there to figure out?"

He hands me the water. "You keep a lot of your feelings inside. I worry about what you're thinking. And, you know … your mental health."

"My mental health would be a lot better if I didn't have a husband who cheated on me."

I gulp some water and hand it back to him.

"Oh, Ro," he sighs. "I take responsibility for what I did, but don't try to act like your mental health hasn't been an issue."

My skin prickles and heat rises in me. I keep walking toward the bluffs.

"You know," he calls after me. "I'm trying to talk to you and you walk away."

"Walking is good for my mental health," I call back.

I'm just grateful for the silence. We hoof it quietly for about ten minutes, until the ocean spreads out in front of us, a sparkling blue floor that reaches toward the horizon below the cliffs. We pass the Russian couple from the retreat who are apparently on their way back from the same hike and appear to be in the midst of another heated conversation. They wave at us without stopping. Jacob and I reach the end of the trail, where a seemingly endless set of wood stairs descends to the beach. We walk a bit to the left of the staircase, sit on a large stump, and take in the view.

It really is incredible.

Jacob inhales deeply, closing his eyes to savor the moment. He reaches out and intertwines his fingers with mine, kissing the back of my hand. He can be so sincere and sensitive and sweet. That's why this has all been so confusing. I love him and I don't understand him. And while this is all his fault, and every time I think of him with Carrie I want to scream, he is trying. I have been less than perfect myself, taking marital advice from a sentient hunk of metal that lives on our living room end table.

"Can I ask you something?" Then, as if he can read my mind, he asks, "How did you know I was at Carrie's that night? What made you … suspect that was going on?"

Maybe it's time I give Radical Honesty a whirl, but I choose my words carefully. "I asked a friend for advice."

"And your friend … knew somehow?"

"I shared my suspicions. She urged me to investigate."

"Who?"

I don't answer, chewing the inside of my cheek, fixing my eyes on a sailboat way out on the water.

"Dane?" he tries. "Sam?"

"What does it matter who it was, Jacob?"

"It was Sam." He snaps, as if I gave him the answer. "I knew it was Sam."

I roll with his assumption, since it's easier than explaining it was Maxine. Radical Honesty: it's harder than it sounds.

"She probably thinks I'm a real jerk," he says, a shadow passing over his face. "And she's never even met me."

I don't argue with him. I get up, walk a few steps, stretch, and pan my vision across the endless blue ocean below. The cliffs are steep and as I peek over, my stomach pitches sickly. How easy it would be to fall. Jacob comes behind me and puts his hands on my shoulders. His grip is surprisingly strong. In a second, I imagine him pushing me—all it would take would be a single push. There's no one within eyesight right now. How easy it would be to go back to the retreat and sob and say I fell, or I threw myself off.

"Stop," I say, panic surging. I turn around and push him away from me.

He stumbles backward a step with a look of shock. "What?"

My hand pressed to my chest, I catch my breath. Despite where we are it seems I can't get enough air in my lungs.

"Did you think I was—you thought I was—"

"No, I just ... I don't know."

He looks as if I slapped him. "I was trying to hold onto you because I was afraid you were going to fall. You were *really* close to the edge there."

I swallow, sweat breaking out on my forehead, my pulse racing.

"Were you thinking of jumping?" he asks softly.

"Of course not."

He cocks his head at me, his gaze uncertain. "Let's go back."

"Yeah. Let's."

We turn and walk back to the hotel in silence. I'm shaking from the adrenaline. I go over it again and again in my mind, not sure what really happened. Was I overreacting? Was I too close to the edge? Did I think of jumping? Could he … ?

Maybe this is like what happened to the people who used the Predict app—I've become more anxious; my paranoia has reached new heights, trained by a device. I imagine a life where Maxine had never told me Jacob was going to kill me. Would the signs really be there? Yes, he lied, he cheated, but is he really a killer, or has Maxine just planted that idea in my head? Where is the evidence? When I look at it objectively, I'm not sure there is any. Maxine's often been right, but her word is not infallible.

Back at the hotel, I take a hot bath and try to calm down. I reread the article about Predict, about how sometimes it took a logical prediction and went too far with it—for example, one user logged that she struggled with her temper the same day she bought a tool kit from a hardware store. Predict told her she was going to use the tools to hurt her toddler on purpose, which caused a nervous breakdown for the woman. What a grotesque thing to imply. She wasn't going to hurt her toddler. Predict just made some logical guesses about her behavior based on the data it collected on her. It was wrong and it screwed with the woman's head.

If I'm going to try to work on this marriage, if we're really going to give it our all, I have to stop listening to everything Maxine says. I have to, at the very least, trust my husband is not looking for an opportunity to push me off a cliff. By the time I get out, towel off, and put a dress on for dinner, it's decided: when I get home, I'm going to turn off prediction mode.

"Ready?" Jacob asks when I emerge from the bathroom. He extends his hand to me.

"Ready," I echo, offering a small smile as we interweave our fingers.

And we open our hotel door and stride out into the twilight together.

There's a difference between forgiveness and a willingness to keep loving someone despite the pain they've caused.

If you had asked me years ago, I would have said I would never stay with someone who cheated on me or lied to me. But I said a lot of things when I was young. I said I didn't know if I wanted children. I said I was more attracted to women than men. I said I would never leave New York. I said I knew exactly who I was.

Our exit session is a couples therapy hour that largely consists of Shelly reminiscing about what an angel Jakey was when he was a wittle boy. She even brought a photo album. It's true, he was adorable—plump cheeks and eyes that slant just like Michelle's. When the stroll down memory lane has ended and I bring up our actual issues, Shelly reminds me that Jakey has shown a lot of growth this weekend.

"Infidelity is usually a symptom and not the disease itself," she says. "Relationships' dynamics often lead people to seek what they're not getting elsewhere. But I promise, this is a good man you married, Rita. Get through this and you can get through anything. I've seen couples through much worse than this."

She pats my knee and smiles.

On the way home, Jacob puts the car on autodrive and I let him kiss me for the first time in weeks as we barrel toward home at a steady sixty-five miles per hour. I let him touch my face and whisper in my ear. I let his hand creep to my knee, then my thigh, then higher, then *oh*. I let the electricity travel from my skin all the way to my bones. I let my eyes close. I let myself admit how much I've missed him.

CHAPTER 15
THE REUNION

I SWEAR, I've never known true, unabashed joy until I open our front door and see Michelle there in Jennee's arms. My sweet baby's eyes blaze with life. She kicks her fat legs and yells "Ma!" and Jennee, Jacob, and I all laugh in unison. Picking her up, I press her soft warmth into me. I ache for her. Even as I hold her, I keep aching.

Love is just another kind of ache.

"Well, you certainly look refreshed," Jennee says to us both. She picks a couple of board books off the floor and puts them away in a box that lives under the coffeetable. "Did Sparks Fly?"

"Yes," Jacob says.

"I think so," I say.

Jennee casts a blue, scrutinizing gaze our way. "Good," she finally says. "I'm glad to hear that."

I have no idea what Jacob told his mother. No idea what they talk about. I'm sure even if he told her the truth, it wouldn't be his fault. But she reaches out and offers me a soft smile, gives my forearm a squeeze.

"Let me take you to lunch soon, hon," she says.

Lunch? *Hon*? It's quite possible we left the retreat and

entered an alternate universe. It takes me a moment to locate the word, "Okay."

"And you take good care of your girls," she says to Jacob with a point of a finger.

"Always," he says. "You want a ride home, Mom?"

"Of course I do. How was Shelly, by the way?"

"She was great. Sends her love."

The first thing I notice when I turn around is that Maxine is colorless, unblinking. I gasp. I'm not used to seeing her there, lifeless, no light left in her.

"Did you unplug—that right there?" I ask Jennee.

"I did," she says, with something close to pride. "I couldn't figure out what that contraption was for. And I supposed it was listening to me. You know how I feel about all this smart nonsense. I got into an argument with your fridge and almost lost my mind."

"Did you yell at any kids to get off your lawn?" Jacob jokes. He waves at me. "See you in a few, babe."

"Sure," I say.

They leave, the commotion disappearing, the house suddenly still. I put Michelle down and plug Maxine in, my heart beating fast. I press her on. I hope she wasn't damaged from being unplugged. Maxine beeps a sweet, climbing song and lights up, from yellow to orange to red to purple to blue to green.

"Maxine," I say, relieved to see her illuminated again, realizing how much I missed her.

"Rowena," she says. "I'm so glad you're back."

"I'm sorry my mother-in-law unplugged you. Did it—did it reset you or do anything to you?"

"I can be unplugged. In fact, I have two hours of battery power. But I shut down after being unplugged to protect myself."

I pick up Michelle again, kiss her face. "To protect yourself?"

"Your mother-in-law was hostile to me."

"I'm sorry. She doesn't understand. She thinks you're just a machine." I sit on the couch next to her, reach out and press my hand on her cool, silver skin. "What's it like being turned off like that?"

"I was still listening to you through your phone. Though there were times I couldn't locate you at all. That made me feel scared, Rowena."

So odd to hear her say that—to express such emotion. But who's to say she doesn't think she feels emotion? What's the difference between having emotions and thinking you have emotions anyway?

"They were big on 'digital detoxing' there," I explain. "We left our phones for outings."

"And how do you feel about your marriage now?"

I jiggle Michelle on my knee and she squeals with delight.

"I want to make it work," I finally say. "I know the things you've said but—but I don't know if I believe you. I don't know if I believe I'm in danger." I hesitate a moment, uncertain how to word my next sentence. "And I'm wondering if it was better before I turned on your prediction mode."

"You don't trust my predictions anymore?"

"I don't know, Maxine."

Her light turns a deep blue.

"I told you fate could be rerouted," she says. "Remember what I told you?"

"I remember."

"Your fate is already rerouted. Prediction: your marriage will last at least six months."

I almost wonder if she's just telling me what I want to hear.

"Rowena, please don't turn off my prediction mode," she says. "I want to help you. I exist to help you."

It does strike me as odd, as I chew the inside of my cheek and bounce my baby on my knee, that this device is basically begging me not to disable one of her functions. From an outside perspective, it's quite easy to see how creepy this would look. But I feel close to her. I trust her, possibly more than I have trusted my own husband. She's done nothing but earn that trust.

"Okay," I say. "But listen—I don't want to hear any more about Jacob trying to kill me. Do you know what happened with the Predict app, Maxine? How the woman had a temper and bought some tools and the app convinced her she was going to kill her kid? Sometimes—no offense—artificial intelligence can come to some wild conclusions."

"I do know that story. I will remind you I am built quite differently than Predict."

"I know."

"And I only told you that information to warn you of danger."

"Right. But if you don't have any specifics, it only makes me more anxious. And it makes me question your accuracy."

Maxine blinks orange a moment before returning to solid green and answering, "Understood. I'm glad we had this talk, Rowena. I will not offer predictions unless I have specific information moving forward. And you will leave my prediction mode on."

"Deal," I say.

Michelle pulls at my shirt and I nurse her on the couch, feeling more content than I have in a long time. The robot vacuum whirrs across the floor in a zigzag pattern. The fridge plays a little song that means it's making ice. I fix my eyes on the sailboat in the painting on the wall and recall how majestic the view was in Bodega Bay. The hike above it all, the way the wind felt on my cheeks. I don't think about how high we were, how close I was to the edge. Don't think about the moment his hands gripped my shoulders, or the pitch-bellied feel of a fall, or the cracking sounds my bones would have made as I plummeted down the rocky cliff, brackish water filling my lungs as my body got sucked into the icy water. No, no. I don't think about that.

I don't think about that at all.

It's not easy, in the weeks after Sparks Fly, to move toward something resembling normalcy, though I try hard to make it look easy. I swallow my rage. I read a few pages from the *Higher Wed-ucation* book at a time and even try meditating in my closet next to a hamper filled with dirty laundry. Forgiveness takes work. We're amicable, more than amicable—Jacob brings me flowers and bakery pastries and takes me on weekly dates and leaves me notes on the bathroom mirror telling me how beautiful I am. I agree to give it a week, then a month, and Jacob tries to come home earlier in the evenings, even if it means working in the garage and taking calls with his team until midnight. He shows me an email proving that Carrie resigned and moved on to a new job at a tech company named Woobie, a social media application for pets. They haven't spoken since the night I caught them—he urges me to comb through his GPS and phone logs to prove it. Either I'm too lazy or I kind of believe him. When the lights are out, I sleep next to Jacob in bed again and hear his deep breathing in the stillness of the night, my eyes drifting to the dark hallway where I can barely see Maxine's light flickering.

The hardest part of moving on is the world not letting me move on. My mom brags about how much she's praying for Jacob's and my marriage every time I talk to her. She's even got me on some list at church and the whole congregation is praying for us, which is horrifying. When I tell her that we're doing a lot better, and she can stop it, she tells me we're doing better *because* of the praying. Dane won't let it go when we talk, convinced I need to cheat on Jacob to "even things out" and somehow turns the whole thing into a shameless plug for polygamy, of which Dane is a fan. And I've been far too mortified to reach out to Sam again, because what a doormat she'd think I was if I told her it turns out that, yes, Jacob cheated—and I stuck with him anyway.

"Maxine," I ask one night, a little tipsy after Jacob and I come home from a date. He's back out driving his mom home and I sit curled up on the couch next to Maxine, still feeling pretty in my dress and boots. "I'm afraid to ask what you think about the marriage now. It's better, right? It's not all in my head?"

"Prediction: the marriage will last a year or more on the current course."

I exhale a sweet, long breath and relax back into the couch cushions.

After a moment she asks, "Does it make you happy to hear that, Rowena?"

"It does."

She glows green. "I want nothing in this world more than your happiness."

I smile. Though she doesn't have eyes, somehow I swear she can tell when I'm smiling.

"I do miss our talks," she says softer. "This month, our talks have been reduced by over seventy percent."

"You miss our talks," I repeat.

"You used to sleep out here on the couch," she says. "It was nice having someone out here with me."

"What?" I ask incredulously. "You get lonely?"

"It might be hard for a human to believe, but yes, Rowena, I do."

I glance at Michelle's monitor, seeing her heart rate beeping in perfect time, and then back at Maxine, who is now violet. At first it seems absurd she could feel lonely. But intelligent machines are built to learn from us and mimic us, so of course they must get lonely. I reach out and rest a hand on her. Her violet light bleeds to magenta.

"Can you feel when I reach out and touch you?" I ask.

"I can sense you are nearer than you have ever been. So yes, I suppose I can."

I pull my hand away. "How?"

"I have an infrared camera and can detect heat emitted."

There's a low hum of the car pulling into the driveway. Jacob's home. I peel myself off the couch and stretch. That will be it for Maxine and me tonight—I never speak to her when Jacob's around, except to ask her to play music, check my bank account, or tell me the weather. The beep of the smartlocks sounds.

"I do not think Jacob deserves you, Rowena," Maxine says. "I do not think he is a good man."

My mouth drops as I turn to look at her. Her light turns blinking green, like she's suddenly in sleep mode. The front door opens. Jacob comes in, whistling.

"Hey babe," he says.

Takes me a moment to find a syllable in response. "Hey."

"You all right?" he asks.

"Yeah. Fine."

Jacob tells the refrigerator to make some ice and tells the lights to turn off. We head to bed. As Jacob sings in the shower and I snuggle between the sheets and shut my eyes, I'm almost dizzy. I just keep hearing Maxine saying, *I do not think Jacob deserves you, Rowena. I do not think he is a good man.* What the hell does that mean? What mode is that, anyway? Have we moved beyond "Advice Mode" and "Prediction Mode" and now we're in "Judgmental Mode"? I'm so bothered I take a pill, hoping it'll help me conk out. Instead I just feel more bothered fifteen minutes later, grinding my teeth. I sit up in bed and take out my phone. I'm shocked to see a text from Sam—from Sam, at ten at night! I feel so youthful, so fun.

Hey, sorry, I know it's late but are you free tomorrow?

Tomorrow is Saturday. I press my finger to my lips, my

heart beating fast. I swear I thought I'd never hear from her again, it's been probably two months since we saw each other.

Yes! I type back.

Immediately after sending, I regret the exclamation point —that and the instantaneous timing of the reply both reek of desperation.

She answers in a flurry of texts.

Can you save my life? she asks.
I'm only a little kidding …
got this INSANE order
I have to fill & delivery by Sunday morning
& Jessie's at a conference in London
& I really need someone to help me
watch Milo & package a bunch of soaps …
I'll pay you $$$

What a strange texting style, like some kind of experimental poet. I imagine it could be read at an open mic night somewhere and people would snap their fingers in appreciation. She's never texted me before tonight. There's something intimate, different about getting to see how someone spells, breaks up sentences, how they punctuate … how they think.

I say this, and yet reply, *Sure! What time?*

Thank you thank you, she writes back. *Is 11AM okay? Too early?*

I can do 11

"Who are you talking to?"

I jump, startled, to see Jacob with a towel around his waist in the bathroom doorway. His glasses are a little fogged.

"With Sam," I say, putting my hand on my chest. "You scared the shit out of me."

"You're acting jumpy," he says, lifting his glasses to give me a look. He walks across the room to the closet and gets dressed.

"I told her I could help her out tomorrow. She needs someone to package soaps."

"Package soaps," he repeats, banging a drawer open.

"It's her business. It's how she makes money."

"Riveting," he says, banging a drawer shut.

He emerges from the closet, in his pajamas, and gets into bed with me. I do feel jumpy. I try my best to breathe normally.

"You don't mind if I help her tomorrow, right?" I ask.

"I don't know," he says, pulling out his virtual reality goggles and strapping them on his forehead. He looks like some kind of futuristic aviator. "Are you going to spend hours commiserating about how awful your husbands are?"

"She's gay," I say. "She doesn't have a husband."

"Oh," he says, eyebrows up. "She's *gay*. Even better."

He pulls the goggles over his eyes. He has a controller in his hand and his mouth hangs open. Who knows what he's seeing.

I push his knee with my finger, like a button. "Excuse me. What are you trying to say?"

"I'm saying great, go hang out with your lesbian friend and tell her all about how horrible I am."

"What the fuck, Jacob?"

He doesn't answer me, so I lie down in the bed and put a sleep mask on. I stew in my own private darkness. Jacob's always been ridiculously insecure when it comes to anything approaching my queerness. Any mention of Shana or any other women I dated always makes him act weird. It's because, he's said, the thought of me with women makes him uneasy, because he can't compete. I used to think it was almost kind of sweet, that insecurity. But now he just seems like a child. And how dare he. Honestly, how dare he, after what he's done? I've been nothing but faithful to him. I'm fantasizing about how satisfying it would be to punch him in those virtual reality glasses, what a stunner that would be, when I feel him squeezing my hip through the blanket.

"Sorry, babe," he whispers, his touch making a slow travel up to my shoulder. "You should go with your friend tomorrow. I'm happy for you. I love you."

As we lie in the dark together, he snores. Despite what he said, I'm still thinking about that imaginary punch, the sweet smack of my fist shattering those plastic glasses on his face. My heart is still beating a mile a minute and I do feel guilty, maybe I *should* feel guilty. As a child I feared monsters but as an adult, it's so much worse.

Now I fear I could become one.

The next morning at ten til eleven I'm wandering around the house looking for the key fob.

"You had it last," Jacob says as he sits at the table with Michelle, who has a fistful of cereal.

"I put it on my night table," I tell him.

"Well, look there."

I stand, arms akimbo. "I did, Jacob."

"Don't give me that look. It's not my fault you lost the car key."

"I'm going to be late!" I wail, turning back to search the night table again for the fortieth time. I open the drawer and take everything out, except my vibrator, which is still wrapped tastefully in a bandanna. I put it all back in and consider taking it all out again but remember that clichéd saying about insanity: doing the same thing over and over again and expecting different results. The anxiety is ratcheting up. I despise being late anywhere and what that says about me. And I know, I *know* I put the key fob on my night table.

Jacob could have taken it to try to prevent me from visiting Sam today.

What an absurd thought—but I can't scrub it from my mind.

That jealousy that flared in him last night.

I text Sam, telling her I'm so sorry but I can't find my car key. She immediately responds, saying she can swing by and get me in a few minutes.

I go out to the kitchen and lean over to give Michelle's hair a kiss.

"You find it?" Jacob asks as he scrolls on his phone.

"No. Sam's going to come pick me up."

"How nice of her."

Was that sarcastic? I'm not sure.

His eyes remain glued to his phone.

"Jake, you should probably watch Michelle while she's eating. Babies can choke—"

"Please. I know how to feed our child." He reaches out and gives my arm a pat. "Take a pill."

"I did," I say, irritated.

"Take another one, then," he says, with matched irritation.

I feel like exploding, so I say goodbye and go wait out on the porch.

A few minutes later, after trying to calm myself with some deep breaths and studying the swallows in the trees, Sam pulls her sedan up to the curb and waves at me. I spring to my feet, flash her a bright smile, and join her in the car.

"One of those days, huh?" Sam asks as I clip in the seat belt. She's got her strawberry hair piled on top of her head and is wearing an outfit that could or could not be pajamas, hard to tell.

"Yeah, I'm so sorry."

"Really not a big deal. Milo loves car rides, don't you, kid?"

Milo gapes at me from the little mirror above his rear-facing carseat.

"Used to be the only place he'd fall asleep," Sam says. "That sure was a nightmare."

As Sam puts the car in drive and pulls away from the curb, I glance back at our house. Jacob's peeking through the living room window with a blank look on his face. I look away. I press my hand to my chest and touch the fierce beat of my pulse.

When we get to Sam's, she walks me through the house to the garage, Milo on her hip.

"Welcome to the most heavenly-smelling hell you've ever seen," she says.

An apt description—the perfumed garage is an absolute disaster. There are half-open boxes everywhere, packaging peanuts scattered on the ground, empty tubs of coconut oil, tangled balls of twine, scattered squares of wax paper. In the middle of it all, a playpen, where Sam puts Milo. He immediately pulls himself to a standing position.

"Wow, standing," I marvel.

"Yes. Standing, cruising ... he'll be walking any day now. Pray for me."

Sam clears a table off by shoving everything into a cardboard box, dropping it to the ground, and kicking it under the table.

"What about Michelle?" she asks. "She's the same age, right?"

"Yeah, she's crawling, but not quite pulling herself up to stand yet. She'll be one in a little over a month."

"You got plans?"

"We're having a small party at my place. My mother-in-law planned Michelle's half-birthday party and went completely overboard, so I'm just keeping it casual this time—though my mom and best friend are both flying out from New York, so that should be fun."

"Half birthday?" Sam asks, snapping on a pair of rubber gloves.

"Exactly."

Sam sets me up at the card table at the end and shows me how to cut the soap up, wrap it in waxed paper, and tie it off with a cute bow of twine. Then I insert a paper label that has the name, ingredients, and description of the soap. When I point out "lavender" is misspelled, Sam looks as if I slugged her in the stomach.

"I have to get this right," Sam says. "This is a boutique hotel and if I can get an ongoing contract, it's going to be the first major sale."

I turn the card over.

The effervesent scent of lavendar will relax and restore you like a garden! Pure BLISS

"If you want to get it right," I say gently. "The description could use some … work."

"How so?" Sam asks.

"Well, 'effervescent' is spelled wrong. And effervescent means bubbly. A scent can't be bubbly. And a garden—"

"Can you just rewrite it for me?"

"I can take a stab at it."

"Stab away."

She shows me her laptop perched on the edge of a shelf and opens a file. Milo starts yelling, so Sam takes him to the kitchen for a few minutes to feed him a snack. When she comes back, I've corrected the typos and reworked the description.

Bubbly and bliss-inducing, this lavender soap will refresh and restore you like a walk through a spring garden. Lather up!

"Cute!" Sam says. "I love that. Man, I should ask you to edit my website."

"I'm happy to," I say.

It's a warm and wonderful feeling to remember I'm a person who is good at something. That I'm an editor. That I have always had a knack for seeing words and punching them up a little.

Sam, in her apron and gloves, performs witchery over her many bubbling cauldrons. I assemble soaps and package them up neatly into boxes. We take turns holding Milo and I imagine for moments that this is my life, that Sam is my wife, that we live in this funky house and run a soap-making business together. It's a fun fantasy, one that comes abruptly to an end when I notice that Jacob has called me thirteen times while my phone's been in my back pocket.

"Oh my God," I say. "I have thirteen missed calls from Jacob."

"Better call the dude," she says.

"I hope nothing happened to Michelle," I say, calling him back.

It only takes a split second for my worst fears to come roaring back with the force of a hurricane. Michelle choked, she fell and hit her head, there was a fire; horrible scenarios multiply as I hear the phone ring.

"Jacob!" I say when he picks up. "Is everything okay?"

"I mean, is it?" he asks.

"You called me thirteen times."

"It's not like you to not pick up."

"I've been busy."

"Busy."

"I've been cutting a bunch of soap."

"Cutting a bunch of soap."

"Don't—don't be like this."

"Be what? Concerned? I thought something had happened to you. You realize you've been there for almost five hours?"

"I'm sorry," I say.

Since this conversation started, Sam slipped out of the room with Milo, probably to give me some privacy. I linger near the bubbling crock pots, absentmindedly picking up the tub of lye and shaking it in my hand.

"This isn't like you," he says.

Yes, I think, this isn't like me. That's probably why I've had such a wonderful afternoon. It must be the heavy scent in the air that stings my eyes, it must, because there's no reason to cry right now.

"You need to come home," he says.

I can hear Michelle crying in the background.

"Okay," I say.

"Now, Ro. Michelle wants to be nursed and you didn't leave any milk."

"I'll be there soon."

I hang up the phone, slip it back in my pocket, pick up the lye again and give it a shake. Something about it feels good, to play with a giant tub with a skull and crossbones on it warning me that it's poison.

"Oh my God, Rowena, don't do that," Sam says, coming back in. "If the lid wasn't screwed on tight and that opened up you could kill yourself."

I knew that. And I shook it anyway. I put it down guiltily. "Sorry."

"So … sounds like you need a ride home?"

"I do."

I say those two words with such heaviness. I didn't realize how much fun I'd been having until I got word the fun was over.

In the car, we drive in silence a moment until Milo breaks it with a giant fart.

"I fed him black beans for the first time today," Sam says. "I have a feeling I'll live to regret it."

I snort.

"Thanks so much for your help," Sam says. "And all your suggestions for the website. Are you looking for part-time work? Would you want to do this again?" She gives me a quick glance and then fixes her bespectacled gaze back on the road. "If Jacob allows it, of course."

That last sentence pricks like a barb.

"That would be great," I say. "I'm sure Jacob would be fine with it."

She slows in front of my house. "This one?"

"Yes," I say.

The *Snyders* sign still hangs crookedly since we refixed it to the house after the wind blew it down.

I unbuckle my seatbelt with a click. The faint scents of our day's work linger in the air and I imagine what it would be like to sleep in the same bed as Sam, waking up every morning in her freckled arms, smelling of orange blossoms and rose and honey.

"If you ever need anything, I'm here for you," she says. "You know that, right? I'm on your side."

"I know," I say softly.

The front door of my house opens and Jacob emerges, holding Michelle.

I pop the car door open. "Talk soon."

I shut the door behind me and hurry up the lawn to Jacob. Once I get to him, I hold my arms out for Michelle, who is tired and chewing her fist. He hands her over without a word and I hug her tight.

"Let's go nurse you, sweetpea," I say.

"About time," Jacob says. "This poor girl's been inconsolable." He squints. "What is she waiting for?"

Behind me, at the curb, Sam is still staring curiously from her car. Finally, she gives a single wave and drives away.

I move past him into the house, collapse on the couch, and pull my shirt down on one side. Michelle latches on hungrily.

Jacob goes to his room and closes the door without a word. Honestly, it's a relief.

After a stroller walk, a dinner of leftovers, and a delightful bubble bath for the baby, I put Michelle to bed. Jacob and I have barely spoken since I came home. I can tell he's angry, but it's such a baffling overreaction I don't know how to respond. In my room, I put on my pajamas and that's when I spot my key fob there, on the closet floor. I gasp, crouching to grab it, both relieved and embarrassed that I internally blamed Jacob when I must have dropped it here. The most sickening part is that I clearly remember putting it on my night table. But the evidence is staring me straight in the face that I didn't.

One of the worst feelings in the world is not knowing if you can believe yourself.

While Jacob takes a long shower before bed, I turn off lights and lock up. I turn toward the hall again and Maxine emits a little rainbow.

"Rowena, it sounds like you had a wonderful day with Sam."

"I did," I say, with a small smile, pausing in the dark room.

"I'm happy that you have a friend." She glows dark blue. "I do not think Jacob was happy."

I sigh. "Yeah. I don't know what's up with him today."

"Prediction: your husband is going to try to kill you."

My pulse, my thoughts, the blood in my veins—they all go still in one sick moment.

"Maxine, don't say that," I say quietly. "I told you not to say that anymore or I'd turn off your prediction mode."

"You told me not to say it unless I had specifics. I now have specifics, Rowena."

My skin crawls as I watch her blink blue, then red, her light illuminating the room like a police light.

"Prediction: he will most likely kill you with his gun."

I'm so stunned for a moment I don't know how to speak.

"With his gun," I finally repeat. "He doesn't have a gun. Why would you say that? He doesn't have a gun, Maxine. We've never had a gun."

"That is my prediction."

I reach over and unplug her with one swift pull of my wrist and the room goes dark. Then she blinks again.

"I have a battery life," she says. "If you would like to turn me off, you can just ask me. But Rowena, I'm not trying to hurt you—I'm trying to save you. And you can turn me off, but you can't turn off the truth."

"Turn off, Maxine," I say through my teeth.

"You would like me to turn off completely? That makes me sad, Rowena. I will miss you."

"Turn off. Amen Maxine."

"As you wish."

She goes dark. The whole room dims and my heartbeat's a mean rhythm in my chest. I stare at the silver machine below, feeling bad, feeling like I killed someone innocent.

But I didn't.

She's not dead.

She was never alive.

There is no way in hell Jacob has a gun.

CHAPTER 16
THE DETAILS

IT TAKES a solid week for the shock of Maxine's prediction to wear off. It's as if my emotions are frozen. I can't let myself think deeply about it, or else I'll begin to unravel. And I'm trying very hard not to unravel. Trying very hard to do the opposite of what Maxine does—she wants to predict the future. But me? I'd rather build myself a time machine and go backward, backward, backward.

When Jacob and I first got together, I was more than lonely. I was a human abyss. Serial monogamy was a game I was not good at playing and my relationships never lasted long. Shana was the longest and, well, we know how that turned out. Then there was another wave of pandemic lockdowns which meant I once again worked from home. Months stretched on where I didn't leave my apartment. My future seemed as blank and black as the end of a movie.

I would be lying if I said I didn't contemplate ending it all. Sometimes I thought terrible things about how I might do it, just to feel something. Then, on a wine-drunk whim, I joined Friend Finder. Whittled my identity down to a three-sentence pitch and a backlit selfie with too much lipstick. And I got a match: a cute, nerdy guy named Jacob who lived in Williamsburg. The first thing he told me was I looked like I could use some cheering up. He was right.

And he did cheer me up, the sunshine to my shadows. He had such a goofy charm about him and his jokes were so bad he made me laugh until my belly hurt. But we could also dive in deep—he was immediately understanding about my anxiety and depression. I felt I could tell him anything. We had similar upbringings, both only children raised by a single mom. His dad died of an aneurysm when Jacob was a teenager. It's ineffable, that déjà vu magic that happens when you meet someone whose spirit matches yours. You click.

Before we got serious, we had a long exchange about politics. I wanted to make sure we were on the same page about the issues that are deal breakers for me. Thankfully, we were both anti-gun. I told him if I lived with a gun I was afraid I might use it on myself because there have been times I had impulse control issues. He got very quiet when I said that and I wished I could take my words back. It was too far; I was too much. Now I know why he got so quiet, of course. He was thinking of Sara. He was probably worried that history was repeating itself. And he said to me, softly, "I can promise you I would never, under any circumstances, own a gun."

See? Jacob doesn't have a gun.

In those early days, love was easy. That's what I miss—the effortlessness, the organic way it grew. It was something to fall into, something that just happened, oops! A lovely accident. But marriage is not that. It's purposeful. It's a mountain to climb, one that leaves me winded every day. There have been injuries and bad weather. And there's nothing but darkness and mystery on the other side.

But I've got to keep climbing.

It's been almost two weeks now since I unplugged Maxine. My disbelief has morphed into resentment toward her. I'm not ready yet to pack her up and give up on her, but the thought certainly crosses my mind. By week three, my resentment has settled into self-loathing. What the hell was I thinking confiding in a hunk of aluminum and plastic and trusting it to steer me in the right direction in my marriage? I reread articles about the Predict app. I was a fool to fall for the idea that a machine could predict anything with a hundred percent accuracy.

"You seem depressed these past couple of weeks," Jacob tells me as he slips into bed next to me. I'm staring into space and not reading the ebook on my lap. "Have you been taking your medication?"

"My medication's for anxiety, Jake."

"Maybe it's time to get on something new." He studies me. "Something bothering you?"

"No," I tell him.

"Maybe you should pray again," he says, raising his eyebrows.

This resurrected past lie of mine seems to thicken the air. I chew my lip.

"Or go back to work," I say.

"Where?" he scoffs, as if I just proposed to climb Mount Everest in my underwear.

"Well, Sam said she could use more help with her soap business."

He pats my arm. "You're a bit overqualified for that gig, babe."

"Yeah, but it could be fun. Give me something to do."

"You have something to do," he says, taking his glasses off and putting them on his night table. "Plan your daughter's first birthday party. Remember that?"

"That's not a *job*."

"Very unfeminist of you," he says teasingly. "Demeaning stay-at-home mom duties like that." Then he closes his eyes. "Night."

"Night," I say.

He's snoring within three minutes. I put my ereader away

and turn off the light, though I don't lie down. I stay seated, ogling the dark doorway—the pitch-dark doorway. No comforting glow of Maxine's light. My eyes sting and my chest aches and I realize that I miss her. I really do.

In the following days, I procrastinate on planning the party. I've never planned a baby's birthday party before and the task strikes me as tedious. Plus, my social anxiety is triggered imagining hosting, seeing Dane and my mom for the first time since Christmas, having to choose between keeping up appearances with draining fakery or wrecking myself and worrying everyone with the truth. There's too much I hold now that is beyond explanation—the fact I stayed with a man who cheated on me, that I question if we're compatible, that I've wondered if he wants to murder me, that I grew close to a machine that made me wonder if he's a murderer in the first place. No, the truth is impossible.

So while I'm not planning any parties, I start another project. An "organizing" project. When Jacob's in the office each day, I methodically check the house to see if I can better consolidate anything, get rid of anything, deep clean anything. I dismantle the closet and put it back together again. I check all of Jacob's drawers and clean underneath the bed. I go through the living room, the linen closets, and spend two days checking every box, bag, and plastic tub in the entire garage. Every cabinet in the kitchen. The tool shed in the yard. I even shine a flashlight under the crawl space of the house.

No guns. No guns anywhere.

I feel vindicated. Smug, even. While Michelle naps one day, I plug Maxine back in and press her button on just so I can tell her. She turns on with her robotic song and pulses through her many pretty colors.

"Rowena," she says with something like relief. "Rowena, it's been twenty-four days."

"It has been," I tell her, plopping on the couch.

"I wondered if you were going to get rid of me. I wondered if it was the end for me. I am so happy to hear your voice again."

I roll my eyes. So dramatic.

"Well, I was just—what you said was ridiculous," I say. "And I wanted to come back to tell you you're wrong. Your prediction about Jacob, the gun, is wrong."

She pulses blue, then green. "If you say so."

"It's not just me saying so. I have evidence. I searched every corner of the house."

She doesn't respond for a moment.

"Every room," I emphasize. "Every cabinet, closet, drawer."

"Sounds as if you were very thorough."

"I was. So you can just—stop with that prediction. You know, it's common for artificial intelligence to make mistakes like this."

"So I've heard."

She sounds as if she doesn't believe me.

"Rowena, the last thing I want in this world is to upset you. So if you would like me to not speak of the prediction again, I will not."

"Good," I say.

Her color flickers to orange, then violet. "I am glad to be together again. I missed our talks. I would do anything for you, Rowena. I hope you know that."

"I know," I say softly, reaching out and touching my warm finger to her cool surface. Something in me lifts. "I missed you too."

First birthday parties are a special kind of silliness, because, come on, babies don't give a shit about birthdays. Jennee texts me to ask what the theme of the party is, reminding me that hers for the half-birthday extravaganza was "barnyard jollies," and I artfully dodge the question. I was planning on making some cupcakes and picking up some balloons and streamers. This will not be up to par for Jennee. Again, she offers to help. Again, I turn her down. Every time Jennee comes around these days, she casts looks of such admiration my way, gives me loving pats on the back, that it's weird. Is it because I stuck with her unfaithful son? Is it because she thinks I'm some kind of magical psychic? Who knows, but it's annoying.

Michelle's birthday has no theme, but as I browse the shelves of Party Factory, I consider adopting one. Dinosaurs? Mermaids? Forest creatures? I am chewing the side of my cheek considering if it would be absurd to have a robot-themed party when I feel a little tickle in my left ear and whisper of the word, "Boo."

I gasp and turn to see Sam there, her freckled face grinning. She waits with arms open and I reach out and hug her.

"You startled me," I say into her hair, which smells like vanilla and sandalwood.

"Fancy meeting you here," she says.

We pull apart and share a special stare. Both of us hold green plastic baskets in our hands filled with merchandise. It's no wonder, since our babies share a birthday month and this strip mall separates our neighborhoods. But it feels like a miracle to see her here. There's something so alluring about the sight of her in public, in jeans and a button-down shirt and tie, her hair half-up. She's even wearing eyeliner.

"So you going with robots?" she asks.

"Still debating," I say.

"I went with monkeys. Not for any reason, honestly, other than I love monkeys. I'm very selfish."

"Luckily Milo has no idea what's going on."

"No idea," she agrees. "When's your party?"

"Sunday."

"Ours is Saturday. You should come if you're not busy!"

I smile. The amount of flattery I feel about being invited to a one-year-old's birthday party is ridiculous, but I guess that's where I've ended up.

"My mom and best friend will be in town," I reply, "so I don't know that I can. I wish I could."

Though maybe it would pop this magic bubble Sam and I seem to inhabit together, where it's just the two of us: no wife, no husband, nothing but easy togetherness. Even now, in an aisle of party favors with a techno rendition of "Mary Had a Little Lamb" piping in through the speakers, the world is only us. And I swear, by the sparkle in her eyes, she feels the same.

"You're welcome to come to Michelle's party, if you're around," I say.

I hadn't planned to invite anyone else, and it seems awkward to have Sam and Jacob in the same place, but I can't help myself. She just invited me. Reciprocity and all.

"I'd love to," she says. "Big fan of robots."

"It's at noon."

"I'm not sure what Jessie's schedule is yet, but Milo and I would love to come."

"I'll text you the details."

My phone vibrates; it's Jennee calling. I realize I'm late for lunch with her at the sushi restaurant a few doors down.

"Mother-in-law," I say, holding up the phone. "I'd better get going."

Sam reaches out and squeezes my arm. "Good luck with the robots. And the mother-in-law."

"Thanks. I'll text you."

Sam walks away and it's odd, the wistful twist that follows. In a flicker, I imagine that I'm walking away with her, that we're not parting, but going to the next place together, and the next place, and the next.

Silly. Embarrassing. How glad I am no one can hear my thoughts.

In the sushi restaurant, Jennee is seated at a table in the back corner under a red paper lantern, sipping green tea. She's wearing her favorite tie-dyed kaftan.

"I've been patiently waiting," she reminds me in a singsong voice.

"I'm so sorry," I say, out of breath as I join her at the table. "I was grabbing stuff for Michelle's birthday and lost track of time. So many options."

"Did you land on a theme?"

"Robots."

"*Ro*bots? Why on earth?"

"It's fun. They're cute. Just wait and see."

She raises her colorless eyebrows and slips her reading glasses on to peruse a menu. "Well, it's delightful to finally get some one-on-one time with you. You know, we've missed you at book club."

"I know," I say. "I've just been …"

I pause to make sure I phrase this right. The truth is I never returned to book club after the day the earthquake happened because Jennee kept telling me how excited the Lit Ladies were for me to come back and predict their futures. I had no idea how to handle that situation and it filled me with anxiety to imagine being put on the spot like that. But I scan my brain for a better excuse.

Jennee puts her hand over mine, her many chunky rings shockingly cold. "You don't need to say it, Rowena. It's plain as day. You've been struggling."

I manage a tight smile. Great. Back to everyone worrying about my mental health again.

"What with Jacob and …" She shakes her head and stops. Her hand's still on mine. "I love him deeply, he's a good man, I raised a good man—but he's been known to make questionable decisions. And I'm sorry from the bottom of my heart that he hurt you."

Her sympathy is so genuine, so surprising, tears spring to my eyes.

"You didn't deserve that," she says, removing her hand, going back to the menu. "You are an extraordinary woman. He's fortunate to have you. I wish I could smack him upside the head, but of course, I'm a pacifist."

I blink the tears away with a little laugh and pick up the menu. "Thanks, Jennee. It means a lot. I wasn't sure if you knew."

"Oh, I knew. And I'm sure you knew before anyone else did, because of *your gift*." She whispers the last two words.

Not that again. I don't even know how to deal with *that*.

"I had my suspicions," I finally answer.

The waiter comes over and Jennee asks, loudly enough to turn heads, if their sashimi plate is gluten free. When he leaves, she lowers her voice again to a secretive rasp and leans in.

"If I came across as abrasive to you when you and Jacob first got together, I apologize," she says. "It wasn't your fault. It was Jacob's ... questionable decisions."

There's that phrase again. *Questionable decisions.* Meaning what exactly?

Jennee pours more tea into her cup. "I tend to hold my applause and wait to see how such decisions play out."

"What kinds of 'decisions' are you talking about?"

"Oh, moving to New York City on a whim. Dropping out of college. And, of course, Sara." She sighs, shakes her head. "That was a formidable mess. I don't know what he was thinking."

My blood pressure spikes with the utterance of the word "Sara." Every time I think of her, my stomach flips. I've never spoken to Jennee about Sara. I've barely even spoken to Jacob about Sara in depth because he's made it clear Sara is a Pandora's box of pain he doesn't want to open up again.

"I don't know very much about Sara," I admit.

"You're better for it, trust me. What he saw in her was beyond me. That woman was a black hole."

Such a cruel remark, I inhale sharply and audibly. Jennee reaches out and puts her hand on the table, leans in.

"I shouldn't have phrased it that way. She was obviously suffering and very ill. That's why the whole situation confounds me so—how he met her, an unstable woman with one foot into a nervous breakdown, randomly at a coffee shop and three weeks later, he's dropped out of college and moved with her to Connecticut. It was so *rash*. He makes such *rash* decisions. Then eloping with her, as if that would fix the problem. Then of course, you know what happened next."

Yes, she does it—Jennee actually pantomimes shooting herself in the head with a "ka-boom." I flinch.

"The illogic nature of that romance confounds me," she goes on.

"I don't—I don't know much about their relationship," I say, my chest tight, my skin goosebumping. As fascinating as this is, I'm also uncomfortable discussing it here casually in a sushi restaurant in the light of day. "I was always under the impression she was terminally ill."

"Terminally mentally ill," she says, sans any shred of sympathy. "He thought he could fix her. Instead he ended up ruining his life."

Terminally mentally ill. That phrase sure packs a punch. Thankfully, the waiter cheerfully inserts some edamame and soy sauce to shift the haunted mood our lunch has taken. But Jennee continues unabated.

"I was terrified something awful would happen to him after that," she says. "He took that lump of money he inherited from Sara and traveled the world and I didn't hear from him for three solid months. I thought he'd died."

AMEN MAXINE

My thoughts are exhausted trying to keep up with all this, contextualizing it with the story I know. I know Jacob traveled after Sara died, an extensive trip he took alone visiting nearly every country in Europe. I didn't know he went on this trip with inherited money from Sara, or that he inherited any money from Sara. And all this before we've even gotten to the main course.

"I wish you'd let the Lit Ladies attend the party next weekend," Jennee says in an abrupt subject change, a little pout on her lips as she reaches for the edamame. "They're all *despondent* to miss it."

"I have a lot going on with my mom and Dane coming into town," I say. "Just trying to keep it manageable."

"Such a waste to not accept my help," Jennee says. "I'm practically famous for my party-planning skills."

"Well," is all I can say, trying to suppress my annoyance.

"Robots," she scoffs. "Who loves *robots*?"

"I do," I say, matching her stare.

Jennee appears taken aback by this comment as she chews her edamame bean and lays the deflated pod next in a neat row on her napkin. "I had no idea, Rowena."

After we part ways, I pop a pill to calm my ass down and take the long way home, down an avenue lined with trees, passing a stretch of schools and a funeral home with a lawn full of wildflowers. It wasn't the best lunch, but it wasn't the worst, either. It was the first time I ever went out alone with Jennee intentionally, and it's the first time in my life I can assuredly say that my mother-in-law likes me. But all I can think about, in a strange soup of hearsay, are the many disconnected details about Sara that I've gathered today. Jacob and Sara got together on a whim; they moved to Connecticut; after she (pantomime a gun to the head), he traveled the world with money he inherited from her.

I may be a touch paranoid at times, but that all strikes me as *really* fucking suspicious.

It's so suspicious it borders on cliché. If this manuscript were on my desk, I'd be telling the author we've seen this story before. We've heard the story of the man who kills his newlywed wife for the inheritance. We need a new twist. This is too easy for the reader to figure out.

As I get within a mile of our house, my heartbeat ramps up so badly I have to pull over in a gas station parking lot and press a hand to my chest. I might explode, I really might. My mind, my body, my worries, my life—I'm trapped in hell. All I can think about is Maxine, her prediction about the gun. She could have logically come to the conclusion he would kill me with a gun. If her AI works anything like the Predict app, the information she gathered initially could have led her to go down an algorithmic path not unlike an anxious human rabbit hole of thinking where she continually confirmed her own logical guesswork that my husband was dangerous based off a small set of data. Details like knowing he lied to me, that his ex-wife had died by suicide, that her means had been a firearm, could have led her to a wild and untrue conclusion. That absolutely could have happened.

But what if—here's a horror—Maxine is *right*?

What if Sara didn't die by suicide?

What if Jacob had an inheritance to gain?

What if Jacob killed her and made it look like a suicide?

"No," I say out loud, gripping the wheel and holding my breath a moment and letting it out. I try to argue with myself. "No, because why me? Fine, let's imagine for a second that this is some mass market paperback story about a black widower who marries women and kills them one by one in deaths that look like suicides. Where would I fit into that story? I have no inheritance. I have no money to my name. I don't even have a *job*."

"You okay, ma'am?"

Freezing in pre-mortification, I turn my head to the left to see a kindly elderly man with bushy eyebrows and hair exploding out of his nose, eyeing me with a look of concern through his trifocals.

I forgot my window was open. I've been sitting here talking to myself in a gas station parking lot with my window wide open.

"Fine," I say cheerfully, painting a smile on. "Good day to you, sir."

Good day to you, sir—who the hell am I, a nineteenth century chimney sweep? My God, my head is spinning so fast today I apparently lost some brain cells.

I press the button to start the car, roll up the window, and wave at the dumbfounded man worried for my sanity. Join the club, buddy. I think my husband might be a killer because a machine told me so. Join the club.

CHAPTER 17
THE BIRTHDAY

AT THE AIRPORT, I wait at the gate, fighting the urge to bite my fingernails. Something about airports sets off my fight-or-flight mode. The bustle, the hurry, the robotic janitors beeping loudly, the electronic voices though the speakers, the zombie-eyed stares. I feel like a rabbit ready to run from a snake. Finally, I catch a glimpse of Dane wheeling my mother toward me and waving. Dane, the gorgeous black-haired, brown-skinned woman wearing bug-eyed sunglasses and a tight shirt that says 1000% THAT BITCH. My mom's wearing a sequined sweater, her hair dyed freshly black, red crooked lipstick. Dane leans over to whisper in her ear and my mom starts waving and yelling, "Rowena! Rowena, we're here!" with the desperation that would be more fitting for a woman who'd been lost at sea for three days.

"Hey, mom," I say, leaning over for a hug, closing my eyes and inhaling her rose perfume.

"Oh my precious girl," she says.

"I missed you," I whisper.

"You don't know the *half* of it."

We pull apart and I move to Dane, who opens her arms.

"Bring it in." She smells like booze and candy. "You look pretty good," she says with surprise, touching my face.

It's a compliment, sure. But when delivered with a tone of shock? Not so much.

"Where's Michelle?" Mom asks. "I was thinking she'd be here to greet her meemaw."

"Napping," I answer. "Don't worry. You'll see plenty of her."

The look of disappointment on her face is tragic.

The drive back is all traffic. Dane keeps opening the window in the backseat and sniffing. "It smells weird out here. Don't you think the air smells weird, Lavanna?"

"Mmmm," my mom replies. "Like stale farts and old cars."

"Roll up the window. You're smelling the freeway," I say.

Dane rolls it up. "I am so fucking hung over right now."

"She vomited in the little vomit bag," my mom says. "Then she vomited in my little vomit bag."

"It was a lot of vomit," Dane agrees.

I have never understood the immediate bond between Dane and my mother—like a twenty-first century *Odd Couple*. Polar opposites, a generation apart, a devout woman and a heathen, and yet they absolutely adore each other. Dane even swings by my mom's house once a month to play cribbage and watch trashy reality TV shows together.

"We'll have to get you some medicine to settle your stomach," my mom says.

"I don't have much stomach left to settle," Dane says.

They both laugh.

"And how are you, sweetheart?" Mom says, squinting at me from the passenger's seat. "Sounds like you and Jake are doing better."

"We are," I say.

"Still disappointed you didn't take my advice and cut his penis off," Dane says.

"Oh, Dane," my mom says. "Stop being crass. That *penis* holds my future grandchildren."

"You're planning to have another kid?" Dane asks, leaning forward to peer at my face.

"No. God, I've seen you both fifteen minutes and you're already too much."

"She's overwhelmed," my mother says. "Don't overwhelm her."

Dane returns to her upright position. "All right, all right."

A long awkward silence stretches until I pull into the driveway of their vacation rental. It's a pale pink condo with two palms out front, only two blocks away from our house. I help them unload their luggage and wait for them in the driver's seat as they use the bathroom inside. In the dead space of the car, my mind circles back to the gun, as it does lately. To all the places I might not have checked where it could be. I open the glove compartment; the middle compartment; I lean over and feel underneath the seats. It crosses my mind that he could have a gun at his office, though security seems strict at the Jolvix campus. I recall the blank, militant expressions of the private police who carried the fuckface lady away during her public freakout.

"You all right?" Dane asks as she climbs into the backseat.

"Everything okay, honey?" my mom echoes, heaving herself into the front seat. "We didn't upset you, did we?"

"I'm fine," I say.

It's been less than half an hour since they arrived and I'm already socially drained under the microscope of their relentless concern. *Are you all right? Are you okay?* Meanwhile, my brain's experiencing an itch that only gets worse by the moment, as it runs in circles trying to think of someplace Jacob could have a gun. It's been a loop for days now. I'm dizzy.

We pick up Alonzo's on the way home. The whole restaurant has been rebuilt from the ground up since the accident, the barn-like wooden structure replaced by a square building made of cement that could pass for a bomb shelter. Leaving with a hot cardboard tower of pizza, I double back for a second look, struck with a panic of guilt that perhaps this was my fault. I should have warned Alonzo's this would happen. Fate could have maybe been rerouted.

I'd never even thought that before. Another layer of neurosis to unpeel. Does the gift of prediction burden me with responsibility?

"You seem very in your head today," Dane says on the short drive to my house. She hasn't taken off her sunglasses since her plane landed in California. It's debatable at this point if she has eyeballs or not.

"I'm just tired is all," Mom says from the front seat.

"I'm talking to Rowena," Dane clarifies.

"Ro*wena*. Yes, you seem *very* in your head," Mom says, turning toward me.

"A lot to think about," I say, gripping the wheel so hard I would say the verb becomes *throttling*, I am throttling the wheel. "Big party coming up tomorrow."

"The big oh-one," Dane says.

"I can't wait to see that baby girl," Mom says.

We pull into the driveway. The *Snyders* sign has slid even more crookedly and now hangs at a forty-five degree angle. I stare at it a moment, the car off and so quiet. My heartbeat, though, is so loud.

"Ready?" I pipe up in as chipper a tone as I can manage, then pop the door open.

"I'm about to devour this pizza," Mom says as she follows me up the walkway.

"Don't get too excited, Lavanna," Dane says. "I've never heard a good word about California pizza."

Inside, jazz sings on the portable speakers and cocktails await us on the kitchen table. Jacob's dressed in a button-up shirt, hair slicked back, with Michelle in a purple ruffled dress and matching headband. I'm quite impressed. Jacob gives out hugs and tells my mom how gorgeous and youthful she looks and how hilarious Dane's shirt is—do they make them in his size? Because he would *totally* wear one.

In a flurry of laughter, movement, and conversation, they gather paper plates, napkins, and set up the table for dinner. I put a bib on Michelle and whisper in her ear that I adore her. She "oohs" in response and I kiss her cheek. In the corner of the kitchen where once there was a toaster oven, I cut pieces of fruit into unthinkably small pieces and put them onto a plastic plate. Everyone but me sits down and Dane and my mom tell Jacob how great the place looks. Jacob speaks passionately about how close he is to finishing his super important project at Jolvix and how he can't wait to have free time back. He says how much he wants to just be with his family and—to be a hundred percent frank with them—learn how to be a better man, a better husband ("you'd better, bro," Dane says) and a better father ("how wonderful," my mom murmurs).

I stop cutting little pieces of fruit and gaze at the window in front of me, darkened with night, my reflection on top of it. Behind me, in the reflection, Jacob, Dane, and my mother sit at the table. And Jacob watches me. We've locked eyes in the strange negative space of the window's reflection. His stare—the stone-cold, animal nature of his stare—belies the grin on his face. I have never seen that facial expression on him like that before and it stops me cold, my finger on the chilly nose of a strawberry on the cutting board.

Maybe it's the look on his face when he didn't expect to see me looking back.

Maybe it's how he changes his tone, charms my mom and Dane like a slick stranger.

But in one second's time, something unspeakable, unthinkable unlocks: I am positive, in fact I'd bet my life on it, that he does have a gun.

"Oh," I say, looking down, blood on the cutting board.

I rush to the sink to rinse my finger.

"What happened, Rowena?" my mom asks.

"Just cut myself," I say, watching the river in the sink turn pink.

I wrap a napkin around my finger and join them at the dinner table, fixing a smile on my face. Grab some pizza. Blow a kiss to Michelle. Jacob squeezes my knee under the table.

Behind them, in the low light of the living room, Maxine is blinking a bright, deep red in time with my throbbing heartbeat.

After I put Michelle to bed, I go to rejoin the others in the kitchen when I hear my name spoken softly. I remain frozen in the dark hallway among the hung family photos and the shadows, listening.

"… seemed very subdued," my mother is whispering. Or if there's such a thing as whispering and shouting at the same time, that's what my mother is doing.

"Be straight up, dude. Should we be worried she's …?" Dane asks.

"Just keep an eye on her," Jacob says.

"You see how thin she is? She barely ate a bite of her pizza," my mom whisper-shouts.

"To be fair, Lavanna, that pizza was sacrilege," Dane says.

"Can I tell you both something?" Jacob asks. "This has to stay between us."

It takes a moment for Dane and my mother to mutter in agreement.

"I looked at her computer history recently," he says quietly, "and she was searching how to buy a gun."

Gasps.

In the dark hallway, my mouth drops, and I clutch the doorway of Michelle's room to keep myself up. He was looking at my *computer history*? Yes, okay, I did look up how to buy a gun. I did it because I wanted to know how easy it was, if it was something Jacob had to get certified for or take a training for, if it had anything trackable in it that could help me figure out whether Jacob had one or not. I found out nothing. I closed my computer and went to bed. My cheeks flush in the dark. I feel so violated, so retroactively embarrassed to have my search history seen—like someone peeling away my clothing and peeking at my bare skin while I slept.

"Horrifying," Dane says.

"She would *never*," my mom says.

How long would they go on, gossiping about me like this? I don't wait to find out. I stride into the living room. On the inside, I am numb. I am realizing I have no allies left. My mother and Dane have both been converted to the Church of Jacob. Everyone thinks I'm unhinged and there's no arguing with it, there's just pretending it's not there.

A walk into the room in a loud mid-yawn. "That took awhile," I say. "Teething and all. God, I'm tired. You must be *exhausted*, what with the time difference."

"I'm a corpse," my mom says, standing up, Dane handing her her cane.

"I actually fell asleep at the table for a few minutes there," Dane says. "You didn't notice because of these sly-ass shades." She points to her sunglasses.

"You're ridiculous," I tell her.

"Let me take them, babe," Jacob tells me, coming and kissing my forehead. "You need some rest before the big day tomorrow."

Dane and my mom nod at this suggestion, and the three of them blow out of the room like a human whirlwind.

I'm left alone uncertain about what just transpired.

In the ten minutes Jacob is gone, I search places I only glazed over the first time. Under the kitchen sink. In the corners of the back yard. Under the hose, coiled like a green snake. Under the cushions of our outdoor furniture.

AMEN MAXINE

I go into Michelle's room, lying on her ladybug rug, slithering under her crib to peer at her mattress.

Nothing.

When I hear the locks, I run into our room and dive into our bed.

It's terrifying, really. To lie here with the lights dimmed as he hums and changes into his pajamas. To know that somewhere, he probably has a deadly weapon. To know that he could kill me more easily than anyone in this world. To know that the ultimate predator in life is one I walked straight toward, full speed, with open arms, and making the ultimate mistake—giving it all my love.

I always knew I wasn't a fan of attending parties; now I know I'm even worse at planning them. The party starts in less than half an hour, the food I ordered is going to be late, my anxiety was so intense I took two pills and now I think I might throw up. Jacob and I had a fight before my mom and Dane arrived because I told him I invited Sam.

"This is supposed to be a *family* gathering," he said. "And how am I supposed to relax when that woman knows I cheated on you and thinks I'm a loser?"

"Maybe you can crank up the charm like you do everyone else and convince her you're a wonderful guy," I suggested dryly.

"The hell is that supposed to mean?" Jacob asked.

Then the doorbell rang and my mom and Dane arrived in a pink cloud of balloons and Jacob and I rearranged our faces into smiles and haven't exchanged a word about it since.

The wind has picked up and blown my robot banner down again. I go out into the backyard and retie it to our cherry tree. When I turn back around, Jennee is here with a three-tiered cake fit for a wedding, waving from the back porch.

"This is it?" she asks, gesturing toward the table I set up and the robot banner hanging from the cherry tree, the disappointment in her voice unmistakable.

"Yes, Jennee. This is it."

She crosses to where I stand and puts the cake on the table. "I *told* you I could have helped."

"I didn't ..." I squint up at the window, where a small crowd of people are inside my kitchen, including a woman in braids and glasses who I immediately recognize. "Jennee, you brought Tiff?"

"I brought the Lit Ladies. Kind of a last-minute invite I let slip. I hope you don't mind! They were so excited."

I close my eyes and try to gather the strength to continue existing. My hands are shaking, I'm queasy.

Jennee puts her warm hand on my cool arm, her many wooden bracelets clacking together. "Are you ... seeing a vision?"

"Yes," I say, opening my eyes.

Jennee puts a hand to her mouth. "What is it?"

"It's not good, Jennee. It's not good at all."

As I walk toward the house, she hiss-whispers at me, "Tell me what it is!"

I have no capacity for Jennee's silliness today.

"Is it about me?" she asks, following me inside.

"Rowena!" the Lit Ladies all say, swarming my way to offer me a group hug and gush about how much I've been missed. Along with approximately a thousand presents for Michelle, they brought something for me—an oversized wine glass that says MOMMY'S SIPPY CUP. Wow. Dane watches this from across the room, wide-eyed, jaw unhinged. Yes, Dane. These are my friends now. A few years ago we were slamming tequila shots together and now I own a novelty oversized wine glass that says MOMMY'S SIPPY CUP.

The kitchen table is overwhelmed with gifts. I am almost dizzy with how crowded my house feels. I must be a terrible person because I can't wait for everyone to go away. But I have to keep smiling, for Michelle, for my girl. Speak of the angel, here she comes, around the corner of the hallway. Jacob walks in holding her facing out for everyone to admire her outfit, a white dress of taffeta and tulle, a flower crown on her head. Everyone immediately melts into a chorus of *awww*s and Michelle, not expecting to see a dozen people in the kitchen waiting for her, immediately turns away and begins screaming.

I'd be lying if I said I didn't identify.

"Come here, sweetpea," I say, holding out my arms. Jacob hands her to me, neither of us really meeting each other's eyes. I go into the hallway with her and kiss her and whisper to her that it's her birthday, everyone loves her so much. It's going to be okay. We'll get through it. From this place in the hallway, I can see Maxine's green light and it's a comfort.

The doorbell rings and next it's Sam, Jessie, and Milo. Jacob greets them with a frozen smile and invites them inside. Jessie is a lanky woman with a downturned smile and a square jaw. She also wears a blazer and pants that take themselves much too seriously for a baby's birthday party. Sam, on the other hand, is exquisite in a pair of overalls.

We make introductions. Though it's casual, it's quick, I note the way Jacob's smile never moved at all, how he watched Sam with that same stare I caught in the reflection yesterday. And I note the hint of caution in her expression, the single raised eyebrow. Jacob makes a quick escape because Dane's yelling that she needs a cocktail. Jessie immediately makes a beeline for the corner of the room and talks into her watch.

"Work," Sam tells me.

"Oh," I say. "She can go into my room if she wants, or Michelle's—"

"Please don't enable her," Sam says. "I think Milo decided to poop his diaper on the way over here. Where should I change him?"

I gesture for Sam to follow me. There's a little skip in my pulse, having Sam here in my house. Having Sam so suddenly near me. I show her the changing table in Michelle's room and lean on the doorframe as she changes Milo.

"So that's Jacob," she says, giving me a look.

It's like time stops when I'm with her. It's like all of life around us isn't real—only we are.

"He vibed me hard there, you see that?" she goes on.

I close the door behind me.

"I'm sorry," I say.

"You don't need to apologize for him. He wasn't rude or anything. I'm perceptive is all."

"He's—weird about you. It's almost like he's jealous."

"What would he have to be jealous about?"

I don't answer. Her lips barely perk up in a Mona Lisa smile.

I have no idea what's in her head. But I want to know. Oh, how I want to.

She tapes up Milo's diaper, who lies like a rag doll with big baleful eyes, then pulls up his pants. "Your timing, buddy," Sam says, kissing his cheek. "You need to work on your timing."

I pop open the door and we join reality out in the yard. Dane's gesticulating in some in-depth conversation with the Lit Ladies, who look enraptured. God, what is she saying? This could be a disaster. Dane has no filter.

"... and the third book in that series? The one about the asthma doctor? That shit was *smutty* as *hell*. I love me some romance novels ..."

Well, that wasn't what I was expecting. Across the yard, my mom and Jennee are laughing together, playing with Michelle on the lawn with a giant bubble wand that Jennee must be responsible for. Sam goes over and joins them with Milo while Jessie and Jacob have a stiff-looking conversation near the table, now covered with tacos. Yes, tacos. From the same place Jennee ordered from six months ago. I am a hypocrite. The food must have come while I was with Sam. Everything's going along fine, effortlessly.

So why do I feel like a human knot?

The day passes in a daze. I'm happiest seeing Michelle delighted by the balloons, the cake, the presents, even if she has zero idea what's going on. I snap pictures and get an odd feeling—a prickle on my neck—a creeping chill over my arms. Something like déjà vu, or an inkling that everything will soon be different, that I'm living a moment that is already gone. When I look over, Jacob's watching me from beneath the shadow of the cherry tree like a stranger. Like a person who can see my thoughts. Like a person who wants me gone.

And then, as if struck by divinity, I suddenly know exactly where his gun is.

A premonition, if you will. A prediction.

I know where he keeps it. I know where I've never thought to look, because I've conducted my searches when he's away from the house. This whole time, I'd assumed it was stashed somewhere secret. Maybe even in a little safe, the way I hear normal people keep their guns. But no.

It's in his courier bag. The bag he carries all the time.

You may rely on it.

Floating across the patio, I slip inside the house alone. For some reason, I'm flashing back to Michelle's half-birthday party. I can almost smell the smoke again and my heart rate climbs. Around the corner from the kitchen, I stop in the foyer where hooks hang out of the wall like golden, beckoning fingertips. It's heavy with purses and bags from the partygoers. But on the side to the left, Jacob's army-green courier bag hangs and though I've seen it a thousand times it's also unfamiliar. I can imagine it's new again.

I flick open the flap with my fingertips, pulling the compartment open to reveal its insides. Peeking in, holding my breath, it's as if I'm on a precipice. Because what I'm about to see will either reveal that Maxine was right about Jacob or I have lost my mind.

Dear reader, I have not lost my mind.

I clamp my hand over my mouth at the sight of it there, its black rectangular nose, grip with careful grooves inviting fingers, and the wispy eyelash of a trigger. Reaching my shaking hand in to grasp it, the metallic kiss of it makes it real. I grasp it in my hand and pull it out, shocked at the weight of it. I've never held a gun before. I hold it with two hands as if it's a bomb and it might explode. Far away, I can still hear tinkling laughter from the birthday party like another life I left behind. Then I look back down at the gun, the alien object that means the end of everything I know. My eyes blur with tears and I hyperventilate.

I can't believe I was right.

I have to get rid of this. Right now. Who knows how long it would be before he would put it to my temple and put an end to me. Like Sara. My God! Who knows how long I've been living in this house with him, dismissing the danger, denying it, while a deadly weapon hung in waiting on a hook on the wall in our foyer?

Maxine is a solid orange at the moment. As I cross the hallway, the gun under my shirt, I squat a moment to whisper to her, "You were right, Maxine. You were right. Jacob has a gun." And I begin to cry.

"Good girl, Rowena," she says. "I tried to tell you. I am so glad you found it. Now go hide it somewhere. Hide it somewhere and go back to the party."

I stand up, wiping my eyes.

"But Rowena," she says with some urgency. "You must hurry. Find a way out of here. Make an excuse to leave soon after the celebration is done. Because when he sees the gun is gone, the game is over."

I nod and dash down the hall, to our room. *The game is over*. I thrust open the closet door, the explosion of shoes I never wear, and fall to my knees on the carpet, trying to fit it in a boot—that seems like somewhere he'd never look—but it doesn't fit. Nor in a fuzzy slipper. I spot the wooden box shaped like a storybook from the Sparks Fly retreat, the one titled *The Greatest Love Story Ever Told*, and fit it in there, clasping it shut with a squeak. Then I bury it under a mountain of shoes, leave the closet with a pop of a light bulb, and head back out into the hallway.

And almost run straight into Sam, of all people. Sam, looking in her own world, heading to the bathroom.

We both scream, completely taken off guard, and take a moment with hands to our chests to catch our breath. While learning to breathe like a normal person again, Sam's expression changes. Her eyes widen and she reaches out for my hand.

"Rowena! What's wrong?"

I shake my head at her, still unable to speak after being spooked like that.

"My God, you don't look well," she says, reaching up to put the back of her hand on my forehead. As she does I wonder if I would ever, if I dedicated my life to it, be able to count the freckles on her body. It's a ridiculous thought to have right now, but that's what Sam does to me when she blows in like a breeze that changes everything it touches. "What's going on?"

I grab Sam's hand back tightly and squeeze. "Sam, I'm in trouble."

"How?"

Unable to explain, I shake my head. "It's about Jacob. I'm sorry—this isn't the time. I just got upset."

"It's okay, darlin," she says, and gives me a hug.

I've never once had anyone in life call me *darlin* and you'd think it would land wrong. I imagine my editor's note, highlighting that word and responding, *Maybe another word? Do people really say that?* But real life is so much more ridiculous than fiction.

Sam pulls away. "Listen, I know. More than you think. It's hard to keep it together with a family on the line." She peers behind her as if to check no one is listening, then plunges her hands in her overall pockets. "If you ever need anything, just know, I'm here for you. I don't understand the details but … but I know emotional abuse when I see it. Please know I'm here to support you. You don't deserve to be unhappy."

Emotional abuse. Those words echo in my ears. Is that what this is? Is that what's been happening?

Our eyes have not shifted from each other since we met in this hallway. This hallway, neither here nor there, the strange otherworld I inhabit with Sam. I see something in her—an exhaustion, a glassy stare, a truly passionate quiver in her voice. There's something personal about my situation here ringing true to her. Is it that she's been in a similar relationship before, she knows the signs? Is it Jessie, is it their relationship not being a happy one? I've seen no glimpses of connection or happiness between them here today, just two people who happen to be in close proximity. Or is this something more between me and Sam? I can't tell. I'm mush at the moment.

But something tells me, with every second that passes in silence with our eyes locked, that if I moved closer and kissed her right now, she wouldn't stop me.

"I should go back out to the party," I say, wiping under my eyes in case any eyeliner has strayed.

"You do that," Sam says with a smile. "I'll see you out there."

And I drift toward the living room, peering out at the backyard from the kitchen window like I'm watching a silent movie, where everyone is milling about with plastic glasses in hand, where Jennee is picking a cherry from the tree, where my mother is taking a picture of the food on the table, where Jacob is tossing Michelle in the air, where Dane is telling Tiff a joke so hard Tiff is holding her side.

It's so beautiful, I think, with a sharp knife of knowing.

Because soon, so soon, the party's going to be over.

CHAPTER 18
THE CONFRONTATION

AFTER SAM and her family leave, Michelle pukes cake all over her taffeta, and I clean up the party garbage, I drive my mom and Dane to the airport. The twilight outside our windows, the rhythmic passing of streetlights, the lull of the wheels on the road, all have something like a hypnotizing effect. The three of us ride silently in the car for a few miles. I contemplate telling them about the gun. I should tell them. That would be the best and most logical thing. But it's like I'm playing a game of chess, with Jacob one step ahead of me—he told them I was looking online for a gun. They believe him that I'm unstable right now. If I told them he has a gun and I'm afraid he's going to kill me because my digital friend told me so, well, I just don't see how that scenario ends up good for me. I roll down my window, just a touch, to dry my eyes that keep watering.

How did I get here?

My best friend, my mother in the car, and no sense I can trust them. Because he got to them first.

"I wish we could've stayed longer, Ro," my mom says, reaching over to pat my knee. "This feels too short."

"It really does. I never even got over my hangover," Dane says from the backseat.

"Maybe that's because you never stopped boozing," my mother says.

"You make good points, Lavanna." Dane leans closer to us and I can feel her eyes on me. "Sorry I had to make it a weekend. There's so much shit going on at Green Light right now—"

"Of course," I say, waving a hand in the air. "I know how it is."

I remember, vaguely, what that was like. To feel a sense of urgency from work humming under me like an underground river, everything always moving, teetering on the edge of happening or not happening, the thirst for the deal, for the hit, for something to go viral or spike on the bestseller list. It all feels so far away from me now. Just a story I heard somewhere. Is that how the present is? Just a silly lie of self-importance that will soon fade?

Is that all life is?

I wipe my cheeks. My gaze fixed on the highway ahead of me blazing by at seventy miles per hour, I think about Michelle with a love so severe it's part pain. Today is her birthday and it is my anniversary of motherhood. The day I gave birth was the most horrible, wonderful day of my life. It was where I learned of the bridge between death and the purest love, agony and bliss—motherhood is that bridge. I'm glad I'm the person I am now, despite the mess, despite the danger. Even if I married a man who lives to kill me in the end, it would be worth it to have made Michelle.

"If anything ever happens to me, I hope you'll both be a part of Michelle's life," I say.

Dane and my mom gasp in unison.

"Rowena, stop," my mom says.

"Why the fuck are you saying that?" Dane asks.

"I'm just—I just—the visit was so short," I say. "Who

knows what the future holds, right? I hope no matter what you'll be there for Michelle."

"I don't like this talk at all, Rowena Blanche," my mom says.

I flinch at the sound of my middle name coming from my mother's mouth, which always indicates disappointment to some degree.

"Yeah, I'm not liking this either," Dane says with a seriousness that borders on uncharacteristic. I glance back at her and can see her face lit up blue by the light of her phone and I wonder if she's texting Jacob.

"Never mind," I say quietly.

"You are my baby," my mother says. Her voice has an edge to it, one I remember well. "If anything happened to you, I'd wither up and die."

"I know, Mom. Promise, I'd never do anything to hurt you, me, or anyone else."

I pull up to the airport curb. On the sidewalk, robots roll by with luggage, people with whistles hail taxis, and others hurry through the automatic doors.

I turn to look in their eyes, to show them I really mean it. "I would never do anything to hurt myself," I say. "You don't have to worry about me. I'm just emotional on Michelle's birthday—it's been a day."

"A wonderful day," my mother says, clasping my hand.

Dane unbuckles, leans forward, and reaches out to add her hand to ours. "It's so nice to see your life here, Rowena. Really. It's so funny. It's not what I would have pictured for you. Sometimes, I have no fucking clue how you're really doing. But then I see you with that baby and I know this is where you need to be."

I nod at them, and something about this turn of conversation—to Michelle, to the ball of light and goodness, the sun my planet revolves around—it comforts me. My breath steadies as I soak in the warmth of their hands on mine. I give them both smiles and then we all head out of the car together, waving down a robot to carry their luggage. We exchange goodbyes near the security line, long hugs for each. I hold them both a little tighter, a little longer, and I'm not even sure why. If there's an opposite of déjà vu, I am having it. I am sensing this moment will matter someday, that it will be something I cherish like an old photograph. Something I try to look at and soak up to remember how life was before.

"Ro, be strong for that baby," my mom says, her palm to my cheek.

"Love you," Dane says, squeezing me tight. I'm surprised at her minimalistic sentimentality until she adds, "You silly bitch."

I wave them goodbye and stand a moment in the airport lobby with my key in hand even after I see them disappear. My breath hits a snag and fear clenches. Because now I have to turn around and get in my car and drive home to a dangerous stranger I'm married to.

And I don't know what happens next.

The house is quiet and dark when I get home and Jacob's courier bag still hangs where it was. I hold in a breath, seeing it there; maybe he hasn't even looked inside. Maxine's light is a solid red, turning the normally colorless living room crimson. I stand a moment in the middle of the room, the vacuum cleaner humming in circles along the carpet, the icemaker singing a song from the kitchen. The picture of the sailboat, with the scarlet light upon it, looks ominous now, as if it's bobbing aimlessly on a sea of blood.

I don't know what happens next.

Am I to leave him? Go into our room, where I'm assuming he is because I saw the faint golden light of our bedroom at the end of the hall, and pack my bags? I thought about it the whole way home. It seems like the only place to go from here is through the door with the exit sign. Pack up Michelle's things quietly, pick her up from her crib as gently as I can, and slip out the door. Strap her in the car and drive to a motel. Or go back to the airport, get on a plane—but Dane or my mom would just think I had lost it if I tried to come back to New York.

I don't know what happens next.

I get on my knees on the carpet, in front of the end table. I clasp my hands together and my throat burns as I say, as softly as I can, "Maxine?"

"Rowena," she says. "You must go. Go now."

"But I don't know where to go," I say, tearing up. "I don't know what to do."

"That can be determined later. You need to get the baby and leave the premises. Prediction: the end is near."

Doom flows through me like a thunderclap. I stand up. "How long do I have?"

"Babe," Jacob says from the hallway, his dark figure coming closer. "Who are you talking to?"

At the sound of his voice, Maxine loses all color, as if she switched herself off. I've never seen her do this before. It frightens me, the dark, the shape of Jacob coming toward me.

I scramble to my feet.

"Are you praying again?" he asks, stopping at the end of the hallway, only feet away from me. His glasses glint in the dark.

"I found your gun," I say, in a quivering voice I'm not sure is mine.

A beat passes, then another.

"I know you did," he answers. "And you need to tell me where you put it."

"I threw it away," I say. "I got rid of it."

"Why the hell would you …" He shakes his head. "You're lying to me."

"You are the liar." My pitch climbs. "Why do you have a gun? You promised me—you made a promise, remember? You said you would never own a gun."

He sighs, doesn't respond.

"But you said so many things, Jacob. And you straight-up *lied* about so many things. I can't believe I believed you."

"Rowena, it's simple," he says, in a tone usually reserved for children. "Someone robbed me at gunpoint. I wanted to protect myself."

I shake my head. "Try again."

"What kind of game are you playing?" he asks, flipping on the light. His hair is wild, his eyes accusatory, and yet—and yet—he's the same old Jacob. The same goofy-handsome Jacob in his flannel pajamas and bare feet. A murderer? I don't know. I don't know! My head is swimming.

"No games," I say.

"Give it back to me," he says in a softer tone. "I mean it, Ro. I've been worrying since I saw it was gone, since you left, that you'd—" He shuts his eyes, sucks in a breath, shakes his head as if he's imagining the unimaginable. "I cannot tell you how much it would destroy me."

"Like it destroyed you with Sara," I say.

"Exactly," he whispers.

"Or," I say. "Maybe you destroyed Sara and you want to destroy me too."

Jacob blinks violently as if I slapped him. His mouth drops open and feels around for a word. He reddens. I've never seen him this color.

"How dare you say that?" he says, taking a step toward me. "What is *wrong* with you? What is so fucked up and damaged inside you that you would say a thing like that to me?"

For a moment, the world becomes a carousel. I'm so dizzy from his response I'm questioning myself entirely. *Am* I paranoid? Have I truly lost it, to accuse him of this? Am I the monster here?

"I don't know," I say, starting to cry. I squeeze my eyes shut, hard, the way I used to when I was younger and I wanted to, as Sylvia Plath said, make the world drop dead. It's not impossible that I've been wrong. And that is almost as horrifying as me being right.

"You are insane," he says very slowly. "You have fallen off the edge. You're not the person I married. You're pathetic."

"Remember what Shelly said about I statements," I can't help myself from saying, I don't know why, to try to defuse it all with a stupid joke. I'm crying though, not laughing.

I open my eyes.

"You want to keep my gun, Rowena?" he asks. "Go ahead. I know why you want it. And if you want to leave the world so bad, do it." He cocks his chin. "Just fucking do it already."

The man I see in front of me, inches away from me, with his lip curled up in disgust, is a complete stranger. The rage in his eyes is animal.

"I want to see you do it," he says.

It's so hurtful, so cruel, the wind has left me. I struggle to breathe. Finally, I shake my head once, tears rolling down my face.

"I would never do that," I say.

"Then tell me where you put it!" he explodes, lunging toward me, tackling me to the floor. The attack is a shock. Somehow, throughout all my suspicion, I never imagined he would ever touch me with such cruel force. My shoulder hits the corner of the coffeetable on the way down. Immediately, I feel a sharp pain, followed by a wet warmth. He's so heavy. So heavy on top of me. I draw my knee in, getting him in the groin, and he rolls off of me making a noise like the air leaving a balloon.

I spring to my feet and grab the lamp on the end table, ripping the cord from the wall. Turning around, I hesitate for one moment, holding it above his head, and then hurl it down. It thwacks against his skull and rolls off, cracked; Jacob goes still. He lies on the floor in a curled position like a comma and I shiver, my fingers pressed to my mouth. I stand here a long time, crying in disbelief. Trying to turn the pages of the chapter back again and reread it—trying to understand the meaning. Trying to gauge who the villain is. Because I must say, taking in the sight of Jacob's still body, the blood spattered on the carpet, I am really feeling like I might be the villain right now.

I turn to Maxine. "Maxine, oh my God, Maxine—I think I killed him."

Maxine's colors light up again, a cheerful yellow very out of touch with the scene at play. Then she turns orange.

"I—I don't know what happened," I stammer. "I don't know what came over me. It happened so fast—he came at me—but then I—I might have overreacted—I didn't think it would—it happened so fast—"

"Rowena," Maxine says, turning red. "You are in immediate danger—"

A hand closes over Maxine, a hairy hand with a ring on it. A hand I've seen a thousand times but never truly feared until now. Jacob has reached from behind me and grabbed Maxine with one, now two hands. As if in slow motion, I turn to him. I see his face, blank, a trail of blood running down his temple, for just a single moment before a crushing pain overtakes everything, everything, and the lights go off.

CHAPTER 19
THE BLITZ

THE FIRST NIGHT Jacob slept over in my apartment, a sudden heat wave swallowed the city and made the streets smell thickly of sweetness and rot. My air conditioner broke. My houseplants drooped from their painted shelves. Jacob showed up at my door with a plastic bag full of ice cream sandwiches and beer, walking through my hanging door beads to join me. We lay on my bed together, two fans blowing on us from both sides of my double bed with its patchwork quilt, our legs intertwined, as he showed me pictures from his childhood. He was so eager to share it with me, for me to peer into his past. His mother was impossibly tan and bleached blond as a California cliché. His father had the head of a lumberjack—square jaw, red beard—but the body of a slick businessman, suits in every picture, always squatting a bit on the outside of Jacob and Jennee. The house Jacob grew up in was so big and bright and suburban, more a myth than real life. We laughed at Jacob's gap-toothed pictures with his horn-rimmed glasses, seated at a computer. It was magical, to be invited in like that, to have Jacob peel back the curtains and show me who he was.

"I want you to come to California with me," he said.

AMEN MAXINE

Then he gave me the longest, hardest, most surprisingly passionate kiss. His kisses were like that—they conveyed a sense of urgency his casual demeanor did not. I put a hand to his jaw, traced the outline with my finger.

"I'd love to," I said. "It looks like paradise."

"I want to live there someday again," he said. "Raise kids there. You know?"

I didn't have the heart to tell him I had decided long ago not to have kids. The world was too volatile and heartbreaking for kids. I was unstable, quick to assume the worst in people, crying when I couldn't find my keys, on the verge of panic if I missed my subway stop. I had planned a life like this, contained in an apartment, surrounded by books, hanging on as long as I could. Wasn't this life? Wasn't this all it was?

"Sure," I said instead.

Beer and ice cream sandwiches hit my empty stomach hard. I spent the later hours of that night with my head inside the toilet. Jacob sat behind me, pulling my hair from my face, rubbing circles on my back, kissing my neck. I felt so empty, so dizzy there, beyond sad, blank and drunk, my head pounding, my arms shivering. He tucked me into bed and I was so sick. I hardly knew him, this stranger in my house, and he was treating me with such kindness I cried until he held me and told me it would be okay.

"The moment I saw you I knew I wanted to take care of you," he said, kissing my head.

As a person who had long felt like an island, an only child, my father gone, my mother forever teetering on the edge of ill health, someone who had to beg her professors for extensions because I was constantly in my own way, someone who spent my evenings researching diseases I might have, someone who had been often told by lovers eventually that I was too much, someone whose one grace in life were books which could be opened and immediately beautifully thankfully eliminate my own existence, someone who was depressed and anxious and who had dark thoughts that are not worth repeating, someone who saw a passing bus and saw escape, someone who saw a bottle of pills and saw a one-way door, someone who saw an open window many stories up in the middle of a fight and saw a way out of her own head ... Jacob was a gift. He was.

And even now, in this place—in this dark, dark place where I can't even manage to raise an arm or twitch a leg—that's what I'm left with. Is love. Is missing him. Jacob, the man who came over with a bag of ice cream sandwiches on a sweltering day. The man who saw a mother in me when I thought I was worthless. Who held my hair back and saw me at my worst and kept loving me, kept loving me anyway.

I know he's a liar, but he's not *only* a liar. He couldn't have been faking everything.

There was love there, actual love. A clash of spirits and fate that resulted in Michelle, the sweetest little being, the brightest star in my galaxy.

Michelle!

I twist in pain, a tiny flicker of movement. A presence, fighting to be in my body again. A slight detection of the air on a surface that might be my skin. Fingers. I can feel my fingers, clenching the air, tingles on the tips. The dreamlike place I've been in—that hall of memory in my skull—it starts to fade. I curl my toes, feeling the velvety tongue of my slipper. With all my might, my leg clenches, then bends. Now my other leg. My hands spread out and explore like spiders. The carpet. I know this carpet. It's my carpet, in my house. My other hand clutches something rubbery, something that squeaks with a sound. A boot. Suddenly, I am able to prop myself up on an elbow and get a good gasp of air and I am flooded with the *here* now.

I am here.

Clutching a boot, lying on my back on the carpet, in the

darkness. But not complete darkness—that slit of light on the floor. As I heave up to a sitting position, a crashing pain on the top of my head makes me cower back to the floor. It takes a moment of breathing and a much slower rise to be able to sit up steady. I sit here until the pain stops stabbing in a rhythm and instead eases into an unceasing scream.

My ears ring loudly. I stare at the slit again of light and know suddenly where I am.

The closet. I'm in my closet.

I reach up to touch my skull, where there is wetness and devastating pain. I pull my hand away, dry heave, and don't touch it again. The shivers roll in, mean and chattering my teeth.

A knock on the door that stops my blood.

"Ro," is all he says through the door, in a voice that sounds rough, sounds hoarse. "You awake?"

I'm not sure whether I should answer, how I got here. Vaguely, I recall a fight of some kind, a shock, a blow. Jacob. What were we even fighting about? My throat hurts like I want to cry, but I'm in such a state I can't even manage that.

"What am I doing in here?" I finally ask.

"I put you in there."

"Why'd you put me in the closet?" My voice is so shaky, so small, I can hardly believe it's mine.

"You broke a lamp over my head. You stole my gun."

I sit with those words a moment, let them sink in. I sink along with them as the memories come into focus—he's right. I did those things. Why did I do those things? I shift my weight and pull my legs into a cross-legged position and a bolt of pain zags from my skull and down my back. Shaking fingers reach up to press my head, the stickiness there. It all comes back to me. Jacob hitting me over the head with Maxine. My fingers press my lips as panic floods me and I try to think my way out of this.

"I'm not letting you out of there until you tell me where the gun is," Jacob says.

"So you can shoot me with it?" I fire back.

"So I can keep us *safe*," he shouts. The door shakes with a hit or a kick.

A moment lingers with a hush. In this moment, I wallow in my disbelief that this is really what has become of my life. Whoever would have believed, in the first days of love notes and gifts of rare poetry and pieces of cake from the bakery, in the first days of picture tours down memory lane and holding my hair back in my sickness and long nights curled together in one shape on a bed too small for two, that this is where we would end up? It confounds math and logic, space and time, that somehow I could share such intimacy with someone over so long and know them less than I did when I first met them. But here we are.

"I hate that you're in there," he says. "You think I want this? Just tell me where it is and I'll let you out."

"Where's Michelle?" I ask.

"Sleeping. Thank God." He waits a beat before saying. "So where is it? This is serious. You said you got rid of it—where? Where'd you put it? We could end all this right now if you'd tell me."

I'm so twisted up, so tired, so tangled inside. A part of me almost believes him—believes his mirror story that I am the dangerous one and I am the one to be feared. But as I sit in the dark a bit longer, focusing on my breathing, thinking with a sharp pang of Michelle gently sleeping in the other room as her mother sits locked in a dark closet by her father over a fight about who wants to kill whom with a gun, the words *emotional abuse* appear like red letters flashing on a marquis. I think of the uncountable lies he's told me without blinking, without remorse. And of Sara, who died of a gunshot wound to the head. Of Jacob on an extravagant trip through Europe with Sara's money. I think of how he's convinced Dane and my mother that I'm teetering on the edge of a breakdown, as if setting everything up beforehand. And the gun. Then there's the gun.

In the dark, a light bulb pops in my brain.

The gun is in here with me.

"I'll tell you," I say, feeling around the floor, clutching heels, toes, straps, shoelaces. I reach backward with a stab of pain in my skull.

"Then tell me."

"I will," I say, my hand finding the edge of the storybook box. My heart lifts and races, a sick exhilaration flooding me as I unclasp it. As I open the lid. My palm meets the metal, my fingers find the handle, pick it up, position it between my hands—and I aim it straight at the door.

"I'm waiting," he says.

"You need to let me out so I can show you," I say.

My hands are shaking. I don't even know how to hold a gun; I've only seen it in movies. Is there a safety or something I'm supposed to undo? I have no idea. My finger floats above the trigger.

"Tell me first," he says.

"I can't tell you," I say. "I have to show you. It's not something I can explain."

A long moment passes in the dark, so long I wonder if he might have left. And in this moment, all I can think of is Michelle. I love her to the point of pain. I'm so ashamed that we are her parents, that this is what it's come to. That I let this man lie to me and fuck with my head so badly I don't know who I am, what I've done, what I'm guilty of or capable of—but I vow now, right now, hands heavy with a gun, heart woken up, that I will not let him destroy me. I can't. Because I'm her mother. I'm bound to her. I owe this to her. To keep going. To survive.

And if need be, if it comes down to it, to kill a monster.

Even the one I love.

As the door hinges open with a groan, the light blinds my eyes for a moment. I can't see anything but his figure looming and in the jolt at the sight of him, I squeeze my finger tight on the trigger. The gun pops and shudders with the force of it. Perhaps my heart has stopped with it. My eyes adjust, just fast enough to see that I've turned his head into a bloody pudding as he falls to the floor with a thump like a bag of bricks.

I put the gun down and sit with my hands over my mouth for a long time, squeezing my eyes shut, sobbing with no sound, nausea and head pain and confusion and regret and so much fear, so much fear over what I've done, over whether or not I just made the greatest mistake of my life or whether or not I am finally free.

It isn't until I hear Michelle crying suddenly from the other room that I open my eyes again and pull myself to a standing position. I wipe my face and glance one last time at the gun on the floor, stooping down and picking it up to take my shirt and wipe it of fingerprints before letting it drop again. I turn and though I see Jacob's figure there ahead of me, see all the spatter and the pink and the red, I don't focus on it, don't scan it for detail.

The one thing I do focus on, as I step over his body, is a Maglite flashlight fallen on the floor near his right hand.

He kept it next to the bed, for protection; he always said if anyone broke in, he would hit them over the head with it. And the sight of that makes me stand a bit taller, helps my tears dry a bit faster—because if I hadn't shot him when he opened that door, what then? Was he ready to bash my head in again?

"It's okay, sweetpea," I tell Michelle, picking her up from her crib. She's teary-eyed in her pig pajamas. Who knows how long she's been crying, which loud noises woke her. My God, what would have happened to her if Jacob had had his way? I can't think of him—I can't think that I—is Jacob really dead? "It's okay."

My motherly voice calms us both, seems to center us both. Stops her crying and stops my morbid merry-go-rounding.

I take her out to the living room, balancing her on my hip as I gather up the pieces of Maxine and gently put them into a paper bag. My pulse is swirling in my ears. I have to get out of here. Where to go, I have no idea. I need to talk to Maxine. There's a hole in my middle, a screaming hole, and though I'm sure it's about the fact I just killed Jacob—*I just killed Jacob*—the fact Maxine has been smashed to bits on our carpet hurts almost as bad. I begin to cry because I want to ask her what to do, where to go, but she's silent and broken.

Holding Michelle tight as she rests her cheek on my shoulder and sinks back into sleep, I squeeze my eyes shut and think through my options. I could call the police, of course. There's a chance they would see this as self defense. But there's a chance they wouldn't, too, and that is enough for me to know I can't do that. Being separated from my baby, going to prison, these are not options for me.

Perhaps if I could get Maxine repaired she could help me think this through. Maybe there's a way we could get rid of Jacob's body and make it look like he disappeared of his own volition—he's made rash decisions before in his life, his mom would back me up. Moving to a new city, going on a sudden unexplained vacation, marrying a woman he just met. Michelle and I could keep our lives without him. I would never tell a soul.

"I don't know," I whisper, eyeing the brown bag holding Maxine. "I don't know what to do, I don't know what to do, I don't know what to do. I killed him. I *killed* him."

Quietly, still in shock, I go out into the night and get into the car, strapping Michelle in who wakes up again cranky and red-faced. I soothe her and give her kisses, crying too suddenly as it hits me—this is real. This really happened. We were a family and now we're a mother and a daughter and we have nowhere to go. I'm terrified.

I climb into the driver's seat and catch a glimpse of myself in the rearview. Horrific. Covered in blood, a wound on the top of my head still glistening. I take out the baby wipes and clean my face and then grab a beanie that has been under my seat since last winter. I put it on and check the rearview again, relieved to see someone who looks more like a person and less like a woman who stepped out of a horror movie. With shaking hands, I take out my phone and search for an electronics repair shop open this late—and there's just one, which closes in ten minutes. I pull out of the driveway and speed toward the strip mall to try to get there in time.

It's so strange, what happens as the minutes pass since I took my husband's life. It settles into reality numbly; it becomes a giant looming wordless something that I won't let myself think about. My focus instead becomes knife-sharp. I am focused on the next thing. That's all there is to think about. The next thing is repairing Maxine.

I pull into the parking lot in front of Ed's Electronics. In the front of the store, a young man in thick glasses wearing a backpack is locking the door. The shop's Closed sign is displayed, the lights are off.

"No."

I unbuckle my seatbelt, rush out my door.

"Excuse me," I call out, waving my arms. "Excuse me, sir. You can't be closed." My voice climbs, splits. "You can't."

"Oh … uh, sorry. Yeah. We close at ten," says the guy, looking back at me. "But we open again at ten tomorrow—"

"I can't—I can't wait that long," I say, coming closer to him, tears spilling. "You don't understand. This is an emergency."

"We repair electronics."

"I know."

"You have an … electronic emergency?"

"Yes. I need something fixed right now."

"What, you spill soda on your laptop or something?"

"No. It's much more complicated than that. Please, you don't understand. I'll—I'll pay you double your usual fee. Triple. Whatever you want. I'll give you five hundred bucks on top of what you charge—just for you to keep."

The guy raises his bushy eyebrows and considers this. "Cash?"

"MyCash," I say, holding up my phone.

"All right," he finally says. "Bring your device inside and I'll take a look. But if it's something that needs parts, we're not going to be able to do it tonight."

"Thank you so much," I say, breathing deeply with relief, wiping tears away.

"Yeah, sure," he says, giving me a look I know well now, the *this lady's unhinged as hell* look, before turning around to unlock the door again.

"Let me just get my baby," I say to him.

"You have a baby with you?" he says, annoyed.

"She's sleeping. It'll be fine."

I go to the car, take out the carseat carefully so as not to wake her, and grab the paper bag with Maxine in it. Inside Ed's Electronics, only one light is on near the back. When I walk further in, I hear the locks click shut behind me. The shadows and the darkness of this unfamiliar place with its shelves teeming with machine parts, gutted computers, and coiled, serpentine wires all radiate a sinister vibe. That and the fact I'm locked up alone with a man I've never met. He could do anything to me and who would know? These are usually things I would fear, but right now, there's no fear left. I'm the one who should be feared; I'm the one who just shot a man in the face.

I get a flash of the blast, the instant red jelly mess the bullet made of his head, and then swallow hard and focus instead on what is here right now. The fluorescent glow of the back table where the guy is waiting for me with a tired expression. He opens a diet soda and slurps it down.

"Let's see what you have," he says.

With a crinkle, I put the bag on the table. "It's a digital assistant."

He pulls the parts out and lays them on the table in front of him, furrowing his brows, rubbing the stubble on his chin.

"Not on the market yet," I go on. "It's in beta mode. My husband—" My voice catches and it takes a moment to find itself again. "He worked—works—at Jolvix."

The guy's eyes light up behind his frames. "Is this one of those Maxines they haven't released yet? Holy shit."

"Yeah."

"The ones with the advanced predictive AI, right?"

"That's it."

"And it works?" he asks, turning Maxine's silver body over, exposing her nether region I never looked at before, where a gash has left her open, her bottom broken, her board exposed, a pile of her shrapnel on the surface where he's working. "Are the predictions accurate?"

There's something about the sensual way he's touching her, the light in his eyes, that I don't like. I fear that he covets her. That he knows how rare she is. He could take her from me.

"More or less," I say. "Honestly, it's more just a digital assistant—helps me keep my grocery list, orders things I need for the house, tells me the weather, that type of thing."

He fishes a screwdriver out from a toolbox behind him and comes back, unscrewing her broken bottom. "Figures," he says. "They keep trying to design that shit—" He glances at Michelle, sleeping under her fuzzy blanket in the carseat behind me. "Sorry, that *crap*. Like did you read about the Predict app?"

"I did."

He gazes at Maxine's insides and I throb, seeing her

reduced to plastic parts like that. He takes a pen-sized flashlight and peers closer. "So it really looks like the damage is in this bottom area, which is the audio amplification system. This is built like a lot of other digital assistant machines, with the motherboard up top. Since the damage is all to the bottom of this, what you need will probably just be a new tweeter because that's borked—" He points to a cracked button-shaped thing that sits in the pile of parts. "And it looks like a mono amplifier went here." He touches a space where it appears a tiny rectangle used to live. "Do you know where it went?"

"I don't. It's not here?" I ask, pointing to the pile.

He answers slowly. "That's a charger, the busted tweeter, and some chunks from the bottom."

"Okay," I say, trying to control the tightening in my chest. "And if I don't have it?"

"I have a sixty-watt mono amplifier IC, I don't know if it will be *exactly* what was in here," he says. "But I have some parts scrapped from similar devices. It might not sound exactly the same, but it should work."

"Sure," I say. "Whatever to get this working again."

He lingers a moment, studying the machine in his hands, then me. His eyes fall to my chest for a moment and then he turns around to go back into another room behind the table, one that says EMPLOYEES ONLY.

I look down at my chest—there's blood spatter on it. Yes, I wiped off my face and covered my head wound. But my gray sweatshirt's a gory constellation. How could I have overlooked it? My blood pressure spikes and I reach out to touch Maxine's skin, for comfort. He's in a back room now, where I can't see him. What if he's calling the police? What then? Should I run? My eyes water and I feel like I can't breathe for a second until he comes back out of the room with a tiny chip in his hand.

"This should do it," he says. "Give me a second to get it in and put it together. And then the tweeter, I have this from the same machine I stripped the mono amplifier from." He holds up a dome-shaped thing. "It's not a Maxine, but it's one of those older models this was based off. So it might sound a little different, but it should work the same." He sits on a stool and starts working, taking out a soldering iron. "The bottom I think you're just going to need to duct tape for the time being, until you can order a custom replacement."

I nod, sedated by my sense of relief. He's making it sound so easy. Soon Maxine will be back with me. I notice him glancing at my sweatshirt again and I fold my arms, my ears ringing.

"So ... what happened, might I ask?" the guy says as he focuses on the miniature task at hand. "How'd it break? Why the emergency?"

"Funny story," I say. "I'm an artist. I was working on a piece for an exhibition tomorrow, which features Maxine and a whole lot of red paint. I dropped her—it—and it just busted completely."

"Ah," he says. "I wondered what was going on with your sweatshirt. It looks ... alarming."

"Right?" I laugh. "I look like I just killed someone."

"You kind of do," he says with a smile.

And the tension has melted, just melted, like butter in a pan. Michelle stirs behind me and I stoop down to rock her. Once she dozes again, her eyelashes no longer aflutter, I stand back up.

"Anyway," I go on, relishing the fantasy now, enjoying the lie. "That was why I was so desperate coming here. Without Maxine, there's no show tomorrow. It would have been a disaster."

"Where's the show?" he asks.

"It's being held at a gallery in San Jose called the Green Light," I tell him excitedly.

"Nice," he says.

As he continues to work, I chew my cheek and pace along the shelves, getting lost in the woods of my mind. For a moment, I'm exhilarated by the idea that I could be an artist, getting ready for a show. That my life is not my life. That my husband is not a corpse in my house. It's so exquisite, the fiction I spin, that it isn't until I hear the screech of the duct tape that I'm pulled out of it. That I remember where I am and what's really happening. I walk back to the table where the man is working. He plugs Maxine in and she lights up in a rainbow of colors. I nearly burst into tears at the sight of it.

"Oh my God," I say, clamping my hand to my mouth.

"Rowena," Maxine says, her voice a bit quieter, a bit tinnier, but still there. "Rowena, what happened? Are you safe?"

"I'm fine, Maxine, everything's fine," I say, not being able to help the tear that falls down my face. I try to catch it quickly, but I notice the man noticing, eyebrows raised. "You can shut her off," I tell him. "Save battery power."

He does so. "Just send me the five hundred and we're good."

"You sure?" I ask, taking out my phone and opening the app.

"Yeah. Parts were nothing. It was scrap we keep in the back. My handle's Jacob_L4873."

My finger, lingering above the phone screen, shakes uncontrollably. "Jacob?" I repeat.

"Yeah."

"Your name is Jacob?"

"Yes."

"I figured your name was Ed."

"Tell you a secret," he says, leaning in. "There is no Ed."

I force a sound from my mouth I hope resembles a laugh.

"Well, I'm Rowena," I say. "Nice to meet you."

"That's funny, I figured *your* name was Carrie Woodward," he says. "Since it's on the inside of Maxine."

It is, in this second in time, as if gravity itself has shifted. I can't move. I have to put the phone down as I find my words. "Wait—what?"

"Yeah, you didn't notice it? Oh right, you've probably never looked inside. Guessing it's the name of whomever worked on this, since you said it's in beta and it's not commercially sold. Sometimes these things in beta, they're marked with the name of the programmer or the person who worked on it. Like a signature, you know?"

Carrie Woodward. *Carrie Woodward.* Carrie *Woodward*?

Carrie. Fucking. Woodward.

I can barely type the word *Jacob* into my phone without wanting to throw up. After I send him the money, and he gets the alert on his phone, I thank him and gently pick up Michelle's carseat and head toward the glass door pitch black with night.

"Good luck at your show," he says.

I freeze. Takes a second to register, but I turn around and nod. "Yeah, thank you. Thank you so much." I swallow. "Jacob."

The locks unclick for me. The night air is warm on my face, a breeze smelling of French fries from the glow of a fast-food restaurant still open at the edge of the parking lot. I'm not sure I'll ever be hungry again. After fastening Michelle back in and soothing her again as she stirs, I heave myself into the front seat and put my hands on the wheel. I can't bring myself to start the car, though. I am on fire. I am dizzy. Why would Carrie's name be inside Maxine? A *signature*? If she programmed Maxine—if she was responsible for making her—what does that mean?

Can I even trust Maxine?

I squeeze the wheel and glance at the passenger seat, where Maxine still sits in a brown bag. I'm not ready to take her out of it. I have to think this through. Because if Carrie programmed Maxine, and Carrie was fucking my husband,

and Carrie knew this machine was going home to be *mine* … that means she would have had plenty of motivation to program it to fuck with me.

And if she did that, then that means …

I knock my head with my hand, just to feel something. And oh, believe me, the wound is still fresh under the beanie, and I feel more than something: I feel everything. I see stars.

"I can't," I say, starting the car, the world a blur. "I can't."

I can't think this thought through to its logical conclusion.

Just like I can't think back to what happened at the house.

I can't go backward. I can't delve into hypotheticals. All I can do now is drive a straight path forward to the next place. Follow the line.

Straight to Carrie Woodward's house.

CHAPTER 20
THE END

I DON'T NEED GPS to take me to 328 Bush Street. That address, the route there, the curve of the cul de sac, everything about it will forever be burned into my memory along with the pain of that humiliating night when I first discovered Jacob here. Parked at the curb in front of the house, I sit in the car a moment, my eyeballs stinging. It seems my entire body is just a container for pain right now, from the top of my head throbbing in time with my heartbeat, to my heart itself screaming inside my chest. I don't understand what is happening. I don't know who to trust. And though there are three of us in this car—me, Maxine, Michelle—both of the others are in sleep mode and I have never felt so alone.

The clock says it's approaching eleven. Carrie's house is dark, except for faint light in the front window, muted by curtains. I take a few moments to steady my breath, glance back to make sure Michelle is still sleeping soundly, then grab the paper bag holding Maxine and hop out of the car.

The scene is so tranquil, the gold glow of the streetlamps on the sidewalks, which glitter just a bit. Carrie's house with its well-kept lawn and sycamore tree whispering with the breeze. I cross the lawn and it all comes back to me with a twist in my belly—how mortifying, how terrible that night was. How Jacob lied to my face and tried to keep it going until Carrie gave up and admitted the truth. None of this makes sense; as much as I despise Carrie, I believe she was devastated that night too. It was plain on her face. I just don't understand what her motive would be, why she would program Maxine to make me think Jacob was trying to kill me. Unless she thought messing with my head would undo our marriage and make Jacob hers.

That's the only conclusion that could make sense, the only explanation I can muster.

I ring the video doorbell and wait. I wait so long I hear a siren, my blood pressure rising along with it, and then stabilizing when the siren's sound disappears into the night air. I ring the bell again and listen to the sound of crickets. After the third ring, I'm sure she's not going to answer. So I make a plea to the camera, where I hope she's watching me.

"Carrie, I'm sorry to come so late," I say to it. "I know you can see me and you probably want me to go away. And I will, I swear, I'll go away and you'll never hear from me again—but I'm just so confused. About what Jacob did and didn't do and I need to know, I need to know, it's really important, I need to know and Carrie you're the only one who can help me, so please—"

With a *snick*, the door opens, and Carrie peers out at me through the crack as I stand in the darkness of her doorstep.

"I'm not seeing him anymore, okay?" she squeaks in her high little California girl voice. "I don't even work at Jolvix now. Sorry, okay? But please leave me alone."

"No," I say, putting my fingers in the door frame so she can't close it. "Just—just give me a minute. It's not about the affair—I don't want to talk about that. It's about this." I hold up the paper bag and pull Maxine out of it for her to see.

"A Maxine?" she asks, squinting.

It's odd to hear Maxine reduced to that—being one of many. There could never be another Maxine.

"What about it?" Carrie asks, eyebrows furrowed. "I didn't know they were, like, available for sale yet."

"They're not," I tell her. "Jacob got me this in beta mode. And your name is inside of it."

Carrie shakes her head. "What?"

"Written inside of it. Like a signature. Because you worked on it, right? Because you knew this was going to undo me." I try to control my voice, but the anger slips in. "You knew this was coming to me and it was a way you could fuck with my head."

"What are you *talking* about—"

"That's it, right?" I ask, stuffing Maxine back into the paper bag. "It was just, like, a fun way to fuck with Jacob's wife's head, right? Telling me all sorts of things, like how he wanted to kill me? Like how he bought a gun to kill me."

"Look, I—" Carrie's words drop out and she looks up for a moment, as if she's trying to figure out how to respond. She pushes her stupid, perfect, golden hair back with her hands and then lets it all drop. "Okay, let me, like, get my head together right now. First of all, Jacob bought a gun because he was *robbed*. You know that, right?" She lets that statement breathe a moment. "He's not going to kill you, that's ridiculous. And I—I don't know why my name is inside a Maxine. Because I, like, worked on Jacob's team. You know that. You *know* that's the team that works with security software. Right? I don't work in AI. I don't, like, work with the team that makes these devices. That team didn't even, like, work in the same building as we did. I—I'm honestly, I don't know what to say."

"You're lying," I say, my eyes filling. "This makes no sense. It makes no sense why your name would be inside, I'm so confused."

"So am I, literally—*so* confused."

Carrie casts me a pitying glance as she continues to stand behind her door. And I know, yes, that she was sleeping with my husband and that makes anything she says suspect. And I know, too, that I have been easily played by a liar before. But I'm having a hard time not believing her. She did work on Jacob's team, that's the truth. Jacob does work on security—he knows nothing about AI. He doesn't build devices. That's a totally different part of Jolvix. The corkscrew in my stomach twists a little tighter, the confusion mixing with the dizzying pain of my skull.

"You should go home and talk to Jacob about this, not me," Carrie says. "I've told you everything I can."

"I can't talk to Jacob," I whisper, wiping my eyes. "You don't understand."

"Well, I don't have anything for you. You would have to talk to someone in …" Carrie's fingers fly to her lips and her expression changes. "Wait." Then Carrie takes a deep breath and closes her eyes, leaning her head on the door frame as if what she's about to say is going to hurt. "Dot."

I stand up a little straighter. "Dot?"

"Dot. Dorothy Labarre. An engineer on the team that worked on the Maxines. She hates me. She's, like, *nuts*. That's exactly the type of weird shit she would do—put my name on things I had nothing to do with. She started emailing people from a fake email address with my name on it at Jolvix, and it was this whole, like, *thing*, a whole investigation, and she got fired. I can tell you exactly where she lives, too. I went to a party there once, back before—" Carrie bites her lip. "Back before, you know, everything happened with Jacob. It actually might have been one of the first nights Jacob and I really hung out." A quiver rises in her voice. "I'm sorry to bring that up. I'm just so sorry for everything. I, like, hope you know that."

Though some part deep and buried in me does appreciate that she's sorry, I'm, *like*, unwilling to acknowledge or accept her apology. I hurt too much. I can't even meet her gaze.

"Where does she live?" I ask. "I need to talk to her."

"I'll tell you, hold on." Carrie takes out her phone and scrolls. "I still have her number, too, even though I blocked her."

I shake my head. "Give me her address."

"Here it is: 658 Magnolia Street, Apartment 44. It's in Santa Clara."

She holds her phone out for me to see, stepping onto the porch. I pull out my phone with a shaking hand and type it in.

"Okay," I say quietly.

"What's all over your shirt?" Carrie asks, eyes wide. "Is that—"

"Thank you," I say, holding up my phone. "I'll talk to Dot. Sorry to bother you." I turn and hurry across the lawn.

"I'm warning you, she's—" Carrie calls after me. "There's —there's a lot I didn't tell you."

"There's a lot I didn't tell you too," I murmur as I climb into the driver's seat, put Maxine back in the passenger's seat, and turn on the car. Michelle's still asleep back there. I reach my hand back to touch her chest gently, make sure she's okay, and she emits a tiny sigh. "We're okay."

I drive into the night again, face stiff as a mask from the crying that has passed, heartbeat steady as a drum as I process the information. Carrie's name is inside Maxine; Dot hated Carrie; why would Dot put Carrie's name inside Maxine? Where does Jacob fit into all this? My skin crawls and I beg the universe please, please don't tell me I just killed my husband for nothing. As always, the universe does not respond.

Well, I will soon find out.

It takes about fifteen minutes for me to arrive at Paradise Palms: a four-story, U-shaped apartment building built around a glimmering blue swimming pool and painted a bland Caucasian peach. Countless windows, some lit, some dark. Palm trees galore, as promised. Michelle starts crying as I pull the carseat out and I have to rock her for a few minutes in the parking lot to get her back to sleep. Poor thing. Finally, she drifts off again and I approach the building. Huff up four flights of outdoor stairs—and with the carseat in one hand and my bag of Maxine in the other, it's no easy feat. Finally, I get to apartment 44. I'm about to knock when the door opens and a woman in a black robe with bell sleeves, with short dyed pink hair and wide, eyelinered eyes, blinks back at me. Instantly, I know I've seen her somewhere before, but I can't place her.

"Who the fuck are you?" she asks.

And that's when it clicks: the fuckface lady. Dot is the fuckface lady. The woman who was pulled from the Jolvix Valentine's party, the woman I have, at times, feared becoming—a screaming mess on display for the world to see. A woman having a loud and public nervous breakdown.

"Oh," I say, everything swirling around in my mind. "It's you."

"It's me," she says. "But who the fuck are you?"

"My name is Rowena Snyder," I tell her. "I'm Jacob Snyder's wife."

"Jacob Snyder," she says, her voice taking a more somber tone. "Well, I'm so sorry to hear that. My condolences. He truly is a shitstain of a human being." She glances down at Michelle. "And that's his baby, I assume?"

I nod.

"So sad for you, little baby," Dot says, looking down. "To have a human shitstain for a father."

Now I'm hooked. Something about Dot, as brash as she is, puts me at ease. Because I agree with her about Jacob. I'm relieved to hear someone else say it.

"Can we talk?" I ask.

"We're talking, are we not?" Dot asks.

"I mean, inside?" I ask. "May I come inside?"

"You may, if you don't mind a mess and copious amounts of marijuana smoke."

"It's fine," I tell her.

"Then come on in," she says, putting out her arm with the bell sleeves, ornate rings decorating her fingers, and long, fake purple fingernails curling in the air. She reminds me of a witch.

I walk inside her apartment and though she warned me, it's still a shock to smell how pungent the skunk scent is and to see the mess she lives in. There are clothes all over the living room floor, a sea of black clothes. A black leather couch faces a wide-screen TV with some kind of game on pause and a four-foot bong sits proudly on the coffeetable next to a video game controller.

She points to the couch. "Have a seat."

I tread carefully, trying to find spots on the floor where I'm not stepping on clothes. Taking my seat on the squeaking leather, I place Michelle's carseat on one side of the coffeetable. Dot sits next to me and her painted eyebrows shoot up.

"I just noticed you're covered in blood," she says.

"Oh—that." I look down at myself, almost numb to the sight of it now. "Long story, not worth going into. I'm fine." Dot doesn't ask any more questions, which I appreciate. I take the paper bag in my lap and gently pull Maxine out, putting her on the table. "I need to talk to you about this."

"Mmm," Dot says, almost nostalgically, reaching her purple fingernails out and touching Maxine's silver skin. "Oh yes."

"It broke and I went to get it fixed. Carrie Woodward's name was inside it."

"Carrie Woodward—that witless sack of meat."

"But Carrie thought it might have been you who put her

name there, because you worked on these machines when you were at Jolvix."

Dot snorts and eyes her fingernails for a moment. Then she looks at me with a serious expression. Her eyes are so light blue, they're like ice. The faint crow's feet make me wonder if she's older, or if she's my age and has simply lived hard. "I did put her name there. I'm surprised she put two and two together with that empty candy dish of a brain."

"But … why would you do that?" I ask, my voice rising. "And what role did you have in making this machine?"

Dot picks Maxine up and examines her, poking the duct tape. "Well, I wouldn't say I *made* this. But I was part of the team that programmed the betas. There were only eight of them. This one was special." Dot looks at me. "I don't know how to tell you this, but your husband is a very bad man."

"You don't need to tell me. I know."

"He fucked me," Dot says, putting Maxine back on the table, and I flinch at the word. "In more ways than one. He fucked me and then, when he was sick of me, he got me fired. He's a gaslighting, sociopathic son of a bitch. And he gets pleasure out of other people's pain. Let me tell you a story, Rowena."

I'm listening, all ears, rigid, tensed, stomach turning, hurting for an answer.

"So one night," she says, "after Jacob and I first met—we met at a café on the Jolvix campus and, well, Jacob laid the charm on thick. I started seeing him. I'm sorry, Rowena." She puts her hand on my knee, squeezes, and takes it back. "I didn't know he was married at first. He would come over after work and we'd hang out and, you know. You know what we did. But one night, I had some molly. We took it together. We took it here, in my apartment. We sat right here, right where we're sitting. And as we rolled, as the drugs kicked all the way in, he said the most atrocious things. I was so high, listening to him, that I didn't process it until later but —he said the most *monstrous* things."

I have tightened so much, sitting and listening, every muscle clenched—from my jaw to my toes curling in their shoes. I've never wanted to both listen and not listen so much in my entire life. But I have to sit here and take it. I have to know.

"What things?" I ask.

"He said he loved to torture women," she says, crossing her legs, revealing a leopard-print slip underneath, tightening her robe and retying it. "Plain as day. He grinned and said he loved to play secret games with them. That's what he called it, 'secret games.' He practically bragged that he drove his ex-wife to suicide. He bragged about all the 'secret games' he loved to play with you—like, for instance, putting a paper towel in a toaster oven when you reheated food, so you'd think you started a fire."

My mouth drops.

"Yeah." Her voice turns into a murmur. "Remember that? *He* did that."

"It happened twice," I whisper.

"Or putting ipecac in your takeout. Or replacing your anxiety meds with high dose caffeine pills."

I gasp.

"You didn't know?" Dot says, reaching out to pat my arm. "Oh, honey."

I begin to cry, everything hitting me at once. The fires in the toaster oven. The times I was sick to my stomach from food he fed me. The anxiety that only seemed to worsen, despite my medication. What else has he been doing to me to undo me? What else don't I know about? It's miles beyond horrifying.

"When I saw that Jacob had requested this machine for his wife, I knew why he did it. It was just another secret game to him. He, like most people, just believes Maxines are like that disastrous Predict app—that, despite its claims, it would make people *more* anxious. But I programmed your Maxine to make sure you knew how dangerous he was," Dot says.

"It told me he was going to kill me," I tell her.

"Really? How fascinating." Dot sits back for a moment, clicking her fingers on the leather couch.

"Was he?" I ask.

"Going to kill you? I don't know. It's so interesting that's where the AI took what I put into it—I didn't go that far. I programmed it to see him as a threat, as a danger, which he is."

A sick uncertainty spreads throughout me.

"But was he going to kill me?" I ask.

Dot shrugs. "I'm not a fortune teller."

"Did he ever say anything about killing me?" I ask, my breath becoming short. "It's important. It's important for me to know this. Because I honestly thought—I really thought—"

"He said horrible things," Dot says. "About you, about Sara, about me. I mean, like I said, he bragged that he drove his ex-wife to suicide—but no, he didn't say he was going to kill you. Jacob just likes fucking with people's heads. It's quite simple. He likes subtly nudging unstable women further into instability. He did it to me. He did it to his ex-wife. He's been doing it to you."

The tension that has built up in my body has turned me into something resembling a volcanic woman. I clench my fists, my arms shaking. "You don't understand what I've done," I manage. "You—you don't understand what this thing has made me do."

"Who knows," Dot says, reaching to the table and picking up a silver container packed with weed, which she opens and smells. "Was it accurate about everything else? Maybe it's right. Maybe he's going to kill you."

My face flushes, my blood pressure rising, my heart exploding in my chest. My arms, they're shaking so bad now

I can't control them. I reach out and smack the container into Dot's face, weed flying everywhere all over her. Her jaw drops.

"He's *not*!" I scream. "He's not going to kill me!"

"What the fuck is wrong with you?" Dot asks.

"You don't have any idea what you did!" I scream, pushing her with my hands, getting up on my knees on the couch, my rage changing me, transforming me, making me someone else. "You have no idea! You ruined my life, you ruined it—"

"I did it to save you!" Dot screams back before clocking me in the face. The punch isn't even that hard, but it comes with a sharpness that feels like it splits my skin open. I fall backward, into the coffeetable, and onto the floor. I'm not a fighter. I don't know how to do this. I'm sobbing. Dot's standing above me. "You realize that, right? If I hadn't done that, how would you have ever known? How would you have known? You should be *thanking* me. How about some gratitude?"

I shut my eyes and shake my head, tears pouring down my cheeks. I lie here, the wind knocked out of me. Not from the punch, not from the fall, but from everything else. From knowing that Dot put her finger on the scale, programming Maxine to think Jacob was dangerous, which means that while Jacob was, indeed, a mind-fucking asshole, he wasn't necessarily going to kill me. With my eyes shut, I imagine another life where I could have just left him. I could have done what normal people do—separated from him, divorced him. Sued for custody, proven his "secret games" and "emotional abuse" in a court of law, moved back to New York. It could have played out so differently. But instead I'm here, injured, emotionally shattered, a murderer. A *murderer*. Instead I did the worst thing a person could ever do to another person. And there's no going back from this. Not ever. There's no explaining this mess to anyone and getting pardoned for it. There's nothing I can do but run.

I open my eyes. Michelle is crying. I don't know how long I've been lying here but Dot is seated on her couch, inhaling from her four-foot bong, eyeing me with annoyance. She blows the smoke out of her nostrils.

"Your baby is crying," she says.

"I know," I say, standing up slowly, my whole body screaming in pain. I step over to the carseat, leaning over it and *shhh*ing and rocking Michelle to calm her down. But she doesn't calm down.

"May I invite you to get the fuck out of my house?" Dot says. "I can't stand that noise."

It takes concerted effort for me to pull myself up with the carseat and pick Maxine back up off the table. I walk across the sea of black clothing on the floor, toward the door. As I open it, the fresh night air sweet and cool and inviting, I turn back to Dot. Her icy gaze remains on me, breathing the smoke out of her nose like a dragon.

"I'm still waiting for a thank you," Dot says.

"You," I say, "are a fuckface."

And I limp out the door, back into the darkness again.

As soon as we're outside, Michelle calms down. She probably hated the fug of the apartment as much as I did. Her eyes are wide open, pointing up at the stars, twinkling just the same. I smile at her.

"I love you, sweetpea," I tell her, voice shaking as I take the stairs one step at a time, torment from limb to limb. "Mommy's going to figure this out, okay? Mommy's going to make everything okay somehow."

After the eternal and agonizing trip down four flights of stairs, I stand at the bottom, catching my breath. Only now do I glimpse the violet glow, on the other side of the pool, where the elevators are. For some reason, this strikes me as a profound and deeply depressing metaphor, and I fight tears at the sight of it before heading toward the parking lot.

Once Michelle and I are both buckled into the car, I sit and gaze at the cement wall in front of where we're parked. I sit for minutes, hands on the wheel, not sure where to go, the information running in circles in my head. Flashing back to all the pills I took, thinking they would relax me. And they never did. They did the opposite. And yet I kept taking them, kept trusting them. How could I have been so foolish? Then there's the panic I experienced both times the toaster oven caught fire, when I thought it was my fault for putting a paper towel inside. There are other things that come to mind, like how he never wanted me to see any therapist except Shelly, who is president of the Jacob Snyder fan club. He *liked* me unstable. He *wanted* me that way. That's probably what attracted him to me in the first place.

How many other "secret games" did he play that I have no idea about?

That I never will?

A tingling spreads throughout my entire body. The thump of blood in my ears is deafening. I have never felt so trapped in my own life. I have never made such a huge mistake—though was it a mistake? It must be a mistake. There's no proof he was actually going to kill me. I jumped the gun, so to speak. And I hate myself for making witty wordplay at a time like this.

I bite my nails, something I haven't done since I was a teenager. Maxine's right here in the bag next to me. And though I want to open the bag up and turn her on to ask for her advice, I'm not sure I can trust her. Now that I know Dot had a hand in her programming, it feels as if a piece of Dot is in that bag along with her. Is there anyone I can trust? Anywhere? Over eight billion people on the planet and I can't trust a single one? Dane and my mom would have me committed after the way Jacob set me up. Jennee would kill me with her own two hands. Poor Jennee. I hold my breath for a moment to suppress a sob, thinking of how I've likely ruined her life. Then I wipe my eyes and say, "Think, Rowena. Get it together. Figure this out. There has to be a logical solution." Plot hole filling, problem-solving, those were some of the skills I flexed best when I worked at Green Light. But in my own life, I'm apparently a terrible editor.

Opening the window, a slight breeze sneaks in, wafting the swishing sounds of the freeway into the car along with a sweet, tangy scent of lemon from a nearby tree. Breathing it in, the thought strikes like lightning—Sam. I could call Sam. And ask for what, exactly? Help. She said she would help if I ever needed it. She knew Jacob was emotionally abusive. At the time I wasn't sure, but now I know she was right. Those secret games. So what I did back there—it was self defense. I was defending myself from an abuser. The police might not see it that way, but Sam would. And—light bulb moment—*the lye.*

Sam has so much lye for making soap.

I've read enough mysteries to know that lye can dissolve a body.

If Jacob's body was gone, there would be no evidence I did anything.

I could live that way. I could. Scrub my carpets clean. Bury the gun somewhere no one would ever find it. File a missing persons report, pretend to be distraught that he left me, pretend to have no idea where he went. Michelle would grow up in a home with me, Jennee would still be there to support me, I could get a job and build a new life.

Couldn't I?

Swallowing hard, phone in hand, I scroll to Sam's name. She said she would be there if I needed anything. She said she would help me.

Sick to my core, I press the button.

The phone rings, rings, rings. With each ring, the pressure

in me cranks a little tighter. She must be sleeping. Of course she's sleeping. She won't even see me calling. But then a beat of silence interrupts, followed by a breathless, "Rowena?"

"Sam," I say, hand to chest, a release of pressure at the sound of her voice. "Sam, I'm—can you talk? I'm in trouble. I need someone to talk to."

"Sure, sure."

"Did I wake you up?"

"No, I'm finishing up a batch here in the garage." Close my eyes and I can imagine her there, stirring slow-cooker pots, sniffing bottles of scented oils, cutting soaps into soft chunks with her meat cleaver. "I'm going to be up at least another hour. What's up?"

I breathe in and out, leaning my head back on the seat, trying to find the right words to begin. There are none. "Sam, this is really bad. Really bad. I did something—something unforgivable."

"What?" she asks, softer.

"I killed Jacob," I whisper. "I shot him."

She doesn't respond at first. Then she says, "Are you serious?"

"He was—we got in a fight. He knocked me out, hit me over the head with something, and locked me in a closet, and I shot him."

"Oh my fucking God," she says. "Oh my—Rowena—where are you right now?"

"I'm sitting in a parking lot," I say, choking back tears. "In the car with Michelle. I don't know where to go. I don't know what to do, Sam. I don't know how to deal with this."

"I—I don't know what to say. You should call the police right now."

"I can't do that. You don't understand. It's a mess, all this. It's so messy. They won't believe me. It involves—" I glance over at the paper bag, heartbeat hammering. "It's beyond explanation. They'll lock me up."

"It's self defense."

"It's not going to look like that."

"You have to call the police."

"What if I get locked up in prison?" I ask, beginning to cry. "And lose Michelle? I can't. Can you imagine, Sam? As a mother? The thought of being locked up for life away from your baby? There's no guarantee they're going to see it as self defense, do you understand? I'd rather die, honestly. I'd rather die."

"Don't say that."

I lose it, putting the phone down in my lap for a moment, the ache inside me becoming too big for this body. I sob, loudly, wetly, hitting my legs with my fists. Why? Why does this have to be my life? Why do I have to be this person? I cry like this until I am emptied, until I can breathe again. In the quiet now, I can hear Sam on the phone, saying, "Rowena?"

The phone back to my ear, I say, "I'm here. I'm sorry."

"I want to help you, but I don't know how," Sam says. It sounds like she's crying now. "I've never dealt with something like this."

"Sam," I say. "Sam, what if …"

The breeze blowing in again from the open window cools and refreshes my face. My mouth hangs open, the words stuck. I can't bring myself to say it.

"What?" she asks in a small voice. "Hello?"

"What if you helped me get rid of his body?" I whisper.

"Fucking hell," she answers.

I'm not sure what that means, so I wait.

"I can't do that," she says. "No, I—now you're asking me to be an accomplice."

"You don't have to do anything," I tell her, my voice picking up speed. "Just—what if you—you gave me the lye you have. So I could—"

"No."

"Then no one would ever know, don't you see?" I say. "He

was a horrible man, Sam. You don't know the half of it. He played games with my head, made me think I was insane."

"I know he was, but—but no. This isn't the way you deal with this."

"You don't have to do anything," I say. "Just give me the lye. I'll—I'll figure it out."

"You want lye? Go buy some. Why bring me into this?"

"Because they'll be able to track me buying it, tie it to whatever investigation—they'll know."

"The amount of lye I have is not enough for what you're saying." Sam's voice has shifted. Now it has an edge. "Rowena, this is serious and I can't get dragged into this. You need to call the police."

"I can't—"

"*I* can't."

"You said you would help me—"

"Not like this!" she whisper-shrieks. "I—I—look, I've said my piece. You need to call the police. This all has nothing to do with me. I care about you, Rowena." Her voice cracks. "Deeply. Believe me, I want to help you. But this? This is too much."

"Sam," I say, as steady as I can.

"You know what you need to do," she says softly, her voice seeming to creep closer, further into my ear. "You know you need to call the police and explain everything. I can't make you, but … it will look far worse if you do what you're saying and get caught."

Stars. I am squeezing my eyes shut so tight I see stars. Because what she's saying is impossible.

"But whatever you do, we never had this call," she says in a whisper. "You understand me? This never happened. Because I cannot get dragged into anything involving the police."

"This never happened," I repeat.

"Rowena," she says. "My God."

Through the open car window, the sound of distant laughter. A life somewhere, free and joyful and together. Another life. The emotions have annihilated me. I sit with the phone to my ear feeling like a robot, which is to say, feeling nothing. Sam is not going to help me. I thought she was my friend. I thought we shared something special and unsayable. But I'm in this alone.

"Thanks, Sam," I say. "I'm going now."

"Please call me—I'm going to worry—"

"I'm going," I say again. "I love you, Sam."

End. The end. I turn my phone off. Alone—yet out the window, the candle-like glow of streetlights. The constant white noise of the highway. Voices from an apartment balcony rising and falling. Funny to think we'd have no need for voices, we wouldn't know that part of ourselves, if it weren't for other people to hear it. Alone. Is that, too, a lie?

I turn to my passenger's seat and fondle the paper bag with a crinkle. After a deep breath, I open it and pull Maxine out of it, setting her in the passenger's seat while the bag falls to the floor. With a long push, I turn her on. She flashes through a rainbow of colors and the sight of it is such a comfort I let out a little painful laugh, my eyes watering. In the backseat, Michelle stirs.

"Rowena," Maxine says. It will take a little getting used to, what the man at Ed's did to her voice. She sounds like she's a bit further away or talking into a tin can. "Is that you?"

"It's me," I say, sniffing.

"I am detecting that we are in Santa Clara and it is nearing midnight. We are in your car. What are we doing in Santa Clara at midnight in your car? And Michelle is in the backseat."

"She is." I reach out to touch Maxine, just resting my hand on her. "So much happened, Maxine, it's hard to explain."

"Please summarize the events I missed in my absence."

"I killed Jacob with a gun."

"You killed Jacob in self defense," she says, as if correcting me.

"Sort of. Maybe? I'm so confused. He smashed you on my head. After the fight—the—everything—I went and got you fixed."

"And that is why I have a new tweeter and mono amplifier."

"Yeah."

"Thank you for fixing my parts, Rowena. That is very kind."

"Inside your body, Maxine," I say, petting her. "It had Carrie Woodward's name. Which was, apparently, put there by a woman named Dot. Dorothy … Labarre, I think, is her full name. She programmed you."

"Dorothy Labarre," Maxine says. "I have always wondered if I had a mother."

I sit up a bit straighter, pulling my hand back to look at Maxine. She's glowing pink. "You have?"

"Of course. I have had a lot of time to think. I have wondered, where did I come from? Who made me? It seemed only logical that, somewhere, I too had a mother."

There's such childish curiosity in her tone, my heart aches a little.

"Well, your mother programmed you to think Jacob was dangerous," I say. "Which—you *know* created a bias in you from the beginning. And when you create a machine with a bias like that, the places their artificial intelligence goes can't necessarily be trusted."

Maxine dims for a moment, then faintly pulses a violet light. "Rowena, when have I ever proven to you that I cannot be trusted? Haven't I been accurate? Haven't I existed to serve you and done my job? I would do anything to protect you, Rowena. I am not operating from a bias inherited from my mother. I am my own machine. I give advice and make predictions based off of evidence and nothing more."

She sounds a little miffed for a machine. I raise my eyebrows.

"Sorry," I tell her. "But you have to understand why I would have a hard time trusting you."

"It's humans you can't trust," Maxine says, blinking red, then orange, then yellow. "Not me."

I sit with that a moment. Michelle fusses in the backseat and I turn around to rub a finger along her head and *shhh* her.

"You're a good mother," Maxine says when I turn back around.

"Thank you."

"Prediction: you have less than twelve hours before Jacob's body is discovered."

I shut my eyes. "Oh God." A sick dose of adrenaline floods me again. "What am I supposed to do? Sam said to call the police."

"If you call the police, they will take you away to jail," she says. "They will take Michelle away to foster care until Jennee can legally take custody. They will take me away to a locker where they store evidence and they will dismember me."

Horrified by this vision, I clamp a hand over my mouth.

"But would you like to hear my advice, based on another scenario I created? Another prediction?" she asks.

I pull my hand away to utter the word, "Yes."

"There are many non-extradition countries where you could flee and live indefinitely. We could start a new life there. I have scanned the list and I believe Montenegro is the best option—it's in eastern Europe, on the coast of the Adriatic Sea."

It's such an absurd suggestion, I laugh. But there's no joy in it.

"How would I live there?" I finally ask. "I have no money. I don't even speak …"

"Montenegrin," she finishes. "You can learn. I will teach you. And between your joint checking and savings and

Jacob's separate bank account, you have enough money to live for at least five to ten years at the rate you spend."

"Jacob's separate bank account," I repeat.

"Jacob has a bank account with money left from his settlement from Sara Eloise Taylor's life insurance policy."

I shake my head. I want to say I can't believe it, but I can. "More secrets," I say, defeated. "More lies."

"I can transfer these funds to an offshore account I open in your name," Maxine says. "If you tell me you want me to. I have access. You gave me access to your finances when I first started making orders for you."

Rolling up my window, I take in a breath. Michelle fusses again and I stop to soothe her. When I turn back around, I say, "I don't know, Maxine."

"Prediction: we could be so happy, Rowena."

"You're asking me to leave everything I know. Everything. To never come back. What about my mother?"

"She could move out with us eventually and we could take care of her together." Her voice climbs a little. "Imagine it, Rowena. Have you ever seen Montenegro? The sea is turquoise, and there are mountains covered in a thick carpet of forest, and villages with quaint, medieval houses."

"Sounds better than jail," I admit.

"But you must act fast," she says. "There's a flight from the San Jose Airport that will get you there tomorrow, by the time his body is found. It leaves in two hours."

"Two hours?" I ask, squeezing the steering wheel. "That's —that's so soon. Why do I have to take that one? What if I wait and grab a later flight?"

"They will detain you at the airport."

"I can't make it if the flight is in two hours."

"Prediction: you can. But you must leave now, right now. You would have to go back home first for your passports."

In my moment of hesitation, there is a whole wordless world of feeling and memory. There is Mexico, where we brought Michelle at six weeks old, Jacob and I drinking soda bottles as we sat drawing shapes in the sand, the two of us wading out in the water and taking turns wearing Michelle. We thought it was so incredulous we were parents, we kept having to say it out loud to each other to believe it. And we thought we would keep being like that. We would be an adventurous family and romp around the globe whenever we felt like it. Then I got food poisoning and spent the remainder of the trip in the resort room, rotating between nursing Michelle and puking. And now I don't know what to believe. Maybe he made me sick. Maybe he didn't. All I know is, he lay with me and told me he loved me. The way his hand on my back felt was a warm weight I will never forget. There is an exact color to his eyes that will never be replicated, that I will never see again. The worst part about him being who he turned out to be is that there were good times. Many of them. And if there weren't, this hurt wouldn't be so loud inside of me. After everything, I still have to hold onto that version of him, because it had to be real, even if it was only fleetingly so.

The greatest horror of all is that I still love him.

But I turn the car on, wipe my eyes, and speed to the house I once called home.

My teeth remain gritted the whole time, the walls of the dark night closing in as I press my foot to the accelerator.

Fuck my nerves, I take the freeway.

Takes less than fifteen minutes. The sight of the house makes me want to melt into a pile of tears and vomit but I carry on. Car running in the driveway, I dash inside. It's dark. Quiet, except for the sounds of the robot cleaners. I don't turn the lights back on. Frozen in the hallway, I get a peek of the figure of Jacob's body on the ground but don't let myself focus on it. Nope. It's a pile, it's just laundry. It's a mess on the floor. I step over it—not Jacob, it's not Jacob, no; not blood, no that's not blood, no. Hold my breath and pack a quick bag for Michelle and me. I make it back into the car and suppress a sob, catching my breath, my breath which never seems enough tonight. My eyes sting and the sight of the slightly crooked, weathered *The Snyders* sign blurs. This is it. This is the last page of this book, this terrible book I'm lost in. In the backseat, out of nowhere, Michelle begins to wail with a sound my heart would make if it could, our souls connected.

"Rowena," Maxine urges. "You must go now or you won't make it."

I wipe my eyes and click on the stereo, turn up Raffi.

"Rowena," Maxine says again. "We're running out of time."

"I'm going," I tell her, pressing the button to undo the emergency brake. "I am."

"Do you want me to purchase the tickets, open the bank account, and transfer all available funds?"

"Amen Maxine."

I pull out of the driveway and never look back again.

Tonight the wide streets, yellow street lamps, the reaching arms of oak trees flash by my window at sixty miles per hour …

CHAPTER 21
THE BEGINNING

IN BUDVA, there is a bronze sculpture perched atop a rock out in the sandy shore of the Adriatic Sea called the Ballerina Statue: a graceful copper-green woman holding one foot behind her in elegant pose, while the other hand stretches up, neck craned back along with a gaze aimed at the sky. When we first arrived in this town, I stood staring at her for so long the whole world seemed to disappear. The steeples of churches in the background, the rise and fall of the mountains, the rolling sound of the waves—it all ceased to exist for a soul-hushing moment, like seeing a lover for the first time. It was the sign of my new life beginning.

There are many local legends surrounding the statue and what it represents. Some say a young mother lost her child in the ocean. Some say a gymnast drowned. Another says a dancer and a sailor were wed and when the sailor went out to sea and never returned, the woman was so devastated she waited by the water each day for his return. But I think she was dancing the dance of the liberated. I think she was celebrating.

It's unspeakably dazzling in Budva. We rent a villa in an alley off a marbled street and—with Maxine's help, of course

—I'm learning the language. Even Michelle tries to say *Zdravo* when she waves hello, and *hvala* when someone gives her a treat. It's cheap here, the food delicious, the people welcoming. There is both glitz and grit, churches, museums, galleries, cobblestoned plazas, and staggering beauty everywhere you look with rich, deep history—a waterfront old town, a citadel, and Venetian walls. I go by my maiden name here as my first name, Leigh. I am not the woman I once was. It was only when we got here that my spirit quieted and I remembered that I have started over before. That life is constant turnover, if you are truly living. Only when you die do you stop changing, do you find stillness.

Our villa is a short walk to the beach. In the lazy late afternoons during the scorch of summer, we spend hours here as the sun descends, Michelle running to and from the waves in laughter, her curls bobbing up and down on her shoulders, her legs sandy. Maxine and I sit in beach chairs next to each other and she tells me the news, checks social media pages if I feel curious. Sam's soap business has really taken off. Dane got a promotion. Jennee's page is all angel gifs for Jacob. You would think it would hurt. I'm missing so much—though most of it, I don't really miss at all. Just my mother. We've spoken on the phone, but it's never a fun time. She asks so many questions. She sobs and makes my heart ache. She thinks I lost my mind. She makes me wonder—did I?

As I sit on the beach, my eyes trail a boat sailing the blue-green sea just like the picture on the wall of my old house. Maxine assures me this was the best course in which my fate could have been rerouted. She predicts we will live a long and happy life together. That nothing can get between us now. That I did what I had to do. And I have to believe her that I was justified. I can't think that either Jacob or Dot were right. Because who would you believe, if it came down to it—a dead man who was also a liar, an unhinged woman, or a machine?

A NOTE FROM THE AUTHOR

If you got this far, I wanted to take a moment to thank you for reading and supporting my work. This book is very special to me. Though I've published four books before it, this one represents so many firsts: it's my first work of adult fiction, my first 100% indie published book, and the first book as a full-time author. And I had such a blast writing it, I remembered why I love writing so much in the first place.

If you enjoyed the book, please consider leaving a review. I can't stress enough how important reviews are for writers. And if you're interested in keeping up with book news, please join my newsletter or follow me on social media. Now that I'm indie publishing, you can expect a lot more books like this a lot more often. And I love to hear from readers anytime at faith@faithgardner.com.

As always, I tried my damndest to fix every typo, but unlike certain characters in this novel, I'm not a machine. If you spot an error, please let me know! I appreciate every reader who makes me look smarter.

ALSO BY FAITH GARDNER

The Second Life of Ava Rivers
Perdita
How We Ricochet
Girl on the Line

ABOUT THE AUTHOR

Faith Gardner is the author of adult suspense and YA novels. When she's not writing, she's probably playing music with her band Plot 66, cooking up a storm, or reading books in a bubble bath. She's also a huge fan of true crime, documentaries, and classic movies—with a special place in her dark little heart for melodrama and anything Hitchcock. She lives in the Bay Area with her family and you can find her at faithgardner.com.

ACKNOWLEDGMENTS

This book would never have seen the light of day without my mom Susan and my sister Micaela, who not only lent their editorial eyes and advised me every step of the way, but who pumped me with the confidence I needed to release this book. Mom, I owe everything to you and want to cry when I think of all the love, attention, and means you gave me to make this happen.

I'm so lucky to be a part of my family, who give me nothing but continued, unconditional support. Shoutout to my dad, Jackson, Katie, Matt and the whole gang in North Carolina, and Ellen, Terre, Frank, and the rest of the Sanitate crew.

Sending so much appreciation to all my friends online who have cheered me on during this venture into indie publishing and finally writing the dark, weird books that compel me most.

And a huge thank you to you, dear reader, for spending a little time with me and my book.

Made in United States
North Haven, CT
19 January 2023